INCOMING LAYNE SHIFT

Alliances are broken and hearts stolen.

BROKEN ALLIANCES SERIES
BOOK 3

SADIE WINCHESTER

To any man who has gone through the process of tattooing his cock...

I learned some things writing this book.

Thank you for jacking up my Google search history.

OFFICIAL PLAYLIST

Below The Belt (ft. Set It Off) - Point North
Body Bag - I Prevail
Brand New Numb - Motionless In White
CONCRETE JUNGLE - Bad Omens
Dirty Thoughts - Chloe Adams
Fire Up the Night - New Medicine
Iris - DIAMANTE, Breaking Benjamin
Kiss from a Rose (ft. Kayla King) - No Resolve
Legends Never Die - Halocene
Punching Bag - Set It Off
Royalty - Egzod, Maestro Chives, Neoni
Song #3 - Stone Sour

EPILOGUE

Wherever You Will Go - The Calling
Your Guardian Angel - The Red Jumpsuit Apparatus

The official playlist can be found on Spotify.

(Tap "Search" in the Spotify app, tap the camera icon, scan and go!)

CONTENT & TRIGGER WARNINGS

This book ends on an **aggressive** cliffhanger. Contains adult content for 18+ readers only. Included, but not limited to, is a list of content/trigger warnings below:

Abduction, Anal Intercourse, Attempted Murder/Murder, Church Altar Sex, Death of Characters, Double Penetration, Emotional Devastation/Scars, MFM Sexual Relations, Non-Con (alluded to, off-page, not MC), Possessive Behavior, Sexually Explicit Scenes, Tattooed Penis, Violence (blood, hanging, gore, guns, etc.)

<u>Disclaimers</u>: There may be light, thematic BDSM elements within the story, and should not be construed as representative of a BDSM lifestyle and/or dynamic.

Your mental health matters.

Please visit SadieWinchester.com or email SadieWinchesterAuthor@gmail.com with any questions regarding content/trigger warnings.

CHAPTER ONE

Continued from Layne Closure Ahead

A large smile came over Gage's face, accompanied by a chuckle of amusement. "Look who it is. After all these years and all the places, I didn't expect to run into my big brother tonight."

Joey's back was straighter than a steel rod, and his chest puffed out defensively. His arm reached out and possessively guided Layne a step behind him as his eyes remained on Gage.

Layne stared at the two men, *two De Luca men*, in her presence. Once Gage dropped the bomb that Joey was his brother, she couldn't unsee it. Their eyes had the same warm brown hues. Their facial structures held similarities that one often would expect between siblings. Both had darker shades of blonde hair. Shit, even both of them had a charm that rolled off of their smiles with ease.

Her eyes darted between them both in shock as she noticed Joey's reaction didn't give off any warm and fuzzy vibes. He never told her that he had a brother, when speaking about his childhood, it had always sounded as though he was an only child. Not once did he mention having any siblings. The way he was looking at Gage right now gave her the impression he had wished that was the case.

"Layne," Joey calmly spoke, "go wait in the car."

She blinked several times. "I'm not—"

Joey cut her off, "I'm not fuckin' asking twice." His words didn't have the usual playfulness to them, causing her to flinch at the harsher tone.

Gage attempted to lighten up the tension in the air between them. "She's welcome to stay, and we can have a few drinks together." He made the mistake of reaching out for Layne's arm.

Without so much as the blink of an eye, Joey snatched up two handfuls of Gage's crisp white shirt and forcefully shoved him. "You don't get to fuckin' touch her!" He released his hold after the strong push of his little brother, which resulted in Gage stumbling back several steps.

Regaining his footing, Gage lifted his hands harmlessly with a smirk. "I didn't mean anything by it. Relax." He chuckled, entertained by Joey's overreaction. His gaze shifted back to Layne, who stood there bewildered and unaware of the history between them. He gave her a sly wink.

Whether or not he knew the subtle move would push Joey's buttons wasn't obvious. What was clear was that Joey wasn't going to put up with it. Years of pent-up rage rumbled to the surface. He lunged at Gage, colliding with him, and they both crashed into a nearby table. A few scantily clad girls shrieked in response to the fight breaking out between the two men.

Upon impact with the table, drinks immediately spilled everywhere while Joey and Gage wrestled with one another. After they both rolled off the table and hit the ground, both of them had a fistful of each other's shirts as punches were thrown.

Both men appeared to be evenly matched with one another. Neither of them were gaining the upper hand in the scuffle. Layne stood back, unsure of how or if she should intervene. If Joey's life appeared to be in danger, she wouldn't have hesitated, but this looked more like brothers hashing out their issues.

The rest of Cassidy's Cave occupants seemed to ignore the battle between the two, rolling around on the floor as if this was nothing but a typical brawl at the club.

Joey rolled on top of Gage, pinning him down as he drew back his fist decorated with the skull tattoo. Seizing the opportunity, Layne grabbed his arm with both of her hands, knowing she needed to if she was going to have a chance of putting an end to this.

"Stop, Joey!" Her fingers dug into his arm, pulling back on it to avoid it continuing its path downwards towards Gage's jaw.

Luckily, he had enough awareness of Layne's presence to not lash out at her as well. Feeling her tug on him again, his heated glare remained on his brother but gave in to her insistence to put an end to the altercation.

He got up off Gage, speaking between clenched teeth, "I don't want to ever see your face ever again." Joey slid his arm from Layne's grasp forcefully. His bloodied hand from his split knuckles dropped to snatch a tight hold of her hand.

The younger De Luca partially sat up on an elbow and used his thumb to wipe away a small stream of blood coming from the corner of his mouth as he watched the two of them. Well, it was more along the lines of watching Layne's ass in those skintight jeans she had on. Fuck, that perfect ass practically had his name on it.

Breathing heavily while recovering from the skirmish, Joey tugged Layne along with him on his way out of the strip club. Her steps were doubled up to keep up with his long strides. She looked over at his face, the tension still pulling at his expression in hard lines.

Once they were all in the Challenger, with Liam drunkenly passed the hell out in the backseat, the silence was damn near suffocating.

Unable to take it anymore, Layne spoke, "Joey, you never told me you had—"

His eyes never leaving the road ahead of them, he stopped her right there. "We're not talking about this." The topic of his brother was immediately off-limits.

Both of her brows lifted in surprise that he thought his statement was going to prevent this discussion from happening. It may have put a halt to it for now, but that was only because they had just pulled up in front of Liam's studio located on the outskirts of Tribeca.

Layne sighed irritably and got out of the passenger seat. She pushed her seat forward and leaned in the back, giving Liam a jab to his arm. "Wake up, jackass."

A sharp snortle came from Liam as he shifted his position in the back. She wrinkled up her nose, and her fist pounded into his bicep once more, this time harder. There may have been a little of her own frustration behind that second hit.

His hazel eyes half-lifted open as he glanced around, grumbling at the inconvenience.

She shook her head and stepped back from the open door. "We're here. Go drink some water and put your ass to bed."

Liam's hand rubbed over his auburn hair, which was already thoroughly disheveled as he tried to shake off enough of the intoxicated slumber to get himself out of the backseat.

Once she saw him get inside the upscale residential building, Layne got back into the car. Her fingers massaged over her forehead, recalling how this evening hadn't gone as planned. From the call about Liam going on a rager at the adult entertainment venue to the drama between Joey and his brother, which Layne never knew he had.

With dread filling her voice, she spoke, "I'm going to have to tell him soon." It was clear that she wasn't looking forward to hashing out more shit with Liam.

Joey scoffed and sarcastically replied, "I'm sure he's going to take it *so* well." He pulled away from the curb to begin driving them back to their home—O'Reilly Manor.

Her green eyes stared over at him. "About as well as you took having a conversation with *your* brother?" She didn't hide the annoyance over his decision to conceal Gage's existence from her. Their late-night conversations had been filled with talks about everything and anything, and he had failed to mention something as simple as having a sibling. It had old feelings of distrust whispering in the back of her brain.

Joey's hand readjusted its grasp on the steering wheel, holding it a little tighter. "Just drop it, Layne."

When did she ever just drop things because she was told to? "No."

Before he got the opportunity to make some comment about him asking twice, she continued, "Don't even start that crap with me, Joey. What the hell was that back there at the club?!"

He reached over and finally decided that he was done with silence and turned the volume knob up to blare the music to avoid any actual conversation between them. The heavy rock tunes filled the car.

While driving back uptown, Joey fought through each of the painful memories at war inside of his head from nearly ten years ago.

Rosie giggled as she ran her hands across the smooth and unmarked skin of Joey's bare chest while he stood there in just his jeans. "You're being so bad! Gage is going to be home any minute."

He gave a devious smirk. "So? Let him see who really knows how to get your pussy wet." His hands continued their descent over her body towards her little white shorts.

Joey leaned in, whispering into the hot, young blonde's ear. "Nothing is going to stop me from giving you the hard fuck you deserve, Rose. Gage is going to have to learn how to share."

He gave a hard blink at the thoughts creeping up of what led up to a horrific day that had been burned forever into his skull. His jaw clenched even tighter, still recalling each detail of Rosie's sun-kissed skin and the sound of her voice when she tried to sound serious but instead sounded as threatening as a kitten mewing.

Out of the corner of his vision, he snuck a glimpse of Layne. She sat there with her arms crossed in front of her chest, watching out the window as each street passed. The street lights flashed across her fair skin as each one passed, reflecting the blank expression she wore when she tightened the screws on her temper. He knew that look on her face too well. She was pissed, and he couldn't blame her.

When they got back home, Layne went inside ahead of him. She didn't bother to wait for him to follow behind her.

After he locked up the front door, Joey found her inside the kitchen with a cold beer in her hand. The way her lips connected with the opening of the bottle, he thought about all the other ways those plump lips could be put to better use.

Layne fully avoided eye contact with him as she leaned back against the counter and took another sip of the hoppy pale ale. Her tongue slipped forth and ran over her lips afterward to collect any remaining beer on them.

Joey stepped up in front of her, caging her in place as he set his hands on the counter on either side of her. His eyes had a soft burn to them as he peered down at her. "I'm sorry."

Refusing to look at him to help maintain her resolve,

she shook her head. "No, you're not. You're thinking about getting your dick blown."

He sighed but didn't argue her assumption that had been right on point.

She pushed away from the counter, but when he didn't move his arms, she pushed against them. Instead of allowing her to pass, he slid an arm around her waist, drawing her up against him.

Joey's hand eased the beer from her hand, bringing it to his mouth and chugging it down. Leaving the now-empty bottle on the counter behind her, he took her face by the jaw to look at him.

"And you're thinking about blowing it." A smirk eased over his face as he soaked in the way she made her irritation look irresistible.

Her insides were beginning to melt as she was forced to meet his eyes. "You're not getting out of this so easily."

Gently, his hand turned her head to expose the line of her neck. Joey leaned over, bringing his mouth up against her fair skin. The short and bristly hairs of his stubble scratched at her as his lips worked over the sensitive flesh, kissing and sucking at it. His teeth pressed into the skin, applying a moderate but brief amount of pressure.

Layne exhaled a light moan as he worked his magic against her neck. Her hands came up to his chest, digging her fingers into the soft cotton of his tee. "I mean it, Joey." Her words had lost their edge to them as her eyes fluttered closed momentarily while his tongue grazed along her throat.

He released her jaw so he could grab her hand and

bring it up against the zipper of his pants to feel the strain his hard cock was putting on it. "You can mean it all you like, Layney. Hell, you can even be pissed, but you're going to take my cum down your throat like a good girl."

The heat of her anger was spreading elsewhere and forming a desire between her legs. Her hand rubbed over the bulge pushing against the front of his pants.

She pushed him back against the pantry door behind him with her other hand. Layne's eyes locked onto his own with a steamy gaze. Her hand roughly jerked on his pants as she tugged them open. She may have been pissed, but she was going to seize this opportunity.

After her petite hand retrieved his throbbing cock from his dark boxer briefs, she dropped down onto her knees in front of him. His hands immediately came down to bury themselves in her silky hair. Her long, dark locks draped over the various lines of the tattoos and dried blood across his fingers.

Now at eye-level with his member, she could see the precum glistening as it spilled over the head of his cock. Her tongue snaked out and licked away the clear liquid from him in one smooth motion. "You better hope that I choke on your cock and forget that you owe me an explanation."

Feeling the velvety stroke of her tongue against his head, he groaned, "Fuck." His grasp on her head tightened. "Suck my cock with that mouth of yours, and we can talk afterward."

Noticing a slip in his initial stance on having a discussion, she grinned and pulled his length into her mouth.

Sucking on him roughly, she didn't waste time drawing him back farther towards her throat. Her head slid back and forth against him eagerly.

He moaned out above her as he watched himself disappear into her mouth. "Christ, Layney, slow down. I want time to enjoy this."

If she didn't have a mouthful of him, she would have smirked, but instead, she hummed against him, causing his body to tense up from another spark of pleasure. She continued at a swift pace as her mouth worked around every inch of him.

Joey's hands attempted to slow her down, but each attempt was met by her tongue dancing along the bottom of his cock and effectively distracting his efforts.

Her oral skills were sending him quickly into overdrive, his moans growing more intense. The buildup of pressure of his arousal was quickly nearing its breaking point. "Layne, ugh. Take it easy…"

When he told her to ease up on him, that's when her hand cupped his balls in the palm of her hand and gave him the money look. Her vibrant green eyes peered up at him through her thick eyelashes as she remained kneeling in front of him.

Seeing her staring up at him like he had the only dick in the world she could ever want, he whimpered right before he exploded. His hips pushed forward, shoving his cock deeper into her throat as thick ropes of seed erupted. Joey released a loud groan while he continued to spasm inside her mouth.

Layne swallowed each mouthful as he came for her.

She felt a sense of pride and satisfaction in her efforts. If he had been a good boy and took the time to have the conversation with her about Gage, she may have drawn out the way her mouth sucked him.

Once the tension eased in his body, she pulled her mouth away and got back onto her feet with her swollen lips in a victorious smile.

She used her fingertips to wipe away a few drops of his seed and her saliva from the edges of her mouth, sucking her fingers clean afterward. "Now, are you going to tell me what the deal is with your brother?"

CHAPTER TWO

Post-blowjob version of Joey was a little more at ease. But still, he stood there staring at Layne as he tried to find the words to respond to her tireless crusade to find out more about Gage.

He tucked his half-hard cock back into his pants, closing up shop with a zip and slip of the button.

"Well?" She pressed him again for a response.

His hand rubbed the back of his neck before he gave a robust exhale. "It's a long story, Layne. Just take my word for it that we're both better off never seeing him again."

She rolled her eyes at him, unsatisfied with his response.

If he didn't want to be exiled to sleeping in Layne's childhood bedroom surrounded by pink frills tonight, he realized that he needed to do better. "Alright." He dropped his hand from its hold on the back of his neck.

"Gage and I had a falling out about ten years ago. One thing led to another, and people got hurt." It was the short and not-so-dirty version of what happened. He stepped closer to her, his hands rubbing over her arms reassuringly. "I just don't want history to repeat itself."

Layne pursed her lips together at the thought of how his so-called long story managed to be summed up in a few sentences. Her eyes searched his face, finding small traces of pain lingering beneath the surface of his coffee-colored eyes.

Dropping the tension in her shoulders slightly, she closed the distance between them with another step. Her arms wrapped around his waist as she looked up at him. "How can you expect history not to repeat itself if you don't tell me what to look out for?"

Joey's hands gave both of her upper arms a light squeeze. "As long as he stays the fuck away, it won't repeat itself."

"With everything that's about to change in our lives, I can't have you keeping things from me. You keep telling me you're all in, but you won't tell me what happened a decade ago?" Now, her tone was shifting to reflect some of the hurt she was feeling from him not trusting her with whatever it was that had him avoiding a few simple questions.

His mouth found her forehead, planting a delicate kiss. He hated that she was feeling any sort of way about the trust they had rebuilt between themselves. It had not been an easy road to pave. Layne had worked so hard on herself to allow him inside her heart again, and he didn't want to shatter it all again. If he did, he wasn't sure that she would ever come back from it. Truth be told, he wasn't sure he would either.

"An innocent girl died," he tried to keep his voice even and emotions withheld. "A woman, actually," he clarified. "Her name was Rose." Rosie had been twenty-three, Gage twenty-two, and Joey had just celebrated his thirtieth birthday.

He stood there trying to find the words to explain how this all went down, struggling to disconnect emotionally enough to explain.

Gage punched a hole in the bedroom wall. "What the fuck, Rose?!"

"Babe, please, just listen." Rosie implored as she pulled her shirt down over her perky and naked breasts. Her hands tugged her white shorts up her thighs. She frowned as she walked over to him after fastening the button at her waist.

Joey sat there in Gage's bed, leaning back against the headboard with an arm tucked behind his head, not even making an effort to get up.

Rosie frowned as she took Gage's hand, squeezing it tightly before raising it to her light pink lips to lay several tender kisses on his unpainted knuckles. "We talked about this, remember? Keeping things open, an open commitment."

While Rosie was looking at Gage, he was looking over at Joey, who was failing at suppressing his shit-eating grin.

"I didn't expect you to turn around and just drop your pants and bend over for him!" Gage gritted his teeth while he gave a deadly glare at his brother.

"Gage," Joey finally spoke up, "don't be mad that she has good taste." He smirked at the additional thought of how sweet her cum had been on his tongue.

A small rumble emanated from Gage, his fists clenching at his sides as he made a step toward the bed where Joey so casually sat with a sheet just barely covering his lap.

Rosie sidestepped in front of him, both hands resting on top of Gage's chest as she looked up at him pleadingly. "There's enough of me for both of you."

With Gage's light brown eyes staring his older brother down, he shook his head. "You just love stirring up chaos, don't you? You're fucking addicted to it."

When Joey returned from the silence of his thoughts, his eyes were met with Layne's concerned expression while they both stood there in the kitchen of O'Reilly Manor. He couldn't put into words the memories that had just crossed his mind.

"It was a business deal gone bad. Gage takes risks he shouldn't. The odds could be stacked against him a thousand-to-one, and he would still think he has a shot. He doesn't think about what the hell happens when the other guy doesn't give a damn about the odds."

He shook his head, already feeling the simmer of fury starting up in his blood as the sequence of events unfolded in his brain.

"You're up." Joey hooked his thumb in the direction of the bathroom, still warm from the steam lingering after his shower. A towel was wrapped around his waist, and droplets of water still scattered over his freshly bathed skin.

Gage nuzzled up against Rosie's side while they lay

there in the king-sized bed that barely fit all three of them. "Are you sure you're not going to join me?"

She gave the sweetest of laughs. "You both have left me barely able to use my legs after all that. All I want to do is stay here and take a nice long nap." Rose smiled and leaned over to lovingly kiss Gage. "Go clean up. I'll be right here when you get done."

Joey tossed his damp towel over the arm of a chair and snagged a pair of underwear, quickly pulling them on to avoid the chill of the air.

As for Gage, he smiled at the beautiful blonde before him and nodded. "Okay, but not before I get you some water and something to snack on. Can't have our girl not getting the care she needs to recover." He pushed the sheets off his lower body and rolled out of bed.

Gage yanked on a pair of boxers and left the bedroom to go retrieve water and some fruit from the kitchen down the hall.

While Gage was focused on his mission for sustenance, Joey grinned as he partially climbed onto the bed with one knee and leaned over to steal a kiss from the woman lying there in complete satisfaction. "You're amazing. I could die a happy man right now."

The heartfelt moment between them was interrupted by the sound of the front door of the shitty apartment they shared in Jersey City being busted open. Immediate shouting filled the small space.

Joey sprang into action, pulling his semi-automatic from the nightstand drawer. "Stay here," he ordered Rose. He ran to assess the situation, but as he made it to the bedroom door, several men in ski masks barged in with weapons drawn.

"Hey…" Layne's hand was resting on the side of his face, lightly caressing her fingers over his week-old scruff. She tried to lure him back from whatever was going on inside his mind.

He finally released a breath he had been holding far longer than he should have.

"We don't have to do this tonight." She saw the struggle he was going through trying to explain his animosity towards his brother. It was clear that this wasn't an issue that ran only skin-deep.

Joey shook his head. "No. You need to know." He cleared his throat, summoning the words to casually describe what transpired that broke the relationship between Joey and Gage De Luca.

"Gage fucked over the wrong person. One day, Gage, Rosie, and I were hanging out at Gage's place. We were all ambushed. We never had a chance to adequately defend ourselves. We fought like hell, but they ended up taking Rosie. She was payment for what Gage had swindled his business partner out of."

He paused as his hand came up to remove Layne's hand away from his face so she couldn't feel the agitation tugging at his jaw as he internally relived what happened next.

Twenty-four hours was all it took for Rosie's return, and even then, it had been too long. Rosie's suffering lasting more than one millisecond was an unbearable thought. Twenty-four hours after she was taken from the apartment, her body was dumped from an unmarked van in front of a veterinarian's office. It was a cruel parallel to how she was treated—like nothing more than an animal instead of the angel she was.

She was still clinging to life when she was found that morning by the receptionist opening up the office. Barely alive was still enough to give Joey and Gage hope.

Both of them were there at the hospital, one on either side of her as she lay unconscious and attached to all the machines. A tube shoved down that dainty little throat of hers as a means to keep her breathing. The sight had been straight torture.

As Rosie's lifeline grew fainter, the anger brewed hotter between both of the De Luca boys, some of it misplaced and targeted at one another. And when her heart could no longer tie her to this earth? Chaos and Wrath were born amidst her loss.

Joey swallowed down the memory, keeping it safely tucked away. Clearing his throat, he shook away the unsteadiness of his voice. "She died from the injuries she sustained. The doctors said it had been injuries consistent with what you would find in third-world countries where captives are beaten and assaulted within an inch of their lives, but never to the point of death. Merely, an ongoing lifetime of torture at the hands of monsters."

She wrinkled her forehead in sympathy, unable to imagine what the poor girl had gone through. "I'm so sorry." Layne knew those words could never ease the pain, but despite Joey's attempt to keep his emotions detached, even she could see how Rosie's death made a lasting impact on him.

He shook his head. "If Gage had been smarter and stopped to think about his actions, it would have never happened. He knew better, but he continued to be reckless anyway. That part of him will never change, Layne."

"This is all your fault, motherfucker!" Gage shouted back in Joey's face. "You were the one that inserted yourself into Rosie and I's relationship. Then, when push comes to shove, you just let them walk out of there with her!"

One of Joey's hands pushed against Gage's shoulder. "My fault?! You decided to play stupid fuckin' games with the wrong people! I did what I could, but I couldn't help get her back if I was a goddamn corpse! I don't recall your unconscious ass being much help either." The sharpness of his words cut through the air.

Gage half-laughed in disbelief. "I would have died for her. I loved her, and you only wanted to fuck her."

Even ten years later, those wounds still wept.

CHAPTER THREE

Last night had been draining on multiple levels, and this afternoon wasn't shaping up to be much better.

"I think it's better if you're not here." Layne looked at Joey as they both stood there in the office located on the first floor of the home they shared. On the exterior, she may have looked confident and at ease, but internally, her apprehension was coiled tightly with her nerves fraying.

He squeezed her shoulders, seeing straight past the multiple walls she had raised all around her. With a nod, he agreed, not liking it, but she needed to hold her ground on this. "Feel free to pop one in his ass if he gets too far out of line." It's what Joey would like to do to Liam regardless of being given a reason or not.

A smile cracked at the corner of her mouth. Joey grinned, seeing a glimpse of one of the things that made his life worth living—Layne's happiness. His thumb and finger took her by the chin and drew her lips into a drawn-out kiss. It was a brief stint in his own personal heaven.

She could feel herself beginning to lose her control over the tough exterior she had spent all morning building up as his mouth took over hers. Layne had come to terms with the fact that Joey was capable of getting past all her defenses with so much as a damn look. However, today, she couldn't afford to have her vulnerabilities on display like a highway billboard.

As much as she didn't want to end the affectionate moment, she eased her face away from his. "Get the hell out of here before I end up a puddle on the floor."

He smirked at her and whispered in her ear. "I will have you begging to be a puddle later."

Layne's cheeks flushed slightly with heat at the thought, and she smacked her hand against his chest. "Go already!" Her teeth pressed into her bottom lip, trying to suppress her smile.

Joey finally listened to her and left O'Reilly Manor to go take care of some business matters of his own. Word had gotten around that his masked alter ego might have had a hand in disposing of one very disliked mayor who had just stepped down from his position. Contracts were rolling in left and right, providing a steady stream of income.

Liam arrived twenty minutes later. He walked into the office they had been sharing ever since Layne had moved into their father's house after hers was burned down by that dipshit ex-husband of hers, Eric Ellis.

A pair of designer sunglasses remained over his eyes to protect his hungover ass from being blinded by life itself.

He had a coffee in his hand as he looked around at the rather empty space. "Where is everybody?"

Layne sat in the chair behind the desk, the blue envelope from her dad she had discovered months ago in her hands. "I told everyone the meeting was canceled today."

Her brother walked over to the desk, and a brow lifted above the top rim of his shades. "Why are you in my chair?" He set the paper coffee cup down on the desk. "And, you what?" His voice was still hoarse from the drunken binge he had engaged in yesterday at the strip club.

"I told everyone we weren't meeting today." Thanks to more financial stability and a few trusted associates, Layne had managed to get the O'Reilly family's business dealings back on track. There was still a lot of work to be done, but at least they were slowly rebuilding their workforce again.

"Why the fuck did I come down here then?!" He yelled at her and then winced as his escalated volume prompted a harder pulse of his headache.

Ignoring his attitude, "Because you and I need to talk, Liam." She stared at him without giving away how apprehensive she was about this entire encounter. "It was driving me insane that you haven't been able to access our primary account."

He groaned in annoyance about this bullshit being brought up again. "For fucks sake, Layne. I will get to taking care of it when I get to it. I have a bunch of shit on my plate right now."

She shook her head and pulled her phone out, dialing the banking institution's number and placing it on speakerphone so he could hear for himself. After a few prompts, a female representative came on the line.

"Thank you for calling Sandy Island Financials. How may I help you today?"

Layne sat back in the chair and motioned for Liam to go ahead and get this taken care of.

He rolled his eyes and placed his hands on the desk. "Yeah, I can't access my damn account. Something is fucked up on your end of the system; this is the fifth time I've called."

She quietly scoffed and shook her head; it was more like the second time he had called.

The banking rep, who sounded like someone's sweet little grandmother who baked cookies every morning, took Liam's personal information. After several long moments, she responded with an apologetic voice. "I'm sorry, Mr. O'Reilly, but you don't have access to that account."

Liam gave a huff. "Someone over there obviously made a big fuckin' mistake."

Layne leaned forward and interrupted Liam before he went on a tirade, stating how important he thought he was. "I'm sorry, I know you said my brother doesn't have any authority on the account, but could you check to see if I do?"

"Of course, I will just need your name and a few other pieces of information to check." The lady seemed pleased to be dealing with someone who wasn't ready to berate her for doing her job.

After taking all of Layne's information, it didn't take

long for her to check it against the account. Layne's green hues never left Liam's face while they waited.

"Ms. O'Reilly, yes, I see here you are the sole authority listed on the account. Is there a transaction you would like to make today that I can help you with?" Now, wasn't that funny? Liam had zero control over the accounts their father had left behind.

As much as Layne wanted to flash a snarky grin at Liam, she refrained since she was trying to handle this situation with as much grace as humanly possible. "No, that's all. Thank you so much for all your help." Her finger tapped the phone screen to end the call.

Liam's face was riddled with confusion. "What the hell? Why didn't you tell her to put me on the account instead?!" He pushed away from the desk and began to pace as his irritability increased.

Her eyes tracked each step he made, knowing that this was about to go from bad to worse. "Li, it's not just the account."

He paused and looked over at her, his jaw hanging open slightly. "What the fuck do you mean it's not just the account?"

She handed the blue envelope over to him, containing everything he needed to know. It held everything she found out months ago and had opted to keep close to her chest until things settled with the business. Going from being on the verge of collapse to freshly stabilized, Layne hadn't wished to shake up the mix too soon.

Angrily, he yanked it from her hand and pulled the contents from it. His eyes quickly read over page after page. The documents contained their father's final wishes and distribution of assets, including some that were never known to either of his children. It was all dated the day before his passing. Layne had full control of all the O'Reilly enterprises.

As Liam stood there soaking in the information, she was predicting a volcanic eruption. When it never came, it was more frightening than if he had flown off the handle.

He finally tossed the collection of papers onto the desk. "You think these mean anything? Nobody is going to listen to you. You don't even have a damn clue how to run things."

She stood up from her seat, her temper prickling at the length of her spine. Layne's gaze hardened as she stared at his body language. Then, it finally hit her. "You knew, didn't you? You've known this entire damn time?!" Her anger was spreading to her limbs now.

His silence and lack of denial said it all. Rounding the end of the desk, she scowled at him. "You've got to be fucking kidding me, right? You knew, and you didn't say anything?"

He shrugged at her. "I knew you couldn't handle things. You're too busy playing house." His dislike of Joey living there or even existing grated on his nerves.

Not taking the bait on his dig on her personal life, she stuck to the topic at hand. "Dad didn't seem to think so. We were on the brink of utter devastation for months, and you kept telling me to keep out of it! We had one foot in the grave, and you still chose to be a selfish asshole?! Even now, we are just barely coming out of that hole that you put us in!" Each word that exited her mouth grew more heated.

The nagging ache of his head didn't stop him from barking back at her. "All of this belongs to me, it always has!"

"Not anymore, it doesn't. Either you can accept that and help, or you can get out of my way." She was willing to give Liam the chance she never got, but hell if she was going to let him think he was going to continue as the head of this organization.

He gave his answer to the idea of sharing leadership by laying his hands on her. Liam shoved her back hard enough that had the desk not been behind her to brace against, she likely would have landed on her ass on the floor.

Layne charged back at him, returning a shove using every ounce of her body weight behind it. He only budged a couple of steps, but she didn't stop there. She gave him another push and immediately followed with her right hook, colliding precisely on target with the hinge point of his upper jaw. The impact knocked his sunglasses square off his face.

If she hadn't been so pissed off, she would have immediately recognized the pop of pain in her hand. Thank God for adrenaline surges.

Liam's face got rocked by her strike, and it only took him a moment to recover and take a swing right back at her. She dipped down, causing his hand to swipe above her head. When she stood back up, she drove her fist up into his stomach.

He doubled over and heaved. Last night's hefty

overindulgence of booze had left his stomach queasy, and her fist assisted in pushing it over the edge as he coughed and expelled whatever was in his stomach onto the floor.

Layne stepped back from him, shaking her hand as that second hit didn't get the full benefit of adrenaline that the first one had. She clutched onto her trembling fist, which was now feeling the intensity of the injury it had sustained upon that first punch.

Her brother coughed and spit out the last bit of vomit onto the floor. He used the sleeve of his shirt to wipe off his mouth while glaring at her. His breathing was ragged while he spoke through the continued waves of nausea, "You should have just stayed in your own damn lane."

She bent over to look at him, resting her good hand on her knee. "Well, it's my highway now. So, you can get off at the nearest goddamn exit." Straightening up, she walked over to the office door. Layne shook her head, leaving him there to contemplate what he wanted to do. Either he was going to answer to her or could fuck off.

Now, the real work was going to have to happen. There was a new face to the O'Reilly faction, and she was going to take back the respect and power that had been lost since the death of her father.

CHAPTER FOUR

Trying her best not to wince in pain while wiggling her fingers, she inhaled sharply instead. She sat on the edge of the examination table in the makeshift in-home clinic that only those involved in the city's criminal underground knew about.

It looked like the room must have been a sewing room in its past life. The strip of wallpaper bordering the top of the walls had vintage-looking spools of thread and silver needles sprawling across it. The colors were faded maroons and olives, indicative of an era long gone.

Instead of smelling like a typical sterile medical office, it smelled like cranberry and spice, reminiscent of the holiday season. The basket of potpourri probably had a lot to do with that. In a way, it made seeking medical attention a lot less overwhelming. It could even be considered cozy.

Dr. Patricia Kimmel continued her examination of Layne's right hand, which was now swollen and bruised, within hours after using it to strike Liam down.

Layne had been using Dr. Patty, as she preferred to be called, for years, especially when it came to injuries that required a no-questions-asked policy. The last thing that was needed was nosey doctors asking about the frequency of injuries sustained by her or anyone else who did work on her behalf. Layne still wasn't sure how much Dr. Patty knew about the O'Reilly business matters, but the woman never dared to ask.

It was the way that Dr. Patty scrunched up her broad nose in disapproval that made Layne uneasy about the forthcoming diagnosis. After landing an explosive hit to Liam's face, Layne suspected something had gone haywire by the snapping sensation in her hand surrounding her ring and pinky fingers, followed by numbness. That was before the swelling even began.

"How bad is it?" She asked the doc, hoping for news that her worst suspicions wouldn't be confirmed.

Gently setting Layne's hand down, she shook her head, her loosely held bun loosened up even further with the movement. Dr. Patty shoved her square-framed glasses up on top of her head of black hair that showed signs of silvery grey streaks coming in. "It's a boxer's fracture, Layne. You'll need to get this immobilized to start allowing it to heal properly."

Layne groaned in annoyance. Of course, of all faces to break her hand on, it would be Liam's. Not to mention, Joey was going to lose his shit.

"How long before it's all healed up? Three weeks?"

The older woman gave Layne a stern look. "Try two to

three months. Minimum. Especially if you want to regain full use of it."

While the doctor gathered some supplies to wrap up Layne's hand, Layne grimaced at the thought of any part of her not being fully functional for that length of time. She had too much going on professionally not to be physically on top of her game.

Layne hopped off the table after her hand was shored up in a soft black splint with her ring and pinky fingers stabilized together.

"Oh, don't forget to take these as needed for the pain." Dr. Patty handed her over a bottle of painkillers. Layne's mouth went dry as she stared at the bottle that was just freely given to her. Her mind went back to that dark spot she had been in after her father's funeral, where she relied on the numbing effects of prescription medication.

Layne nodded at her briefly. "Thanks." She pocketed the pills into her leather jacket. They felt like they carried the weight of a two-ton bag of bricks. Despite the pain stemming from her fifth metacarpal, she wasn't sure she could bring herself to allow the relief to enter back into her system.

She began to leave when Dr. Patty lightly touched her arm. "Before you go," the look in her eyes shifted into those resembling a concerned mother. "Please, be careful out there. As much as I know you don't like coming here to see me, I also don't want an increase in our visits. There's been something brewing in the air, and I don't like the feel of it." Well, that wasn't ominous at all. For a woman who relied on science, it was out of character for her to tap into unsubstantiated gut feelings.

With a partial smile tugging at her lips, Layne shrugged casually. "You know me, but I will do my best to avoid any more visits for a while."

When she finally left the modest home that housed Dr. Patty's unlicensed medical practice, she pulled out the plastic pill container and looked it over. The temptation was literally in the palm of her hand, staring her down. It whispered such beautiful promises to her like a devil on her shoulder. She squeezed her palm around the cylindrical object and cursed under her breath.

As she passed by a trash receptacle on her way back to her car, she chucked the pills inside. It was going to be a shitty and painful couple of months.

Layne sat in the backroom of McGregor's after texting Joey to meet her there for a quick bite to eat for a late dinner. She hoped that being in a somewhat public setting would help keep his reaction to the turn of events on the milder side. Thanks to her ownership interest in the pub and the seedy nature of its patrons, there was a lot of discretion as to what transpired there.

When she saw Joey walk in, wearing a rugged pair of jeans and a slate gray shirt under his leather jacket, she lost her train of thought of how she was going to explain to him how she ended up with a broken hand. His blonde hair was a bit out of place, which usually was an indication he had just removed his motorcycle helmet.

He laid his eyes on her, immediately noticing the black brace on her hand. His cocoa-colored eyes filled with darkness. Striding over to her, he gently lifted her arm while his muscular body vibrated with the need to inflict violence on her behalf. "What the hell happened?" The tone of his voice indicated he was ready to go break the hand of the motherfucker responsible, or worse.

Attempting to brush it off, she murmured, "It's not that bad." She eased her arm out of his hold, but it only prompted him to look her over for any other potential injuries she may have sustained. His hands roamed over her body only to find nothing else to feed his desire to inflict suffering.

"I'm fine, Joey," she attempted to reassure him again. "It's just a minor fracture from trying to put Liam in his place. It was worth it."

Not seeing any other obvious wounds, he sighed and drew her in with a hand on either side of her head and laid a kiss on her forehead. "How did he take the news?"

She shook her head. "He already knew."

"What?" His voice dropped in disbelief as his hands fell to the tops of her shoulders. "What do you mean he already knew?"

Trying not to get herself all riled up again, she took a deep breath. "He's known. He's known this entire goddamn time that everything was supposed to be under my control."

"Two-faced, selfish motherfucker, I'm going to fuckin' kill him!" Joey stepped back from her and began to pace across the floor. His fingers combed through his long-cut dirty blonde hair as he wracked his brain on all the ways Liam tallied up a long list of shitty deeds.

Layne retrieved her glass of golden ale with her left hand, the engagement ring on her finger lightly tapping against the glass as she did so. Her eyes watched as Joey worked through his thoughts and feelings. Taking a few sips of the beer before setting it back down again, she finally decided to try to get him to settle down.

"Look, he can either get on board or not. The guys I signed on to work the daily operations know who is calling the shots. The few who pretended to respect Liam's authority will go where the money is." And the money was definitely not in her brother's hands. Eric Ellis's inheritance, liquidation of assets, and life insurance payouts were to thank for that.

Out of habit, she went to prop her hand on her hip but hissed as the pressure elicited a sharp burst of pain in her hand despite the brace. She dropped her hand down to her side, trying to control her exhale through the discomfort.

It was the sound of her reaction to the pain that shook Joey from his spiraling thoughts. He paused mid-step and turned himself to head back to where she stood. He looked down at her, his brown eyes holding a soft command to them. "Sit."

His eyes were met with her own delicate green hues. "I don't need to—"

"Shush." His finger trailed across her lips. "Did it sound like I was asking? I will force your ass in that chair if I have to."

A glimmer of mischief reached her eyes as her mouth formed a small smirk while she thought about him making good on his word. It made other parts of her body ache in such delicious ways.

Joey's hands dropped to her hips, firmly grasping them and guiding her back until she was at a chair. His tone dropped to a light rumble. "Layney, sit down."

It wasn't difficult to follow his orders, the way he had spoken them had made her legs weak. Her ass found the seat of the chair, and now her head was tilted up at a greater angle while she stared up at him.

"Good girl." His hand brushed over her cheek before he rewarded her with a gentle yet brief kiss. "Stay here while I get us some food." Before he left, he slid his jacket from the fit shape of his upper body, draping it over the back of his chosen chair. The short sleeves of his shirt allowed all the designs of his tattoos sprawling over his arms to be on display. All the rich shades of red roses stood out against the darker ravens and skulls.

He disappeared for a few minutes to head out to the main area and put in an order for food with John, Sean's backup, when he had the night off. When he returned, she was still where he had left her but nursing her beer as her only option to self-medicate.

"What did you get me?"

Joey grinned and pulled his seat up closer to her. "The same damn thing you always get."

Layne smiled. "Cowboy burger, medium-rare, extra bacon, and barbeque sauce on the side?"

He rolled his eyes as if he didn't have her very specific

order memorized by now before he nodded. "Yeah, and I told them I didn't want to hear you bitch about it being overcooked again."

With her injured hand useless and throbbing with constant pain, she kept it resting on top of her thigh. Joey took notice of how much she was babying it. "What did Dr. Patty give you for the pain?"

She shook her head. "Standard shit that will knock you on your ass for a week. I just tossed it in the trash."

With a sigh, he leaned over and squeezed her thighs reassuringly. "You can't just sit here and suffer. I won't let you go down that dark road again, but there's no reason for you to constantly hurt." Watching Layne being in pain was one of the few things that had him feeling like it was worse than death itself.

"I didn't want to risk it. Besides, with Liam now being on notice that he either is with me or he isn't, there's too much to let my brain get all foggy. Then, there's all the work that's going on with trying to reestablish power in the city." Layne did her best to brush it all off as no big deal. All that she had said may have held some truth behind it, but the biggest factor was her prior history of using painkillers to take care of more than just the physical pain.

Before he could try and convince her otherwise, John came over with two plates of food. Layne's burger and Joey's cluster of buffalo wings. Their conversation paused while he delivered the food to their table before he left again.

She felt Joey's eyes on her still, despite their food having arrived and sitting in front of them. She held half of the messy burger in her left hand while she stared back at him. "What?"

He smiled deviously at her. "Nothing. If you're not going to take anything, I'm just thinking of all the other ways I can make sure you feel good." Joey reached over and slid his hand along her inner thigh. "I want your body aching for far better reasons."

Putting her burger back down on the plate, she gave a playful frown. "You know, now that you say something, it really does hurt. *A lot.*" He was one drug that she didn't ever want to break the habit of.

"Oh? Well, I can't have that. I have just what you need." He rose from his seat and took her uninjured hand, leading her back to the men's bathroom.

Once inside and ensuring there were no other occupants, he locked the door. His hand settled on the small of her back and pulled her back to him, not allowing her to stray too far.

Joey pressed her back up against the door as his face dropped down closer to hers. His eyes were full of lustful thoughts and intentions. His hand wrapped around her throat just under her jaw. "You remember the last time I had you in a bathroom all to myself?"

Layne whimpered at the memory. How could she forget? She had been out on a date before Joey ambushed her on the way to the ladies' room. His hand had brutally brought her to the cusp of an orgasm that had threatened to leave her entirely undone, and then he abandoned her there on that ledge. It had left her in an epic state of frustration.

"Mmhmm," she responded, already breathless just from

having his fingers curled around her neck. It drove heat down into the pooling sensation of desire in her core.

His smirk showed off how much he knew his actions were affecting her. "Good. This time, I'm going to show you just what I really wanted to do to you that night."

A chill of excitement flooded across her body. Her lips parted in speechless awe. Joey took advantage of her open mouth by claiming it with his. Immediately, his tongue dove inside to seek out her own.

He stepped up against her, letting her feel the heat coming off of his body and the way his jeans were failing to conceal his arousal. When she tried to grab onto him, she forgot about the restricted use of her hand. The movement drew a protest from the fresh injury, and her gasp of pain got swallowed up by the kiss they shared.

Joey pulled back, releasing her throat, his hands carefully guided both of hers away from him. "You're going to keep your hands to yourself. I want to show you exactly what you do to me simply by standing here looking so fuckin' beautiful."

Her teeth bit into her lower lip while she grinned. "I can't make any promises."

His hand slid up the back of her neck, getting lost in the tangles of her chestnut waves of hair. Closing his fist around a handful of it, he tugged her head back as his lips dragged up along her throat. Once his mouth was at her ear, his gravelly whisper came forth. "If that's the case, I can't make any promises I will let you come all over my cock like I know you want to."

A delicate little moan came from her at the mere

thought of how badly she wanted him buried deep inside of her. Her hands fought the urge to latch onto him again.

Joey nibbled along her lobe for a second, waiting to see if she was going to adhere to his instructions. When she refrained from putting her hands on him, he smiled and pulled her by her hips until he had her positioned at the counter where all three sinks were lined up.

His hands spun her around so she was facing the large mirror on the wall behind the sinks. Layne met his eyes in the reflection before she felt his hand run up along her spine. It gradually placed pressure on her until she was hinged at the hips and bent over the edge of the counter.

Joey's fingers hooked onto the side of the black leggings she was wearing and rolled them down past her thighs. He squatted down with the motion, the warmth of his breath caressing over the bare skin of her ass before he laid several kisses across it.

The fact that she was still going without panties had his dick twitching excitedly in his pants. It was simply knowing he would have immediate access to her pussy without so much as a damn piece of string that passed for women's underwear these days.

As he laid those kisses across the roundness of her behind, she felt his hands glide up the backs of her thighs. Her knees quivered in response, threatening to give out at any moment.

When he stood up, he slid his hand between her legs, allowing his fingers to stroke along her slit. "You're goddamn soaked, Layney." He gave a broad smile while he single-handedly began to undo his belt and open up his pants.

She pushed her hips against his fingers, craving more. "Joey, stop fucking around. You know I can't take it when you tease."

He pushed two of his fingers into her, Layne's arousal allowing for smooth entry. "Don't lie, Layney. You can take a hell of a lot. I've seen this cunt of yours take anything I've ever given it." Joey's fingers slid in and out of her, drawing out the sweet sound of her moans with each movement.

Layne stayed glued to her place, bent over the counter while his fingers stroked those parts deep within her. When he removed his hand entirely, her moan dissolved into a whimper. Before she could protest, Joey had his cock out of his pants and shoved deep into her pussy in one quick movement.

Her body gripped around his length from the second he entered her. Joey groaned as his dick immediately throbbed as her walls encased him. He grabbed her at the waist and began to fuck her from behind, her ass presented to him like the prettiest little gift of encouragement to keep going. He moaned out, "Mmm, fuck…"

"Yes, God, yes!" Layne let the pleasure quickly take over her body, allowing everything else to fade away from her mind.

Joey continued to slam into her tight cunt, each thrust of his hips becoming more urgent and full of need. "Beg me for my cum, Layney. I need to hear how much you want your pussy filled with it until it's dripping down your damn legs." His voice grew breathless as his desires began to approach the apex of pleasure.

Her body trembled at the sound of his words. Each stroke of his cock deep inside her body, pushing against her sweet spot, had her coming more and more unraveled. With the mirror in front of her, her eyes looked up at his image reflected in it.

"Joey, please, I need your cum deep inside of me. I need to take all of it." Her gaze witnessed his heated expressions, and it had her quickly losing herself. All of Layne's body tensed up as she shook from the violent orgasm that ripped through her as she screamed out.

The moment she spilled over into her climax, Joey gave several more frantic thrusts into her as he breathlessly moaned out at the sensation of her body's warm fluid coming over his rigid cock.

He growled out a curse as he gave one final slam of his hips up against her, driving his length fully into her before his seed erupted. Each spasm of his cock releasing more of his cum until he finally felt the sigh of satisfaction settle deep in his chest.

Layne dropped her head down until she felt the cool counter against her cheek. Still panting after that explosive release, she couldn't even manage to get her words into a coherent sentence. "I… Wow. Everything."

What broken hand? The sea of ecstasy made it feel as good as new.

CHAPTER FIVE

A few mornings later, Layne rolled over in bed, expecting to find a large, warm body next to her. Instead, she was just met with the small mound of the cold white bedding Joey had tossed aside.

She frowned as she opened her eyes and found a small piece of paper left on his pillow.

Have to pick up a package for a client. Be back in an hour to have my breakfast. - Joey

P.S. I'm never late.

Layne grinned in giddy anticipation, damn well knowing that between her thighs was going to be ready for him the second he walked in through the door. He had been finding creative ways and sneaking in every opportunity to distract her body from the pain of her fractured hand.

She slid out of bed, wearing a cropped light blue

camisole with a matching pair of shorts. After taking care of a few things in the bathroom, she left the master suite and went downstairs to find a cup of coffee left on a warmer for her.

It looked like he was doing his best to stay in her good graces, and she wasn't complaining about it. The coffee was only a small gesture in comparison to how he had been trying to help her organize and restructure how she took over the operations of her family's business. The stressors of her new role, plus the added injury to her hand, had been leaving her already short fuse even quicker to blow.

Liam had been radio silent since their blowout, likely licking his wounds and having a pity party for himself between Kristill's legs. After he puked all over her office floor, she had to toss the maid a little extra money to come in on her day off to clean up the mess he had left behind. Layne could handle some bloody violence, but vomit? Hard pass on the sour smell alone.

Before Layne could let the first drop of caffeine hit her lips, the doorbell echoed throughout the house. She set the mug back down on the center island in the kitchen before leaving to answer the door.

When she swung open the front door, an unexpected face greeted her on the other side of it. She blinked a few times at the scruffy-jawed man with eerily similar brown eyes as Joey.

Gage stood there with a broad smile at the sight of Layne answering the door in her pajama set and her long brown locks of hair in wild waves, indicating she had gotten out of bed not too long ago. "Well," he licked his lips as his eyes wandered, "good morning, love."

Layne stared at him in both surprise and confusion as to why he was standing there on her front step. "Gage? What are you doing here?"

His hands were tucked in the front pockets of his dark blue jeans, and a pale green shirt that seemed one size too small for the ripped lines of his upper body. A long chain hung from his neck. At the very end of the chain was a small coin-like charm with the spread wings of an eagle and the letters *SPQR* at its base and a laurel wreath curved around the outer edges.

The short, dark blonde hair on his head was styled casually to appear as though very little effort and thought had been put into it. His smile reflected how at ease he was feeling enough that he attempted to step inside without an invitation.

Having gotten used to the soft brace on her right hand, she immediately put her left hand against his chest to put a halt to his advance into her home. He didn't press onward, but he did look down at her hand and grin. Taking his hands from his pockets, he wrapped one around her fingers and examined the platinum and black rhodium diamond ring on her slender finger.

"My brother give this to you?" He lifted a far too curious brow.

She ignored his question. It was none of his damn business. "You haven't told me why you're here. How did you even know where I live?"

Finally releasing her hand, he raised a finger to her

while a hand slid into his back pocket. When he pulled it back out again, he held her credit card between his middle and pointer fingers. "You dropped this the other night at the club. A few online searches, a few questions asked of chatty ex-neighbors, and here I am."

Despite that, he was now smiling oh-so-proudly, Layne plucked her credit card from his hold and kept her eyes full of suspicion. "Thanks."

Gage leaned over to attempt to catch a glimpse of what lay just past the front door of her home. "Nice lookin' spot. Looks like Joey traded up."

She stepped to the side to try and block his view of the interior of her home. Though, it was a moot point given how he easily saw right over the top of her head, given his towering height that matched Joey's. "Why are you still here?"

He chuckled and raised both hands in front of him innocently. "Settle down, sweetheart, I'm just being friendly."

"The fuck you are." She leaned over and slapped her credit card down on the thin side table to the left of the door before she crossed her arms in front of her chest.

Amusement sparked in his eyes as he leaned one forearm against the doorframe. His eyes noticed the way her arms pushed her breasts together in that cute little camisole she had on. "Oh, there's a bit of a brat in you. Now, I get it." It seemed his brother's taste in women hadn't changed much.

"Get what?" Her patience was quickly running out as she released a sigh of frustration. "I swear to God, is there a gene in your family that causes you to be irritatingly arrogant and cocky?"

He laughed in response to her observation. The way he did so had a deep and rich tone to it that seeped in past her barriers. It made something inside of her flutter with excitement. Layne quickly tried to pitch those feelings to the side and focus on how he had interrupted her morning coffee.

His charming smile didn't leave his face as he rubbed his hand over his jaw in thought. The sunlight glinted off of a few silver rings decorating his fingers and also highlighted the inked letters 'WRATH' just above his knuckles on the back of his hand.

The way he was now staring at her while he did it was getting her even more flustered. Layne shook her head. "Alright, congrats, you've found me and returned my card. Either move along, or I will—"

Gage shoved his way inside, firm hands catching her off guard when they grabbed just below her shoulders and moved her to the side. "Hey!" She squawked. His foot kicked the door shut behind him.

After his hands released her, he began to wander deeper into the house. His head nodded to himself as if he was impressed with what he was seeing. He stopped right outside the dining room, which was currently a mess with plastic liners, buckets of paint, ladders, and various other tools. The memory of Mick's death there needed to be erased along with the outdated decor.

Gage motioned at all the hardware. "Doing some renovations? You know, I'm pretty good with my hands, or so I'm told." He smirked at her.

Layne strode after him, her bare feet padding quietly against the tiled floor of the main hall. Fuck the pain in her right hand; she shoved his shoulder with it to turn him partially to face her as her left hook came at that smug face of his. If he wanted to invade her home, he was going to get an unwanted visitor's welcome.

He gave a brief look of surprise as he pulled his face back before she could make contact. Gage's grip wrapped around her left forearm, twisting her around until he had her back pulled up against the front of him with her left arm twisted behind her back. The strength of his other arm wrapped across her and squeezed tightly.

"Take it easy, killer." He chuckled.

Layne wriggled in his hold. "You have no idea." She wouldn't mind adding him to her body count at that moment, even if he did smell like an intoxicating combination of spices and soothing vanilla.

Gage leaned over and gave her a quick peck to her cheek before letting go of her, nudging her forward away from him. "So, where is Joey? I was hoping to catch up, make amends and all that shit, then maybe even bring him into a business deal I'm working on."

She took a few steps forward when he released her, then spun around to glare at him. "What makes you think I know where he is?"

He waved off her question. "You're going to play that angle? My brother doesn't start getting hot and throwing punches over a one-nighter. Though, I am surprised he was willing to get on one knee." He shrugged at the thought of Joey popping the question to any woman. Maybe the woman standing in front of him was that great of a lay. He wouldn't mind taking a tour of everything she had to offer to see what had Joey getting all possessive over.

"He's not here." As if on cue, the front door creaked open. Joey stumbled in, his hand clutching onto his side. A large patch of red soaked into the white fibers of his shirt, and his blood covered the hand he was using to apply pressure to the area.

Layne looked over her shoulder at the sound of the door opening. When she saw him trudge in with a grimace on his face, her face fell, and her heart sank right along with it.

"Shit," she uttered as she ran over to him. Her hand grabbed onto his arm, though she wasn't sure what good it was going to do if he fell. His weight was easily twice her own and would take her right down with him, and hard. "What the hell happened?!"

Joey groaned as he looked up at her, trying to brush it all off. "Son of a bitch brought a cracked-out friend thinking he was getting out of handing over the package…" His eyes caught sight of Gage standing off to the side.

His pain turned to anger with the flip of a switch. "What the fuck is he doing here?!" He tried to straighten up but immediately doubled back over again as pain shot through his body. Layne stumbled under the weight as her arm tried to at least keep him upright.

She shook her head. "Don't worry about him right now. I'll shoot him on your behalf if I have to. Let's get you in a chair."

Gage snorted. "Hopefully, your aim is better than your swing." Then, seeing the struggle between the both of them, Gage took pity and approached. "Move," he commanded as he encroached on Layne's space at Joey's side.

It only took a brief moment for Layne to assess that Gage didn't have any malicious intent in his eyes before she allowed him to take her spot. He took up Joey's non-injured side, wrapping Joey's arm around the back of his shoulders to help take the burden of the weight.

Layne left to grab a chair out of the dining room, returning to meet Gage and Joey halfway across the foyer. She set the chair down in front of Joey. "Here. I will go get supplies." Moving quickly, she disappeared to gather any first aid supplies they might need.

Gage eased Joey into the chair. Immediately, Joey let out a sigh and leaned back. With Joey's jaw set in a hard line from both the searing pain in his side and his anger, he leered at his younger brother. "What the fuck is wrong with your hearing? Have you gone deaf in the last ten years and didn't hear me when I told you to stay the fuck away?"

Squatting down, Gage began to peel back the shirt to try and see how bad the damage was underneath. When Joey didn't move his hand to allow him to take a look, Gage sighed. "I heard you, but you think I give a shit? At least let me check this out and see how much of a pussy you're being right now." He had seen his fair share of wounds from fights breaking out in the various establishments where he worked as head of security over the years.

"Fuck you." Joey relented and eased his hand away to allow Gage to further lift the bottom of his shirt up to expose the injury.

Despite all the blood surrounding the area, making it difficult to determine the full extent of the damage, it was obvious that the slash was the deepest, right above the waist of his black pants on his side.

Layne returned, a bin of various medical supplies in her hands. She knelt at Joey's side to see the laceration for herself. Her emerald hues looked up at Joey, silently saying everything she was thinking. His stubborn ass should have called. He should have been more careful. The last thing she wanted was to lose him.

She pulled out disinfectant, but Gage plucked it out of her hands. "No offense, but I think someone who has full use of both hands automatically makes me more qualified." He motioned to the black brace on her right hand.

Joey grumbled but didn't protest, allowing Gage to proceed.

Almost an hour later, Gage removed his gloves after applying a bandage to the freshly stitched wound. During the course of the hour, Layne had tried to break the awkward tension between the two of them every so often by asking Joey questions but only received one or two-word responses.

"All set." Gage stood and offered a hand to help Joey up out of the chair. It was either hard-headedness or pride, but Joey pushed through the pain, still very much present, and stood from his chair on his own accord.

Layne gently hugged Joey's uninjured side as she looked up at him. "Why don't you go upstairs and get some rest?" Seeing the distrust painted over his face of leaving her alone with Gage, she rolled her eyes. She reached up and grabbed his face to turn and look at her. "I can handle getting him out the door."

As a means of reassuring him and maybe even sending a message to Gage as well, she stood on her tiptoes and brought her lips to Joey's. Kissing him long and slow, she allowed the taste of him to linger in her mouth. Once she felt some of the tension in his body fade, she pulled back with a sweet smile, promising more to come.

After Joey was upstairs, Layne turned and looked at Gage as the sweetness of her smile shifted into a conflicted look between gratitude and sheer irritation he was still lingering. "Thank you for helping."

Gage grinned, finishing her unspoken thoughts, "But, get the fuck out?"

She tried to hide the smile pulling at the corners of her mouth, but she wasn't quick enough, and he caught sight of it. He already knew from that glimpse that he wanted to see just how big of a smile he could get out of her in the future.

Layne walked him over to the door. He turned after stepping foot onto the front step to look at her. "I still need to talk to him about a few things."

Scoffing at the thought of Joey willing to entertain the notion of having another talk with Gage, she shook her head. "Good luck with that."

Trying to re-engage his charm and smooth-talking, his eyes looked into hers. "Well, that's what you are - luck. I'm sure you can find a way to convince him to come down to Cassidy's and have a chat. What do you say, lucky charm?"

"Why would I do that for you, of all people? After everything that's happened between the two of you." She didn't make any effort to diminish the skepticism in her tone.

He tilted his head slightly with a curious note in his words. "And, just what did he tell you happened?"

She crossed her arms in front of her chest and gave a small shrug. "Everything I needed to know."

"I very much doubt that, but my offer applies to you as well. If you ever want to know what you're in for, come see me." He gave her a harmless smile.

"Bye, Gage." She shut the door in his face.

Layne turned and looked at the main staircase that led upstairs. A small voice in the back of her head wondered what else there was behind the animosity between the two De Luca brothers.

CHAPTER SIX

Finally, after several weeks of pain and torture for them both, Layne's hand was free of that godforsaken brace. In her opinion, it had wreaked enough havoc and inconvenience for a lifetime. While her hand wasn't fully healed yet, per Dr. Patty, she at least had full functionality of it again. She just had to promise she wouldn't go around punching anyone else until it was completely healed. It was a tough sell, but she agreed she'd do her best.

Joey's knife wound was healing up nicely. As much as neither of them wanted to admit it, Gage had done a good job stitching up the laceration. As a precaution, Dr. Patty also provided some antibiotics. Nobody wanted to drop dead from an avoidable infection; this wasn't the Middle Ages.

The forced downtime allowed her to continue laying out strategy and resilience plans for the O'Reilly organization. She had a newfound appreciation for all that her father had been in charge of. Having not been raised to take on this role, she felt lost more often than not, but no less determined to reestablish the respect her last name used to demand.

Layne found herself in the office standing before the most senior associates who worked for the O'Reilly faction - who now worked for her. She had been meeting with all of them in smaller groups, but now she had all of them in the same room with her to make sure her message could be heard loud and clear. She wanted to be able to stare at all their faces to make sure nobody was missing the memo. From here on out, it was Layne in charge of how things operated. Nothing was to be done without her being made aware of it. The way things operated under Liam's piss-poor leadership would no longer be the standard.

Bringing all her boss bitch energy, she looked at the faces of the group of men with eyes on her. All of them came from various backgrounds but had one thing in common: criminal intelligence. Could she have hired every thug looking to make a quick buck to beef up her work-force? Sure. But she didn't want just anyone executing her vision for this organization; she wanted people who knew what the fuck they were doing.

"With all that said, anybody who disagrees can see themselves out that door right now. I am not going to tolerate disloyalty, inadequacy, or excuses. If you can't or won't put everything on the line to honor all this enterprise stands for, then get the fuck out. My dad set forth stringent expectations for all those who reported to him. You can expect that those standards have now been raised when you report to me." It wasn't going to be easy taking back power across the city, even more so knowing that all the other factions would consider her an emotionally weak female undeserving of respect.

The fierce green of her eyes shifted as she scanned each of the men there in the room with her, looking each one in the eyes while assessing their body language to determine how reliable and trustworthy they might be in the long run. The only person missing was her brother. The invitation for him to take a spot reporting to her had gone without a response. It seemed someone was still feeling a bit butthurt that he might have to take orders from Layne for once.

When no one made a move to leave the room, she nodded and leaned back against the edge of her desk. Her arms crossed in front of her stomach as she got comfortable. Layne began to dish out instructions to have her crew make the first moves under her reign.

First up was Jonathan, the most diplomatic of the bunch. He had worked in politics, covering up scandals and making illegal deals behind closed doors for years. He wasn't much of a fighter, but he could talk a deaf man into listening. "Jonathan, you go rub elbows with the other faction heads and try to smooth things over with the change in leadership. Make it clear that what was flying the past few months is no longer the case. Anyone who has a problem with that can take it up with me directly, and I will be more than happy to paint them a very clear picture of what I won't be tolerating."

Next was Ethan. He had nearly as much of a temper as

she did but a far more intimidating stature. The man was built like one of the NFL's top defensemen. He had started his career out as a professional bodybuilder competing in fitness competitions until he branched out into shakedowns for whoever gave him the largest commission. "Ethan, you take your guys and begin cracking down on overdue payments. I don't want there to be a single penny still owed to us."

Finally, one of her favorite hires was Sammy. He was a perfect blend of both Jonathan and Ethan. A smooth talker, but the man could get damn scrappy in a fight. Either he was brawling his way out of shit situations or using his words to manipulate others. "Sam, please see to it that Diego is relieved of his duties at the Brass Mirror. I can't be having someone operating that site who can be easily bribed by someone like Eric Ellis." May the bastard be rotting in hell. "I need someone with a backbone running that operation."

One of the others, Thomas, stood from his seat. He was well into his fifties and had seen some shit during his time served in this industry. She had determined anyone with that level of wisdom would be an asset as an advisor and mentor to the others. "Layne," his tone full of caution, "this isn't going to be a smooth transition given how weak the O'Reilly reputation has been."

She nodded. "I'm aware. That's why I'm doubling down on everything. If anyone thinks they're going to find themselves getting second chances, you can make it clear in no uncertain terms that I have a one-strike policy. Don't pay? I will take what you owe and more in any way I see fit. Ignore the boundaries of the O'Reilly territory? You will be struck down without hesitation. I'm not here to play games." Lord knew that she couldn't afford to fuck around.

Skeptically, Jonathan looked at her. "That goes against all the rules of engagement we have with the other factions, politically speaking."

Layne gave a harsh laugh that rattled the atmosphere. "You mean it goes against the unwritten and outdated rules? What good were those rules when I was being shot at when this business was circling the drain? Fuck their rules. I'm making my own now."

She shook her head in irritation, recalling all the struggles over the past year when she should have had all of this under her control and not under Liam's inept ass.

"Anything else?" She glanced around the room, waiting for anyone to speak up. When she was met with heads shaking and a lack of affirmative responses, she waved them all off. "I want reports coming back on everything; I don't care what time of day it is. If it can't be spoken over the phone, you better be knocking on the door."

Her hand waved off the men that she had hand-selected to be the foundation of building a stronger O'Reilly empire than had ever existed before. Money may have gotten them in the door, but now she would see just how much money talked when it came to them taking action on her behalf.

The men filed out of the room gradually, some chatting amongst themselves about more mundane things like sports and financial markets. Finally, it was just Layne left there in the office, and she felt like she could drop the façade of being a confident and fearless leader.

She stepped away from her desk, walked over to the window, and peered outside at the traffic coming and going down the street. Her brain felt fried, and her lack of personal engagement on the front lines of the business had left her feeling useless. Getting lost in her thoughts, she hadn't even noticed a presence coming into the office.

The strength of Joey's arms wrapped around her waist from behind. It was at Layne's behest that Joey not be part of her meetings with her leads. This business was already too male-oriented; if he were to participate, they would be too quick to look to him and ignore the little lady in the room. She needed to build the foundation first that she wasn't just a pretty face pretending to be the head of a criminal syndicate.

Layne leaned back into him and allowed a sigh to escape. "I was never prepared for this. Liam always got the insight on how to run things."

"Look what good that did him. He had his chance." He didn't hide how unimpressed he was with her brother on both business and personal levels.

She was on the same train of thought. "That's because he's a fucking idiot."

Turning her around by her hips, Joey looked down at her with a grin. His hand cupped her chin. "And that is what will set you apart from how he handled things." He lowered his mouth onto hers, coaxing her into a more at-ease state.

When their kiss broke, he smiled at her lightly. "There is another matter of business we need to discuss, Layne."

She furrowed her brows together, wondering what other details needed to be ironed out that she must have overlooked.

"You're not just running side jobs for Liam or your dad anymore. You're running the whole damn show." He set his jaw in a hard line as he thought about the harsh reality he was going have to admit to out loud. "That puts a massive target on your back. As much as it pisses me off to say it, even I have my limitations on what I can do to keep you protected. We need to consider seeking out someone who can professionally see to it that you're safe when I'm not around."

Her face fell at the thought of anyone other than Joey hovering over her every move. "And you're going to trust another human being to do that?"

Now, it was Joey's turn to frown. "I didn't say it was going to be easy finding someone, but it has to happen. I will check around and see if anyone is worth talking to about the job."

Not being on board with this idea, Layne shook her head. "I have always been able to take care of myself. I'm not going to just trust some stranger breathing down my neck and hope that they have my back when it matters most."

To prove a point, Joey knocked her feet out from underneath her while pushing her back. Instead of letting her back hit the floor, he caught her with his other arm. With his spare hand, he pointed his index and middle fingers at her forehead. "Bang."

She tried to mask the surprise on her face as she stared up at him, but her slightly wide eyes gave it away. Her hand pushed his fingers away that were aggressively pointed at her. "Are you planning on taking me out yourself? Playing the long game and finally finishing the job for Franzetti?" Layne narrowed her eyes at him.

He pulled her back upright onto her feet. "No, but it's people like me that I'm worried about, Layne. Do you think they're going to give a shit about where you are or who you're with? You'd be lucky if all they do is fire a single round into you. I wouldn't be able to live with myself knowing I had the chance to put safety measures in place to prevent it."

The stubborn side of her wanted to fight him on this and tell him he was wrong. She pressed her lips together, ready to push back on the issue, but her phone began to ring in her pocket, disrupting her from debating with him. "This conversation isn't over yet."

She stepped away from him as she pulled out her phone and answered it. "Yes?" Layne stopped mid-step as the caller spoke in her ear. "What?" She was pretty sure she had to have heard the person on the other end of the line incorrectly. "Oh, for fucks sake. I will be right there. No, don't do a damn thing."

Layne pressed the red button on the screen to end the call. Returning her phone to her pocket, she balled her hands up into fists and pressed them to her forehead as she shut her eyes tightly. She wanted to scream at the top of her lungs in frustration. Instead, she muttered, "I'm going to kill him."

After approaching her, Joey lightly tugged on her wrists to pull her hands away from her face. "What is it?"

She opened her eyes and shook her head in disbelief. "Liam got his stupid ass arrested."

CHAPTER SEVEN

For the sake of avoiding any unnecessary entanglements with Joey accompanying her to the police station, she left him behind while she handled this on her own. With Joey's criminal record and history with the department, the last thing she needed was for them to receive any unwanted attention or harassment.

As for Layne, the only charge formally tied to her record was an old misdemeanor of public lewdness after a night of drunken debauchery on her twenty-first birthday. It resulted in a slap on the wrist and a wink in her father's direction.

When she arrived at the 1st Precinct of the NYPD, there was a lot of foot traffic outside the primary entrance. A podium was set up, and surrounding it were several officers in their blues, various media outlets with cameras and recorders, and what could only be assumed to be assistants, civilians, and other interested parties.

A woman with short, ashy blonde hair that was a little

too long to be considered a pixie cut was standing at the podium. From the appearance of her dress blues decorated with extra stars and service stripes, it was the Chief of Department of the NYPD.

The woman's voice carried a warm yet commanding tone. "Spearheading this new initiative, it is my honor to introduce you to New York's newly appointed Police Commissioner, Vincent Saito."

There was a round of applause from the surrounding crowd as a man in his late forties approached the podium in a navy suit paired with an unoriginal white collared shirt underneath. His shiny black hair was just long enough to comb over to an off-center part. From the slight slant of his eyes and his skin tone, it appeared that he had a mix of both Asian and Caucasian heritages.

Everything about him was clean-cut and nearly too squeaky clean to be any sort of appointed official. This guy looked like he spent weekends coaching his kid's soccer team, feeding the homeless, and honing his golf skills on a country club green.

He shook hands with the Chief and gave a sparkling smile to the people, and if there had been a baby present, he probably would have kissed it, too.

Stepping up onto the curb towards the back of the crowd, Layne paused and began to watch whatever bullshit this guy was about to spoon-feed everyone.

Commissioner Saito repositioned the microphone in front of him before resting his hands on the edges of the podium. "Thank you, Chief Graham. It is with great pleasure that I would like to announce this city's greatest step towards cracking down on organized crime. With increased funding from an anonymous donor and partnership with the Federal Bureau of Investigation, I am proud to announce the Unwind and Un-organize Initiative."

Layne raised a brow as she crossed her arms in front of her, her interest piqued. Every new commissioner that was appointed always rolled in with vows to do things differently. Each one of them ultimately just made a show out of their empty promises.

She listened intently to the man speaking to the masses about how he was going to crack down on organized crime in Manhattan. It was mostly the same shit she had heard before from law enforcement: more training, zero tolerance, and supposed accountability.

After the rundown of specifics on this new plan that was going to be implemented across the city over the next twelve months, Commissioner Saito began to take questions from overeager journalists.

One woman raised her hand high, trying to capture the attention to be called on. When the Commissioner pointed at her, she gave a hopeful look and an excited smile. "Commissioner, as we all know, there is a concern about officers being swayed to look the other way and investigations being swept under the rug. Criminal behavior doesn't just stop at the front door of the NYPD. How are you proposing to put an end to that?"

To his credit, the new guy on the block took a moment to look thoughtful before selecting a response from a likely preplanned list of answers. "We hold all our officers and detectives to a high standard of integrity. If there is any reason to believe that integrity has been compromised, I will personally ensure that those involved will be harshly reprimanded." Yup, same old bullshit.

It would take time for any of this to get past all the red tape and bureaucracy, but Layne added the mental note to keep an eye out for any potential headaches this could all bring. It wasn't just a worry for her but for all the rampant and corrupt underground criminal factions.

Deciding she had enough of listening to all the political grandstanding, she walked around the sea of people until she squeezed by enough to get into the main entrance of the precinct.

Once inside, she went through the mundane and drawn-out process of trying to get information from the clerk sitting at the front desk. After having to repeat Liam's name nearly three times, present her identification twice, and be given the stink eye, she was finally escorted back to the holding area.

Despite Layne having triple-checked, she had removed anything that could be construed as a weapon from her body before arriving, a small pang of paranoia nagged at her after she went through the metal detector. Fortunately, the machine remained silent, and the officer guided her to a cell that held several men, one of whom was her disheveled-looking brother.

From the state of his hair, he must have been tugging at it and leaving it sticking out in every direction. He was in a pair of jeans and a loose-fitted tee, all of which had seen better days. Clearly displayed across his face was the stress of his situation.

"You have five minutes," the officer warned her, but when she looked at the man's hands, he subtly flashed his five fingers twice, indicating she had ten minutes. Corrupt cops were one of her favorite assets during times like these. Layne nodded in acknowledgment before stepping up to the bars, keeping Liam from being a free man.

The second he saw her, he stood up from the small bench and quickly approached. His hands each wrapped around a bar as he looked relieved to see her. "Layne, finally, you made it."

She stared at him, and while her face may have appeared emotionless, she was anything but. Layne wanted to tear him a new asshole for the stupidity of getting himself locked up.

Beginning to pitch his story, he blurted out the start of his excuse. "This is all a big fuckin' mistake."

Layne shook her head in disappointment. "Shut up, Liam. I don't want to hear another word from you until I'm done saying what I came down here to say."

Liam's hands tightened up on the bars in front of him while his lips were tightly pressed together in a strained effort to keep his words to himself.

"You know what some of the charges they have pending against you are? Assault of a police officer, driving under the influence, possession of a deadly weapon, resisting arrest. Oh, and the real cherry on fucking top? Bribery. Were you just trying to see what they could throw at you?" The second he opened his mouth, she lifted a finger to indicate she wasn't done speaking yet.

"Since you're unlikely to get out of here on a Desk

Appearance Ticket, let me put this clearly for you so there is no mistaking what I will and won't be doing. I will not be posting bail for you. You can go to your arraignment and pray that the judge forgot his anti-senile pills that day. I will make sure that you don't have the dumbest fucking attorney show up to represent you." She stared at him without any hint of jest in her expression.

He gave a shake of the bars in his grasp before hitting one with the side of his fist. "Fuck you, Layne! You know damn well that Dad would have already gotten me the hell out of here."

Her eyes widened in disbelief before she scoffed. "Oh, really? What good would that do you, hm? You'd just turn around and do it all over again. Dad *knew* he fucked up with you. That's why things are the way they are right now, with me once again cleaning up your fuck ups. Only this time, you're not getting back the chance to sabotage it all again." Sometimes, the best truth was the harsh truth.

The anger in his voice rose as he glared at her from within his cage. "You need to bail me out! It's my damn money, too." He clenched his teeth so hard she hoped his face got stuck like that, or he cracked a tooth, preferably both.

Remaining the calmest she felt in years in dealing with her brother's bullshit; she shook her head again at him. "No, it's not. You spent every last dime on pieces of ass and who knows what else. We nearly lost everything! *Everything*, Liam. As far as I'm concerned, you don't have a penny to your name until I say you have earned it. If this is the lesson you need to learn to get your ass to that point, so be it."

Her feet brought her a step back from the cell, maintaining eye contact with Liam as he seethed at her with a deep-seated sense of loathing and hatred at that moment. She didn't care if he never spoke to her again after this, she was tired of his messes and inability to take responsibility for himself.

"I will let Walt Elkins know you will need representation at your hearing. It's the best you're going to get from me." Walt was the latest addition to Layne's growing team of assets. He was an expensive lawyer to keep on retainer, but his track record was noteworthy. Enough so that she felt confident that Liam wouldn't get raked over the coals, even if he did deserve it.

She let out a tired sigh. "When you do get out, come find me. If you want any part of this business, this bullshit has to stop."

Layne turned on her heel and walked back down towards the end of the hall, where an officer opened up a door that led out of the holding area. The echoes of her brother's voice reverberated off the walls and into her ears.

Liam yanked on the unyielding bars again, this time with explosive frustration. "Bitch! I hope you fucking get eaten alive out there! You won't make it a month in this business without me! The others will never give you any more respect than they would a damn whore!"

When he noticed that his outburst wasn't capturing Layne's attention, he unleashed a raw yell. "Fine! Go! Go fuck that freak, but he's only with you for the money and power! He will be nothing but a goddamn cum stain on our name, just wait and see!"

She paused at the doorway, her back to Liam as he hurled those last vile words. Layne gave a hard swallow, trying her best to deflect the pain of the verbal attacks. One would have thought she had learned to ignore her brother's wielding of words as weapons by now.

In a perfect world, she had always hoped that with enough time, maturity, and healing, he would find his way to being a better person. She didn't expect anyone who worked in the realm of underground violence and crime to be a saint, but she did expect more from someone she shared a bloodline with. Maybe it was a lot to hope for, but a small piece of her had tried to hold onto that optimism for as long as she could.

With every bit of self-control she had left, she locked her jaw shut to prevent spewing forth her thoughts, which were not meant for public ears. Especially not when she found herself in the middle of a police station.

She glanced over at the officer waiting for her to leave through the open door. Steadying her voice to hide how shaken she felt inside, she nodded at the man, "Thanks."

Layne left the holding area, left her brother, and had to tell herself that this all would pay off in the long run. A girl could dream, right?

CHAPTER EIGHT

er boot-clad foot slammed into the stomach of the poor sap lying on the cement floor in front of her. "Then, he says I'm not going to make it a *month*!" It wasn't clear if she was recounting the visit with Liam to the victim on the receiving end of her brutal kicks or to the watchful man at her back.

She huffed as she felt suffocated by the black mask stretched over her face. The heat of her breath trapped behind the fabric created a sheen of sweat across her face. Layne couldn't imagine how Joey made a habit of wearing his for long periods of time. The rest of her donned all dark clothing from the slim-fitted pants with enough stretch to allow for movement and a black tee underneath a jacket.

Ever since she started making moves to lead the O'Reilly organization, Joey had insisted she take some precautions to protect her identity. It wasn't the big baddies that worried him, but also the saints of the world looking to help the so-called good guys. Honestly, she just figured Joey got turned on seeing her wear it.

As a result, she had been doing her best to remember her similarly styled skull mask that covered the lower half of her face from the bridge of her nose down over her chin. The white toothy smirk of the skull had crisscrossed ribbons in orange and emerald colors to honor her Irish descent.

Layne brushed a strand of her dark chestnut hair away from her face, attempting to incorporate it back into her ponytail as she exhaled an aggravated sigh.

The man in front of her was sniveling as he rolled back and forth with his arms wrapped around his stomach. "I swear, I don't know nothing about no deals between Russ and Italo," he cried out pathetically.

This worthless low-life was supposed to have information on Russell Spencer, the same jackass that had worked with one dead Andrew Correlli and thought the O'Reilly legacy should be defunct by now.

Word on the street was that Russ had been working with a mid-grade crony, Italo Giorgi, to assemble a meeting of the minds of various criminal units across the city. Layne hadn't been extended an invitation, and she doubted it was an oversight. She was pretty damn certain that Russ was still hung up on their last discussion where she promised he would make the top of her shitlist if he crossed her again. The difference now was that she was the one in charge of O'Reilly Enterprises, and he had to answer to her, not to her jackass brother.

She had come here to personally extract some information from this piece of shit after one of her more reliable resources had suggested he was potentially useful. So far, she hadn't gotten anything from him except vague non-answers. "That's not what I fucking heard." Her temper was already at full flare before this idiot made the decision to lie to her.

Behind her, also bearing witness to Layne's attempt at relieving some stress while demanding answers, was Joey. His face was concealed by the very mask he had worn when he had first encountered Layne after Franzetti's goons had abducted her and brought her down to the docks.

He leaned back against the exposed steel beam of the third floor of the warehouse, which was currently under construction. The bulk of his muscled arms crossed in front of his chest as he stayed out of her warpath. From head to toe, all six-foot-two of him was dressed in black. The collage of tattoos on his arms were covered by the long-sleeved black shirt, and his broad thighs were in a pair of cargo pants with a utility belt around the waist.

At the root of his reasoning for being there were mostly good intentions in ensuring her safety now that she was leading the charge at the top of the O'Reilly ranks. The less honorable side of him just wanted to get his dick hard by watching her sport that dark mask and bring a grown man down to his knees. It did something primal to him, knowing that lesser men bowed before her and begged. Yet, he was the only man capable of getting her to drop to her knees before him. Call it ego, alpha male bullshit, or whatever else you'd like, but he got off on all of it.

He spoke up, "Look, man, this isn't looking good for

you. I'd just tell her what she wants to know." Joey was hoping it would help the man have a moment to see the light to the path of his salvation.

Layne squatted down and pulled her Glock from the back of her pants, yanking on the slide to make it clear it was hot with a round in the chamber. The man stared at her with wide eyes that let you know he was one hiccup away from shitting his pants.

While trying to maintain an even tone, she stared right back at him. "We've been at this for over an hour. You need to give me something to work with here. A name, a place, some chick that overheard something in the middle of a blowjob. Help me out."

The man perked up a little bit and nodded his head quickly. "Oh! I know someone who might know something."

She rolled her eyes, hoping this wasn't going to be another trail to another dead end. "And…?" Layne urged him to continue as she gave a slight wave of her gun for him to continue speaking.

"Italo has a girl. She works at this fancy nudie bar. Um… uh… Katie's, n-no, Cassidy's Cave! That's it! He gets a private room with her every Thursday night. Does a lot of his meetings there, too." He nodded in excitement with his eyes full of such hope that he had given Layne something to go on.

Layne glanced back over her shoulder at Joey at the mention of Gage's strip club. It's not where either of them wanted this trail to lead to. Looking back at the quivering rat of a man on the ground, she pushed her hands against her knees as she stood back up. "Was that so hard? Thank you."

The man breathed out in relief. A false sense of security claimed him as he relaxed back against the floor.

Without warning, Layne fired a single shot that found a home directly in the man's temple. He had never seen it coming. At least he had died without fear, that was more than some people got.

She went through the motions of ensuring her firearm was safely tucked away again. Her right hand curled into a fist and stretched back out several times as the kickback from the shot drew an ache in protest. The freshly healed fracture still did not leave her without its occasional reminders.

Joey didn't even flinch at the sound of the gunshot echoing inside the room full of exposed beams, stacks of sheetrock, and scaffolding. He came up to her, easing her gaze away from the body on the floor. "Look at me, Layney."

Even with his fingers guiding her by her chin to look away at the price this man just paid so she could have her information, her eyes struggled to tear themselves off the morbid sight.

"*Layne.*" This time, the demanding depth of Joey's voice asserted itself more forcefully to draw her attention. Her eyes finally looked up at him. The hypnotizing darkness of his chocolate hues drew her back from what was going on inside of her head.

The violent edge her voice had possessed over the past

hour had eased down into something softer and more delicate. "I couldn't risk him tipping anyone off."

He tugged down his mask now that it was just the two of them there. "I know. I would have done the same thing." Joey's fingertips traced along the trail of ribbon across the front of her mask until he found the edge and eased it away from her face.

She became more aware of her breathing as her body recognized the tender trace of his touch. "Joey, now isn't the time…" her voice apologetic, ready to wave off whatever advances he was about to make.

He leaned down, and his hands grabbed her right underneath her ass and lifted. His cock was already straining to be free from the confines of his pants. Getting her back up against the beam he had been leaning on earlier, he had her legs naturally spread for him to press himself up against her center.

His fingers roughly dug into the backs of her thighs. "The hell it's not. I want nothing more right now than to fuck you after watching that."

Layne's hands grabbed onto the top of his wide shoulders, feeling the muscles rippling underneath as he supported her weight. She groaned as his hardened bulge pressed against her core.

After she wrapped her legs around his waist, linking her ankles together, his hands glided up her sides, rough palms sliding up underneath her shirt against the smoothness of her bare stomach.

With a lustful blaze in his look at her, his hands stopped just short of the bottom of her satin bra. "Go ahead and tell me." His husky tone bore the weight of a dare in it.

Her body not only felt like his hands were lighting her on fire but incapacitating her. Layne's emerald eyes looked right back into the depths of his. She was hardly able to swallow down her own saliva that was pooling in her mouth at the thought of what was positioned at the apex of her thighs.

"Tell you what, Joey?" She asked, genuinely wondering what he wanted from her besides a good hard fuck.

He inched his mouth closer to hers, leaving just enough room for a single breath. "I want to hear you tell me you're going to stop being my good girl and taking my cock any time I want to give it to you." Joey's hips rolled up against her to make it unquestionably clear what he planned to give her, whether it was the time for it or not.

If any words were spoken in the universe that could have caused her self-control to self-combust, he had just spoken them. Her heart rate was picking up speed, and the dead body on the floor no longer registered in her awareness.

With a sharp inhale at the push of his body, reminding her pussy how much it was throbbing, she shook her head while her teeth bit into her lower lip.

The tiny gesture of how she drew in her lip only increased his need for her. Closing the gap between their mouths, his lips connected with hers possessively. His teeth then sank into her bottom lip to draw it away from her own bite. Sucking on her lip to savor her taste, he lingered there for not nearly enough time for either of them.

"That wasn't an answer. Are you going to stop being my good girl, Layney?" His hands grasped onto her ribcage, his thumbs caressing over the delicate skin just below the swell of her breasts. It was all too easy to feel how quick and shallow her breaths were in reaction to him.

Layne caught herself shaking her head again and was quick to push the words out. "No, I will always be your good girl."

A sensual growl of approval escaped past Joey's lips when she confirmed what they both already knew. His mouth came to the side of her neck, lavishing it with electrifying kisses as one of his hands slid over the cup of her bra. His fingers pulled the cup away from her breast so he could wrap his hand around the mound of her flesh.

Layne's hand slid along his shoulder and up the back of his neck as she tilted her head back until it was pressed against the beam behind her. The soft pink lips of her mouth parted as she let out a quiet moan of approval.

Joey pushed himself roughly against her core despite the clothing on each of their bodies. His hand pushed her body down so she could feel how hard his cock was for her. As his mouth consumed the taste of the skin of her throat, his fingers took the stiff nipple of her breast and twisted it between his fingers. His hips still slowly trying to dry-fuck her.

Her arousal was soaking through her panties as she felt the desire reaching peaks that had her other hand dropping down to frantically pull at the button of her pants. Before her fingers could dip inside to provide some self-provided satisfaction, Joey's hold set her breast free, dropped to grab her wrist, and pulled it up above her head.

He raised his head from her throat, his lust-drunk expression drawn across his face. "Not yet. I have first dibs on that wet cunt of yours, Layney."

Fuck. She had some idea of how much Joey got turned on while she worked, but this was a whole new level of his domineering side, and she was here for it.

"Then fucking take it." Her voice was breathy as she leaned forward and crushed her lips against his hungrily. She was met with his tongue pushing past her lips to invade her mouth. His hand tightly held onto her side inside her shirt while his other dropped her wrist and grabbed the side of her face. His fingers curled around the back of her neck, keeping her head exactly where he wanted.

The ding of the elevator on the other end of the wide-open space echoed through the air. No one should have been in the building at this time of night. Yet, here they were, loaded with weaponry and keeping company with a rapidly cooling body on the floor.

Immediately, their faces split from one another. Layne dropped her legs down from his waist as Joey set her on her feet. His fingers made sure the first thing he did was pull Layne's mask up over her face as a measure to keep her safe, no matter the cost.

"This way." His hand latched onto hers tightly, pulling her in the direction opposite of the elevator doors. By the time they got to the door leading to the stairwell, he had his skull-faced mask also back in place.

Running over to the door to the emergency exit with

Joey, she slipped into the stairwell first, with Joey close behind her. Her feet quickly carried her down the steps, his heavy set of boots sounding off quickly behind her.

When the fresh night air washed over them as they exited the building, she saw Joey's black sports bike parked right where he had left it in the alley just several feet from the door they just emerged from. He jogged ahead of her, snagged the sole helmet off the seat, and tossed it at Layne before mounting the bike. His hand retrieved a pair of protective riding glasses from his thigh pocket, sliding them over his eyes. A second later, the purr of the engine filled the air.

Her hands caught the helmet, immediately pushing it down over her head. Her hand grabbed onto his hard bicep as she hopped on behind him. After her ass was in the seat, Layne's arms were tightly wrapped around his waist as she adhered herself to his back.

As Joey pulled out of the alley, Layne looked, and her gut filled with both dread and relief as they sped by the front of the warehouse they had just fled from. Two NYPD patrol cars sat out front with their lights flashing. There was no way that they were there by coincidence. Someone had tipped them off.

CHAPTER NINE

Inside the modest apartment belonging to one Rebecca Zappa, the two girls hung out in the cramped living room. The limited space was filled with papers scattered across the coffee table, boxes of samples of various wedding paraphernalia, and a laptop off to the side.

Rebecca rapidly tapped the top of her pen against the pad of paper while she mulled over the thoughts inside her head and stared down at the doodles and diagrams in front of her.

Layne lay across the dark brown leather sofa with her head supported by the arm of it, a bottle of beer hanging out in one hand while the other rested on top of her stomach. Her hair swept up into a messy bun on top of her head, a comfy pair of black leggings on her lower half, and a distressed scoop-neck turquoise tee hanging off of her upper body.

"You know," Layne spoke up, "does it *really* matter

where the flowers go?" She turned her head to look over at her best friend. This entire wedding planning was all Rebecca's jam and not something Layne had given second thoughts to. Did people actually care if flowers were low on the table or up on a pedestal? She didn't.

Her blonde bestie's jaw hung open after a small gasp, her pen immediately ceasing its movement. "Of course it does!" she exclaimed. She set the pen down on the pad with a dramatic sigh. "I'm not going to let you downplay your own damn wedding day, Layne. It's going to be extravagantly beautiful, perfectly executed, and all you need to do is show up and say, 'I do.' You deserve it after all the shit-storms you've had to endure."

Rebecca knew better than to bring up the horrific circumstances surrounding Layne's first marriage—if one could even call it that. Signing papers that were questionably legal with Eric had been nothing but a cold and emotionless business transaction. She knew that Layne deserved better than that. Even if she still had minor reservations about Joey, she could agree that he had been taking care of Layne more than any man ever had. That was no easy feat.

After taking a small sip from the amber lager, Layne gave a light smile at the notion of seeing Joey standing across from her, ready to commit to being in her life forever. The thought of seeing him dressed in a tux, in a church of all places, began to remind her of the last time he had gotten all cleaned up for her. A memory where she ended up on the hood of his car left a heated desire beginning to pool in her lower stomach.

Disrupting Layne's thoughts was the sound of the front door to Rebecca's apartment giving a small click as the handle turned and swung open. Joey pushed his way in with several bags of food in his hands. He nudged the door shut behind him and carried the bags over to the nearby kitchen table, where he unloaded all of them.

"When you said you ordered lunch, I didn't expect to be picking up an entire damn buffet." He griped as he shoved his sunglasses up on top of his head to rest on his slicked-back dark blonde hair.

Rebecca gave the biggest smile ever, trying to exude as much innocence and sweetness as possible. "You're the best. It wouldn't be girls' lunch without options. Besides, we both know that Layne needs the reminder to eat every once in a while before she gets too cranky." That earned a piercing glare from Layne at the minor dig.

"Does that mean I'm officially out of the doghouse?" He raised a brow at her.

She gave a shrug of her shoulders and a playful grin. "Ninety percent there."

Joey looked over at Layne, who was lazed out on the couch. "She's a tough one to win over." He nodded over at Rebecca before coming over to the end of the sofa where Layne's head was resting.

"Nearly as tough as you are," he murmured as he leaned over her. His hand ran along Layne's throat until it cupped under her jaw to tilt her head further back so he could greet her mouth with an upside-down kiss. The several-day buildup of scruff on his face was lightly abrasive against her skin.

The magnetic draw of his mouth left her wanting more as her back arched slightly at the sensation. It wasn't until Rebecca cleared her throat that the two of them wrapped up their moment of affection together, leaving Layne with a sheepish smile on her face.

Joey rounded the edge of the couch and took a seat at the end where Layne's feet were, lifting them momentarily to lay them back down in his lap. "How's the planning going?"

That earned him a rolling of eyes from both girls for different reasons, but it was Layne who chimed in first. "She's in full, level five-thousand wedding planner mode. At this rate, I expect members of a royal family from a country I've never heard of to be attending." Her snark and sass were in full swing.

Rebecca, on the other hand, shook her head in denial and looked at Joey for backup. "Help me out here. I've already explained to her that showing up to the courthouse and having a kegger afterward is not only *not* what she deserves but sends the wrong message socially."

Layne shifted, so she was now propped up on her elbow. "There's nothing wrong with that plan!"

"Except it's not what you want." Rebecca fired back quickly. "Do you want me to go into the many in-depth conversations we've had over the years? I will be more than happy to share your extremely detailed dream wedding plans involving Jackson Holloway in the ninth grade. *Including* the wedding night."

Her eyes widened. "Oh my God," Layne groaned as she sat up. "Don't you dare," she warned before looking over at

Joey. "Look, you've even said it yourself, it's a piece of paper."

Suddenly finding himself in the middle of this, Joey sighed and looked over at his future wife. His incredibly stubborn future wife. His hand gave her foot a gentle squeeze. "I did say that, but that was different."

Goddamn, if he didn't want to bring Eric Ellis back from the dead just to snap his neck all over again for the number he had done on Layne. The bastard never deserved to have his name next to hers on that marriage certificate.

He straightened up in his seat, directing his eyes right at Layne. "Layney, I want you to have the day you deserve. I want everyone to know that you get the best of everything, including the best of me. Let's show the world that we aren't paper-thin." He let those words sink in for a moment.

When she began to show signs of backing down, the tightness easing away from her shoulders and a softness flittering across her eyes, Joey flashed her a smirk. "Although, I am interested in what you had in mind for the wedding night."

Layne sat up, grabbed one of the throw pillows tucked against her side, and tossed it at him. "Not a damn chance!"

He easily dodged the square pillow with a chuckle. "We'll see."

After an afternoon of planning, well mostly of Rebecca

laying out options and drawing out opinions from Layne, Joey drove Layne back home.

"Have you heard anything about Liam?" He glanced over at Layne in the passenger seat while they sat at a red traffic light.

Looking up from scrolling through some messages on her phone, she shook her head. "Only that he had his arraignment hearing. He was denied bail, so he will have some time to sit and think about his actions behind bars. Walt thinks it was a politically driven decision by the judge." She shrugged, trying to appear unfazed and indifferent.

"You still did the right thing, Layne. Sometimes, the best thing is to be in lockup. When I did my time at Rikers, it was shitty, but I fucking learned what I needed while I was there." It had been a hellhole of an experience for Joey, but it gave him the resources and contacts to learn some of the best tricks of the trade. Not to mention, it made him smarter, so next time, he wouldn't make the same fuck ups.

She felt a deep breath fill her lungs before she released it, trying to absorb the words of reassurance he was attempting to give her. "I know. I just had hoped things would be different, ya know? It's only him, and I left in this family, and I expected more."

The light turned green, and Joey proceeded, taking them towards their destination. "Blood makes you related, not family. Liam hasn't been your family since I've known you." Perhaps a harsh iteration of the truth, but from the outside peering in on the O'Reilly household, Liam only gave a shit about one person—himself.

Trying not to dwell on the topic, she shifted things over to the subject of another troublesome sibling. "So…" Her voice trailed off as she tried to find the best way to broach the topic.

Joey glanced over at her briefly while trying to maintain his focus on the road. "So?"

"I think it's a good idea if you hang back tonight." She did her best to keep it sounding as much of a neutral decision as possible. It was Thursday, and if luck was smiling upon them, Italo would be at Gage's strip club for a weekly private dick rub.

Immediately, his upper body stiffened in the driver's seat. His hand jerked the steering wheel and cut off several other drivers before pulling off to a side street where he double parked the Challenger. "You've lost your damn mind. Not happening." His chocolate eyes looked over at her, full of unyielding assertiveness.

The sudden maneuvering of the vehicle and near collisions nearly caused her a heart attack and shook all her efforts to keep her voice calm. "Christ!" She glanced around at where they were parked on the street before staring back at him. "You really think that you can hold your shit together if Gage is there tonight? Honestly?"

He reached over, his hand curled around the back of her neck to make sure he had her full attention. Joey wanted her to hear his words loud and clear. "Gage isn't my concern. You are, and you aren't going there without me. Do you understand?"

The warmth and the strength of his hand on the back of her neck had tingling sensations coursing down her spine and spreading down each of her limbs. His words carried the weight of a man who was hellbent on getting his way.

"Don't make me ask twice," he added.

She nodded at him. He accepted her acknowledgment by leaning over and briefly locking his lips onto hers to ease away the sternness he had thrust upon her moments ago.

"Good," was all he said afterward before he sat back in his seat.

Great, it looked like they were both going to Cassidy's Cave tonight. She just hoped that Gage wouldn't hinder their efforts and Joey could keep his personal shit with his brother on lockdown.

CHAPTER TEN

As it turned out, Thursday evenings weren't very popular at the strip club tucked away into the outer edge of the Hell's Kitchen neighborhood. It was just shy of one o'clock in the morning, and a bouncer wasn't even posted outside the blacked-out glass door.

The neon letters above the entrance were a symbolic mixture of what you'd find inside, with 'Cassidy's' in a swirly pink feminine font and 'Cave' in more masculine blocky blue letters. The color combination was reminiscent of a tuft of cotton candy you would purchase at a fair. Though, the treats inside this establishment were much more carnal.

Layne held the door open long enough for Joey to follow in closely behind her. The second they stepped foot inside, the heavy scent of various floral perfumes and freely flowing booze was overwhelming. Music played in the background, something sensually upbeat with a husky-sounding female singer that Layne didn't recognize.

Dancing half-assed to the tune was one platinum blonde on a circular stage before a sole male patron seated at a table in front of her. Given several empty cocktail glasses at his table, a gold wedding band laid next to them, and the sullen look on his face, the poor guy looked like he had been having a day.

At the bar was a scantily clad bartender, wearing nothing more than a black bra filled with a pair of obviously fake tits and a pair of hot shorts that may as well have been painted on. She was leaning back against the liquor display behind the bar, and right next to her, standing at the cash drawer, was a now familiar figure.

Gage had on a pair of faded blue jeans that were fitted just enough to do justice to his tight and drool-worthy ass. A black dress shirt covered the hard muscles of his upper body; the sleeves rolled up to his elbows, showing off several tattoos, which included several roses. He counted a wad of cash in his hands and tucked it back into the drawer before pushing it shut.

The woman bartender nudged Gage's arm and said something to him, prompting him to turn around. Setting his deep brown eyes on Layne first, one side of his mouth lifted as he gave a cocky smile. His sights shifted to Joey standing next to her, his smile then faltering ever so slightly.

He left his spot behind the bar and approached the two of them. "You finally convinced him to bring his stubborn ass down here?" His brow lifted curiously at Layne. Gage's arms crossed in front of his chest; it became clear he was wearing a white tank underneath the dress shirt where the silver chain of his necklace hung just underneath.

Joey didn't waste time in responding. "We're not here to see you." His voice strained to keep things as amicable as possible.

"Really?" Gage looked around at the sparsely populated club and then back at Joey. "Not too many other people here to see." He grinned at Layne. "Just couldn't stay away, could ya?"

Over his cocky attitude, she brushed off his question with a roll of her eyes. Layne hoped there was at least one other customer there. "Are any of your private rooms occupied?"

Something entertaining must have crossed Gage's mind as he gave a sinful little smirk while his eyes briefly surveyed what Layne was wearing. The way she wore her ensemble had his cock coming to life inside his jeans. It wasn't just what she had on, but it was the way her black pants fit her toned legs and wrapped around her hips. The curve of her body up to the swell of her breasts in the snug black long-sleeved shirt with a low scooped neckline had his thoughts sinking south quickly.

Layne's dark hair was woven into an intricate French braid, leaving Gage with thoughts of wrapping his hand around the tail of it and pulling until she submitted to him. He would happily occupy a private room with her, given the chance. It made him wonder just how much of a brat she would be in the bedroom or if she knew how to behave when given a thick and hard reason to.

"Just one, but we can make it two." He finally responded to the question with playfulness dancing across his words.

Joey gave a growl, earning him a look from Layne to simmer down. He shifted his stance, his arms flexing under the moment of tension. He had opted to wear his go-to outfit for his jobs, the all-black tactical attire that made him more easily blend into the shadows. The only thing that was missing was his mask—for now.

She approached Gage, painting a sexy little smile on her face as she stared up at him with her best big ol' innocent doe eyes. "Gage," she spoke with a gentle voice as her finger trailed up the center of his chest. The tip of her finger ran along the exposed skin below his collarbone until it hooked under the chain of his necklace. Twining the cord of metal around her finger, she pulled it into her grasp so she could pull him forward to come closer to her face.

Her face was inches away from his as he voluntarily leaned down at her beckoning. "Does it look like he's the type that wants to share?" Layne referred to Joey, standing just a few steps behind her. "Just tell me who is in the private room."

Layne's question earned her an unexpected chuckle and an amused grin from Gage. He weighed the risks and benefits of taking advantage of the proximity to those deliciously pouty lips of hers, ultimately deciding to bide his time. "Oh, you'd have to ask him about that one." His eyes flicked at Joey with a wicked grin.

The response had Layne's hand loosening up on the chain enough to allow it to fall from her fingers as she hadn't foreseen that answer to her question. Her lips separated partially in confusion and the inability to find the words to respond.

Gage straightened up, putting some fresh air between them before he pushed any more of Joey's buttons tonight. "It's one of my regulars, Italo Giorgi. Comes here every week. Brings a few of his buddies, and my girl, Danielle, provides the entertainment. He's usually in there 'til nearly three in the morning most weeks."

Joey's hand came onto Layne's shoulder, grasping onto it possessively, sending an unspoken message to his brother. "Clear the club, Gage." A fierce look in his eyes made it clear that this wasn't a request. The fewer witnesses they had, the better.

She stood there assessing the tension between the two men before stepping away to scope out the club to get a count of who was currently present outside of the private room.

When she returned, the two guys were still standing where she had left them. She arrived within earshot only to hear the tail end of the conversation between them.

"Layne isn't Rosie," Joey said. "She's—" his words cut off sharply once he noticed Layne approaching. Whatever else he had intended to tack onto the end of that sentence was left unsaid.

Despite what he thought, Layne had overheard enough for the seed to be planted in her mind about whatever was going on during the conversation she had interrupted. However, they weren't here to talk about past issues. She had business to take care of.

Her emerald hues stared at the two of them. "Are you two done here? I have shit to do." The words spewed forth more harshly than they should have.

"Sure," was all Gage responded with before he stepped away. He dismissed the few remaining employees on the clock, which in turn prompted a very disappointed and sad middle-aged man who had been the sole recipient of entertainment during this slow evening.

Layne didn't look at Joey while she tried to focus her brain on Italo and what was going on in that private suite. Who else was in there? What information was she going to be able to extract? What did Rosie have to do with anything that Joey and Gage were talking about?

After all was said and done, Gage returned with confirmation. "That's everyone."

The second that Layne made a move to head back toward the private room, Joey's hand stopped her. Easily, his hold swallowed up her elbow in his grasp, ceasing her from continuing forward. Her eyes glanced down at his inked hand and then his face, wondering what the hell he was doing.

His other hand reached into her pocket and retrieved one last important item. "You don't know who else is in there." When he lifted his hand, her mask hung from his fingertips.

She snagged the mask and began to stretch it across her face. "Oh, good. I wouldn't want anyone to mistake me for Rosie." Layne knew she shouldn't have jealousy over a dead woman she hardly knew a thing about. Yet, there was something in the way Joey had spoken her name to Gage that still had her insides twisting with insecurity.

Layne pulled her arm from his grip, not bothering to wait for any sort of reaction to her bitterness. She stormed off to the area where she had noticed the private rooms where only one door was visibly shut. At least she could put her feelings to good use; it would make things much easier.

While the urge to just kick in the damn door was strong, there was no sense in expending extra energy on making a dramatic entrance. She twisted the doorknob, and much to her surprise, it fully rotated, indicating it remained unlocked.

Right as Joey was approaching with his own dark mask now in place, she swung open the door to reveal the occupants inside.

Well… fuck. There were four people inside that room suddenly staring back at her. That didn't include who Layne assumed to be, Danielle, given she was the only one with tits out and a strand of yarn for panties. Taking a good look at each man cramped into the room on the velvet sofa, she didn't recognize any of them. Each of them wore cheap and grungy clothes, indicating they weren't rolling in the big bucks. Low-level thugs.

Layne leaned her shoulder against the doorframe, using her small and innocent size to look as unassuming as possible. Behind her back, she spread out four of her fingers and gave them a wiggle. It was the signal to Joey of how many potential threats she saw before her. "I'm Danielle's replacement for the evening. Which one of you assholes is Italo?"

When she was met with silence and uncomfortable stares, she shrugged and pushed away from the doorframe. "The strong and silent types, eh? I can work with that." She motioned for Danielle to come closer. When she did as she was told, Layne gave her one more instruction. "Go home."

The dancer hesitated, so Layne repeated herself more firmly. "Get the fuck out." The woman with a face full of makeup and glam nodded and slipped out of the room.

That's when someone finally found their voice and stood up. It was a lanky-looking man who had spent too much time underneath a tanning bed. "Yo, what the fuck, bitch? You into some kinky-ass shit with that mask or somethin'?" He squared his shoulders and thrust his chest forward to look like he was something titillating to look at.

She made sure to keep her eyes out for any other movement, but knowing Joey was out of their sight a few feet away, she had very few concerns.

Finally, she decided it was about time to stir the pot and see which one these asshats were going to react. "I told you, I'm looking for Italo. Actually, I'm looking for any one of you who might have been talking to Russell Spencer. Does that name ring a bell?"

Ding, ding, ding! That was the winning ticket. The second Russ's name was dropped, they all began to scatter like roaches running back to their hidey holes when the lights got turned on.

It was the man who first stood up that reached her first. The skinny bastard tried to push her out of the way, and instead, her hands latched onto him and propelled him into the hallway headfirst toward a wall. Upon contact, he was dazed and dropped to one knee.

Two more guys ran out behind her, encountering the looming presence of Joey. He clotheslined one who fell to the floor like a sack of potatoes, then grabbed the other by his throat before greeting the center of the man's face with a harsh punch. The impact shattered the bones of the guy's nose.

The last one? He ran by Layne just as she was bending over, grabbing a fistful of the first man's hair and slamming his head into the wall one more time. Her eyes caught sight of the straggler who darted past her. "Damn it, we got a runner!"

Without a second thought, she released Mr. Crispy-Fried Tan guy who was now blessed with a massive headache. She immediately chased after the last guy, who at least had the sense not to run toward Joey. Layne could appreciate his decision to take the opposite path. Joey was nothing less than fearfully intimidating, even without his mask on.

While securing zip ties on the wrists of both of the men he had incapacitated, Joey looked up to see Layne rounding the corner out of his sight in pursuit of the fourth man. "Gage!" he barked over his shoulder for his brother.

Layne sprinted as fast as the short length of her legs would go. The man she was chasing after was quick but not agile. He slowed down each time he had to shift the movement of his feet to avoid running into various pieces of furniture and other obstacles as they entered the back storage area of Cassidy's. It allowed Layne to cut down the distance between them.

There was a backdoor exit straight ahead of them, and if he made it out that door, he was going to be likely as good as gone. Before she could make a final push to get close enough to him to prevent that, a metal bat swung out straight into the man's gut. The attempted escapee lost all the breath in his lungs at the unexpected strike that came from off the side and left him lying on the floor.

She tried to skid to a stop right as Gage came into view, wanting to avoid running right into him. He tossed the piece of sports equipment off behind him, figuring this guy was as good as down for the time being. Immediately, he held his hands up, catching hold of Layne as she failed to slow her momentum in time to prevent the collision with him.

Her small body landed up against him without so much as shifting his weight on his feet. Gage grinned proudly at her as his hands remained locked on her arms. "Do I get a token of your appreciation for coming to your aid?"

Still trying to catch her breath from the chase, her eyes looked up at him in disbelief that he thought he deserved anything other than a thank you. "*Please.* I would have had him."

He leaned over and whispered in her ear, looking for any excuse to get closer to her. "Keep telling yourself that, sweetheart." Even with a little bit of sweat gracing her skin, he took note of the scent of her perfume lingering underneath it. Gage could already imagine how amazing the mixture of daisies, rain, and her sweat would smell on his sheets after giving her a night filled with his type of pleasure.

The scent of spiced vanilla invaded her senses, with Gage leaning in so close to her. She squirmed in his hands to avoid the temptation to lean in and let herself get wrapped up in it. Her arms eventually broke free of his loose hold. "If you want my appreciation, you can drag his ass back to the others."

Layne didn't wait for him to agree, she just began walking back to where things had kicked off just outside of the private room. Gage pulled the man who thought he was running out of here to his feet and dragged him back to where Joey had the other three all in their zip tie constraints. He shoved the attempted runaway towards his brother to take care of.

"Have any of them said anything useful?" She eyed the collection of lowlifes before her. Gage hovered at her backside as Joey stood on the other side of the group.

Joey tightened the last tie and gave a shove to the fourth man to join the rest of his comrades on the floor. "No, just a lot of pissin' and moanin'."

From behind Gage and Layne was the sound of a door swinging open. Shit, none of them had checked the bathroom. A man wearing clothes with a little more class emerged from the men's room. He was dressed in a pair of khakis and a dark purple polo.

Layne spun around to fully give the man her attention while Gage just peered over his shoulder. She started to step out from behind Gage to take care of this new situation.

There was little time from the moment the new guy came out from the restroom to the point where he saw the gathering of his pals on the floor, a woman and man both masked up and the club's owner.

Gage tried to keep his voice friendly. "Italo, man—shit!"

That's when things took a turn for the worse. Italo immediately withdrew a gun from the back of his pants, raising it in Layne's direction.

Then shots rang out.

CHAPTER ELEVEN

Italo squeezed the trigger with the intent to eliminate one of the masked individuals closest to him–Layne.

The second the jerkoff had revealed the firearm, Gage saw it being lifted in line with where Layne was. Gage stepped toward Layne, who was fortunately still within his arm's reach. Protectively, he wrapped his large arms around her, drawing her in tightly to his chest as he turned his back to Italo so his body curled over Layne's petite form like a shield.

He ducked down, covering as much of Layne's body as he could, paying particular attention to her most vital parts, like her head and upper body. Tightly, using his strength, he clutched onto her like a man fearful of losing a rare treasure to the depths of the ocean.

She had no time to react from the moment Italo became an active threat and when she was suddenly yanked into Gage's tight embrace. It had happened so quickly that all she could ascertain was that she was cloaked in safety. While the protective hold that Gage had on her was damn near suffocating, it was far better than suffering a potentially fatal gunshot wound. One experience in the whole being shot department was more than enough for her.

Layne felt Gage's body flinch around her as the sound of the bullet bursting into flight echoed in the air, her hands were pinned between their bodies, not allowing her to grab for anything defensively. Being pressed so close to his chest, she couldn't see shit. All she could do was huddle up with him and listen to the sound of his heavy breathing. Quickly after the first shot, that's when she heard a second round fired, which caused a slight ringing in her ears and was followed by a heavy thud.

It all felt like it transpired over the span of minutes, but it had only taken mere seconds. Even as panic set in at the sound of a body hitting the floor, and she began to struggle and push against Gage, he didn't allow her a single inch of freedom.

Once Gage looked up, Joey was holstering his pistol, and behind Gage was one less regular patron of Cassidy's Cave.

Joey immediately came over to where Gage was crouched down, his arms locked around Layne. He met eyes with his brother, not needing to say anything as a look passed between them. It was a look from Joey that held something with the least amount of hostility than it ever had in recent history with Gage.

His voice held a gravelly texture to it as Joey spoke. "Let me see her."

Layne was still squirming against Gage's chest, only easing up as she felt Gage pull her up with him as he stood. He loosened his arms from around her, allowing her to create space for herself. However, Joey didn't give her the chance as he immediately pulled her into his arms, surrounding her with the familiar woodsy scent of sage and leather.

The hug was brief but just enough to erase the concern from them both. Joey pulled back and looked her over. "Are you okay?"

She nodded and did the same inspection to Joey to confirm he was equally unhurt. "I'm fine."

Now that the adrenaline-filled moment was over, Gage looked at his arm, which had a burning sensation nagging at him. As he moved his arm to take a look, he gave a quiet hiss of pain, noticing a small tear in the curve of the shoulder of his shirt. "Goddamnit, this was a new fucking shirt," he grumbled.

Gage undid the series of buttons on the dress shirt until he peeled it from his torso. It revealed the white tank top that clung to each line of his bulky muscles and exposed the series of tattoos creeping up his arms. The lines of ink curved into images of roses and various sharp-edged weapons.

He inspected his shoulder, where there was a small wound, a line of blood creeping from it. Thankfully, it was only a graze. If he hadn't pulled Layne to him, it was quite possible she would have been struck down. He would accept this minor inconvenience over the thought of her perfect body being damaged.

When Layne noticed Gage stripping his shirt off and revealing where Italo's bullet must have skimmed past him, she had a mixture of feelings fill her up inside. Guilt that he had put himself in harm's way for her and awe that he hadn't even thought twice about it. Sprinkle a little gratitude on top of all that, and she found herself seeing him through a slightly different lens. That lens especially didn't look half bad when she saw how the thin fabric of his tank top adhered to his fit form and the cut of the muscles of the steel-like biceps that had been clenching around her moments ago.

Interrupting her thoughts while her eyes had been lost on his younger brother, Joey spoke. "Now that we're down a lead," he motioned over to Italo's still body, "hopefully, these four are feeling chatty."

Layne looked over at the group of men all on the floor with their hands bound behind their backs. Some looked worse for wear, especially the one with the smashed nose courtesy of Joey's fist.

Killing Italo was not in the plan for tonight, and it put a major hitch in her plans. She tried not to be pissed about it, given they didn't have much of an option when guns were drawn. Pulling away from Joey's hold, she walked over to the group of men, all with different expressions on each of their faces. One still looked to be in pain, another looked defiant, one appeared to be terrified he would be shot next, and one was in shock and mentally checked the fuck out.

"The first one of you to give me something useful about Russ Spencer will be the only one walking out of here with both legs intact." Her eyes narrowed at them dangerously; she wondered who was going to break first.

Layne had been pleasantly surprised that the man who had appeared full of steadfast contempt was the first to crumble. He had sung like a canary the second Gage had fetched her the metal bat he had used earlier, and Layne used it to give a love tap to the lackey's kneecap.

Ended up that Russ had been working with Italo to begin setting up a series of intimidation tactics on known businesses that either supported Layne or straight up were on the outer edges of her territory. Of course, Italo needed the help of pettier criminals who were willing to engage in violent acts for less of a monetary incentive. That's where all four of these men came in.

She had made good on her word, leaving the man's legs uninjured. He only left the strip club with a broken arm and a promise from Layne. If he so much as tattled to Russell, there was no place he could hide that she wouldn't be able to track him down and creatively find more ways to impart pain on him.

The other three? None were so fortunate. Each of them left still sucking air into their lungs, but they all earned a bashing of their legs to have them hobbling or crawling out of there.

Layne locked up the front door after the last of them was gone, exhaustion weighing down on her. The two De

Lucas were stationed at the bar, giving her the space to carry out her methods. Gage had offered to assist, but Joey convinced him that Layne was more than able to take care of this on her own while they sat back.

Tossing the bat to the side, she removed her mask and walked back to where Joey and Gage were standing, noticing each of them tracking her movements. What she noticed pressed against the zipper of Joey's pants wasn't unexpected, given how he felt about watching her assert herself. It was the outline at the front of Gage's pants that she hadn't expected to notice, and it was incredibly difficult not to have her attention drawn to it.

Well, shit, that was a hell of a sight to see in front of her. Trying her best to ignore that she had seen the dually magnificent sight that had her imagination swirling, she took up a seat on one of the stools.

Joey reached behind him, grabbed a glass of whiskey, and handed it over to her. It earned him one of her delightful smiles. "Thanks." She took the glass from him and wasted no time in emptying its contents into her mouth, swallowing down the burn happily after all of tonight's events.

Gage leaned back against the bar top on his elbows. "I took care of Italo. His body won't be found until someone takes a fine-tooth comb through whichever landfill he ends up at." One perk of Manhattan was the metric tons of trash the city generated got transported to one of many sites, some as far as South Carolina or even overseas in China.

She nodded, impressed that he was willing to help clean up their mess. Layne set her empty glass down on the bar.

"I appreciate it." Her emerald eyes looked at his exposed shoulder. "How's your arm?"

He shrugged indifferently. "I'll live. Not the worst I've ever had, and the ladies love a good battle scar." Gage winked at her.

Joey poured another finger-high amount of the amber booze into Layne's empty glass. "Layne," he started with an even tone that sounded like he was about to discuss a trivial matter. "Gage and I were talking."

She sat up straighter in her seat, not liking how guarded he was making his voice. Anytime he started a conversation with such calm, it usually meant she wasn't going to particularly like what he had to say.

"About what?" She turned to set her gaze on Joey, who was now removing his mask and shoving it into his pocket. He rubbed his hand down over the front of his mouth, knowing that this had the potential to be met with a lot of resistance. It also had the risk of Layne trying to send him to sleep on the couch.

He offered her the refill of whiskey, but she refused to take what was only being handed to her to help ease the impact of whatever he was about to drop on her. Joey slowly inhaled and set the glass to the side.

"We already talked about you needing an extra set of eyes on you. I don't want to trust just anyone looking out for you. I need someone I can rely on, and finding anyone in this business that even comes up close to the caliber of protection I need for you…"

Joey didn't even have to finish his thought before Layne jumped to the conclusion. Her eyes darted to Gage, who, to his credit, wasn't wearing a smug smile for once. "Are you kidding me? Gage?!" She shook her head. "No." This should have been a point-blank decision from her and the discussion done with.

"Layney—"

She cut him off before he tried to pull out his charm to smooth this over. "Ever since he's come around, all you've been doing is telling me how reckless he is, and you don't want him around. Now, you're doing an entire one-eighty on that?"

Gage nodded. "She has a point. I'm about as reckless as you are." The sarcasm was in full swing on his words.

Joey shot his brother a glare before stepping up to Layne, taking her face in his hands. "It's just for the time being. If he does anything to give me pause, he's gone." He pressed his forehead to hers, lowering his voice. "You don't have to like it, but I'm not asking you to. I'm telling you, this is what has to happen."

Met with Joey's face in close proximity to her own, she gave a small frown, displaying her dissatisfaction with his decision overriding her own. His ass was already in the doghouse from his comment to Gage earlier, and now he was dropping this bomb on her, and she wasn't happy about it.

"Hope you find the couch comfortable to sleep on." She grumbled, knowing trying to argue with him on this was going to be pointless. It would have resulted in hours of back and forth, eating up energy she didn't have to expend.

Joey's lips pressed onto hers with a heat to melt away her agitated demeanor. When he pulled back, he smirked at her. "Couch is going to be just fine when you're underneath me taking my cock all night."

His words sent a spark of desire straight down between her legs, distracting her from realizing how soon she was going to always have a De Luca at her side.

CHAPTER TWELVE

All of Layne's abdominal muscles down the length of her torso were on fire. Her forearms were pressed firmly into the gym mat underneath her, supporting the weight of her body. The short span of her body was suspended in a rigid plank inside the home gym around the corner from the kitchen.

Her forehead donned a scattering of sweat droplets as she squeezed her eyes shut. She had to have been holding this plank for at least thirty minutes. Her body was beginning to tremble as her muscles felt pushed beyond fatigue.

When her eyes opened to take a peek at the timer between her wrists, she was sorely mistaken. The last bit of air in her lungs was forced out in a huff as she dropped her body down flat onto the mat with a groan. Almost two minutes. Her hand slapped the timer off as she laid her cheek against the cushy texture of the mat.

Layne lifted her head to look in the mirror affixed to the wall ahead of her. She saw Joey's reflection where he was seated on a weight bench at the back of the room. He finished the last shoulder press in his set before he set the heavy dumbbells down. "You're thinking about it too much." He said it like he knew exactly what was going on inside her head.

She groaned as she continued to lay there. "What else am I supposed to be thinking about when my stomach won't stop screaming at me?"

Joey stood and walked past her to the mini fridge filled with bottles of water. Her eyes watched each movement, appreciating that he had done his workout in a pair of navy gym shorts, sneakers, and nothing else. All of his tattoos were exposed for her to admire as they sprawled across the hard muscles of his body, which were currently coated in a light layer of salty perspiration.

While he pulled two bottles of water out of the fridge, Layne shifted her position so she was up on her knees and sitting back on her ankles. Her hand reached out to take the water Joey offered her. Twisting the cap off, she welcomed the sting of the icy temperature of the first sip filling her mouth before being swallowed down.

The only other thing plaguing her mind besides her abs being on fire was what had been said at the strip club the other night. "We still haven't talked about the night at Cassidy's." She finally initiated the topic that she had been unable to just let go of. Lord knew she had tried to forget it, but the words spoken between the two men replayed over and over in her mind.

Joey had already chugged nearly all his water down in a matter of two large gulps. "Gage is going to be your shadow when I'm not around. There's nothing else to talk about." Perhaps it was wishful thinking that Layne wouldn't press the issue about the other elephant having a tea party in the room with them.

"You know damn well that while I disagree with it, that's not what I'm talking about." She pushed herself up onto her feet. "What did you mean that I'm not Rosie?"

He sighed and sucked down the last little bit of water before tossing the bottle a few feet into the open trash can. "Nothing, Layne. It's self-explanatory. You aren't her." Joey did his best to play it all off as nothing but a matter-of-fact observation he had made.

He must have thought she clunked her head and suddenly was stupid enough to accept that explanation. Her eyes narrowed at him as her temper kicked up a notch. "Don't fuckin' go there, Joey! You don't just drop the name of a dead girl randomly and make a comparison like that for the hell of it. What did you mean by it?"

There was nothing but silence from him in response, and the tension in the air was palpable. Layne locked her eyes on him, waiting for him—begging him to explain himself.

Losing faith, he was going to clue her in; she began to walk away from him toward the door. "You know what? If you're not going to tell me, I will be spending enough time with Gage, and I'm sure he'll be more than happy to share."

As her hand started to draw the door open, Joey rushed over to her, shoving it back shut again. The look on his face was a flurry of emotions ranging from panic to desperation and even agitation. "I don't get why you're so hellbent on this. It's all shit from the past. I'm doing my goddamn best to let past shit go with Gage, so why can't you just drop it?"

Her hand jerked on the door again, and to no avail, it remained shut as his hand made sure of that. "Because I see the look in your eyes when you say her name. Because there's clearly something I'm not being told. Call me fucking crazy, but I thought it's reasonable to expect you aren't going to be keeping any more secrets from me." Her anger pricked at the back of her neck in response to the emotionally charged topic at hand.

Joey looked down, and for the first time, she saw a pinch of shame in that handsome face of his. "Because it's not fair to you." His voice lost its edge as his fingers pinched the bridge of his nose while gathering his thoughts.

"She was our girlfriend." The proclamation was seemingly harmless on its face, and it left Layne wondering why the hell he had been so hesitant to say something.

"Who was dating her when everything happened?" Layne didn't quite put it all together on his first attempt at an explanation.

The depths of his cocoa eyes pulled up from looking at the floor, and when they connected with hers, he made it clearer. "We both were."

Oh. *Oh.* She hadn't been expecting that. Any responses she had expected to say to him hadn't been prepared to learn that he and Gage had been seeing her at the same time. Her mind began to jump through a series of thoughts and emotions. Rosie had been with both the guys, and at first, that unveiling was a surprise. Then, Layne was filled with something that was an even bigger shock. She found herself envious and thought about how Rosie had been one lucky bitch.

Furthering down the web of thoughts, she thought back to her first meeting with Gage and the fight that broke out. Joey's possessiveness had come exploding at an all-time high. After mentally going through the story of his history with Gage, she was able to fill in some of the gaps and unspoken truths. Fast forward to their most recent meeting, where the odd response from Gage about asking Joey about sharing suddenly made sense.

All the puzzle pieces clicked into place in her brain, and she was unsure of how long she had been standing there stuck inside her head. What does one even say to this? Joey must have been having his own internal string of thoughts, and fortunately for Layne, he spoke up first.

"Layney." He reached out, taking hold of her arms gently. "I didn't want to say anything because I didn't want you thinking—fuck, I don't know." Joey found himself frustrated that he couldn't cohesively put together a decent explanation for her. He wanted to give her what she deserved to hear without leaving her full of disappointment in him. Even worse? He couldn't fathom losing the trust she had in him.

Out of all the emotions that were rolling through her, anger wasn't one of them. When she looked up into his face, she found herself looking for answers. "Did you love her?"

His Adam's apple bobbed in the center of his throat as

he gave a hard swallow. "Gage will tell you that I didn't, but I did, in my own way." He moved his hands up to draw her face into his hands. "Not in the way that I love you, though, Layne. You are the spark that keeps my heart pumping blood through my veins."

She shook her head at him. "You don't have to defend your feelings, Joey. I will always be here making sure that you know you will always have my heart." Layne wrapped her arms around his waist, stepping up against him. "I will love you so hard for the rest of your life that you won't ever have to worry about losing that spark."

When Joey saw the curve of her lips as they lifted into a smile, he fell into a sense of ease and relief. His mouth sought hers out, and before he could fuse their lips, Layne pulled back with a smirk. "One question, though."

His brow arched at whatever was nagging at her brain. "Hm?"

Layne's eyes looked at him, full of curiosity. "Did you both… at the same time?"

He responded with a dark chuckle. Coyly, he responded to her, "Did we both, what?" Oh, he was going to make her say it just to see her reaction.

It could be counted on one hand the number of times Layne blushed from a mere thought. Now, here she was, fucking blushing. The spread of pink on her cheeks made her either want to hide her face from him or punch him so he didn't get the chance to see how flustered she was.

Joey could have made her life all the easier by stating the question for her, but he was enjoying seeing the warm blush spread over her fair cheeks. He began to walk back toward the weight bench, tugging her along with him. He dropped his hands down onto her hips. "You're going to have to be more specific, Layney. Now, be a good girl, and don't make me ask twice."

With his hands now locked firmly on her, he spun her around so her back was to him and the bench in front of her. Joey used a hand to bend her over so that her firm ass was nudged against the front of his shorts, where it was clear his cock was very much coming alive with excitement.

She had nowhere to run and hide from her discomfort at the question niggling at her. Her teeth scraped over her bottom lip as she looked back over her shoulder at him. "Did you and Gage both have sex with her? Together?"

His eyes filled with a mischievous twinkle, and his grin spread wider. Joey's fingers stretched the material of her workout pants down over the curve of her ass until she was bared to him. "Mm, of all the questions you could ask, and you want to know if she got stuffed with two cocks?"

Not releasing his tight hold on her, he dropped down to his knees behind her. A growl rumbled in his chest as he saw just how wet she was talking about him and Gage sharing Rosie. He leaned forward, his tongue dragging along her slick pussy, drawing in a long line of her taste into his mouth.

Layne moaned out as his tongue snaked out and sampled her arousal. "Yes…" Her hands grasped onto the edge of the bench her forearms were resting on.

There was a slight saltiness that enhanced her sweetness from the leftover perspiration from her workout that had made it to her center. He groaned out, "Fuck, Layne. You're the best-tasting post-workout I've ever had." His hands grabbed her thighs, spreading them wider for better access to her needy cunt. Joey hungrily put his mouth on her again, this time his tongue diving inside her.

The swell of pleasure immediately had her squirming against him as she made a sound of approval of the sensation. One of his hands left her thigh and found her throbbing clit. With just one swipe over it with his finger, she wanted to collapse down on him.

He swirled his tongue inside of her tight pussy to collect more of her flavor before he pulled back enough to talk. "She got whatever amount of cock she wanted from us." Joey's finger circled over her highly charged nub again, extracting more gorgeous moans from her throat.

She felt her knees shake underneath the weight of pleasure collecting low in her stomach and expanding throughout the rest of her body. Layne cried out as she felt Joey give one last lick of her folds before his presence and his touch both left her momentarily.

Before she could whimper as the sinful sensations ceased in her body, she felt Joey behind her again. Now, he was standing, and his shorts were down at his feet. The swollen head of his cock teased her entrance.

"Fuck, Joey, I need you in me," Layne begged with a neediness to chase back after her release again.

His hands braced her hips, holding them steady for him. "Just me, or are you thinking about how it'd feel to have more than one dick inside of you?" Pushing forward, he began to invade her pussy with his hard length. Her body tightly encased each inch of him.

Out of desperation to be filled with him, she tried to push her hips back to take all of him. Joey held her still so that he had full control of how much of him was inside her perfect cunt. "You can say it, Layne." His words were filled with encouragement.

Her breaths came out quicker as he took his entry nice and slow. Listening to how his words were spoken instilled a sense of confidence and safety to confess. Layne nodded. "I'm thinking about how good being filled up would feel."

Joey moaned out behind her as he sank into her until he was pressed flush against her round ass. His cock glided into the warmth of Layne's body, which felt like the closest thing to heaven he would ever get. Hearing her admit to getting turned on by the thought of getting two cocks had his dick hard as steel.

Her body rocked forward gently as he seated himself inside her. She cried out, enjoying the full sensation his size always gave her. Joey pulled back and thrust back into her, this time more vigorously. "Fuck, yes!"

All the thoughts of the many combinations of how two guys could ravage her already caused her to succumb to her body's trembling. The cusp of her orgasm swiftly approached as Joey began to ram himself into her.

Getting lost in his thoughts, he envisioned Layne as she was now but with her pretty mouth filled with dick, swallowing down a large load of cum while her pussy got filled. The imagery had rekindled a desire in him that he hadn't felt in years. His hips slammed against Layne over and over as he replayed those fantasies in his mind.

The sound of their bodies smacking against each other filled the space of the home gym; Layne was now screaming out in absolute ecstasy as her climax took her body hostage. Her release exploded as she came hard and furious for him. Her vision blurred at the edges from the instant state of immense bliss her body fell into.

Layne's inner walls squeezed Joey's dick so tightly he swore he would be lost inside her forever. He gave a raw growl as his cock pulsated before his seed shot deep inside her body. He gave small grinds up against her ass as he continued to fill her up with more of his thick cum.

After several moments of heavy breaths filling the air and the cloud of intense orgasms subsided, they were both seated on the floor. Layne was settled into Joey's lap with his arms wrapped lovingly around her waist. He kissed along the line of her exposed shoulder. She leaned back against his bare chest in total contentment.

"You will always and forever be mine, Layne. Don't you ever forget that," he murmured against her skin. Even if he were to ever share her, that would never change.

CHAPTER THIRTEEN

After their—ahem—post-workout stretches, Joey informed Layne that the following day, he had to drive out to Newark over in Jersey for the day. That meant Gage was going to be stepping up to the plate. She wasn't sure if it was better or worse now that she knew the truth about Rosie.

Up in the master bedroom, Layne yanked her forest green shirt down over her head and torso. Her hands retrieved her long tresses out from underneath the top, allowing them to fall freely over her shoulders. "I could just go with you." She glanced at herself in the full-length mirror on the back of the bedroom door to make sure her outfit was up to her standards. Being the face of a criminal empire meant being aware of one's image.

The long-sleeved shirt clung to her body, accentuating every curve, including a peek of her cleavage from the sharp v of the neckline. The dark hue of the green helped to make her eye color pop amongst her other features. The hem of the shirt stopped just above her belly button, revealing the fit muscle tone of her stomach. Layne partially twisted, pivoting her hip to check out her best asset in her low-rise jeans. The swell of her ass proudly showed off all the hard work and squats she did to maintain it.

Joey's hands wrapped over her shoulders as he came up behind her. He brushed her hair to the side, revealing the length of her neck. Lovingly, he laid a path of kisses from the crook of her neck up to her ear. "These aren't the type of people that welcome outsiders. Especially ones with a goddamn ass that begs for some dick." His mouth captured the bottom of her ear lobe, teasingly sucking at it before he drew his lips away from her skin. Those dark brown eyes of his glanced down to admire the plunge of her shirt and the view of her supple cleavage.

The strength of his cut arms wrapped around her and squeezed. "Besides," he continued. "It's a good opportunity for you and Gage to get to know each other a little better. See if he's up to the challenge of keeping up with you." He smirked at her, knowing damn well Layne wasn't an easy assignment to keep tabs on.

Layne turned in his arms, coming face to face with him with a grin. "So, does that mean I can hop a ride on the back of a bike with some stranger to ditch his ass?" Her hands slid around and grabbed a handful of his ass as she recalled how their first date kicked off.

His hand came up below her chin, his thumb running

across it, barely tracing along the bottom edge of her lip. "If he fucks up that badly the first day on the job, I will beat the shit out of him. And if you pull that crap on him…" Joey's voice held the edge of a soft warning. "I will find your ass and take you somewhere secluded where no one will ever find us."

"A vacation? I accept." Her smartass comment was coupled with a playful grin.

Before Joey could get more than a grumble out, the doorbell of O'Reilly Manor pierced through the air of the house.

"Probably Gage." He looked down at his watch. "Asshole always runs at least five minutes late. I will meet you downstairs." Joey leaned over and brushed his mouth over hers quickly before leaving to go down to the first floor to let his brother inside.

When Joey pulled open the front door, Gage stood there with a smile and a pair of aviator sunglasses on his face. "Hey. Reporting for duty." He mockingly gave Joey a salute.

"Come inside, you're late, jackass." Joey was taking a big but calculated risk by letting someone other than himself watch after the woman who meant everything to him. It didn't mean he had to be happy about it, either.

When Joey stepped back from the entrance, Gage came inside, his hands tucked into the dark tan pants he was wearing. "I have to admit, I never expected you to be living the swanky Upper Eastside life."

"Shut up." Joey was already sensing a headache

approaching with his little brother making stupid comments. He pushed the front door shut and moved to stand in front of him. "Ground rules."

Oh, this was going to be good. Gage didn't typically have rules set for him; he was the one who set them. With an amused smirk, he pulled his sunglasses from his face and hung them on the neck of his black long-sleeved tee. He looked directly at Joey. "I'm all ears."

With all seriousness in his face, Joey stared at Gage. "What she says goes. The only exception is if it involves you taking your eyes off of her, do you understand me? If she has so much as a papercut when I get back, I swear, Gage…"

The younger De Luca chuckled and raised a hand to stop Joey's impending threat right there. "Relax, I basically took a goddamn bullet for her. I think that should earn me a little trust, yeah? Besides, keeping my eyes on her—" he paused his words as Layne appeared on the stairs. "Not going to be a problem." Damn, the sight of that woman had him ready to face a firing squad for her.

Layne made her descent down the staircase, her ankle-high boots giving quiet little taps against the floor. She had chosen a light jacket to go over her shirt, making it easier to conceal several weapons on her body.

Noticing Gage's lustful gaze past him, Joey turned to see Layne approaching them both. He took another quick look at his watch, realizing he needed to get on the road soon unless he wanted to be late. His hand gripped firmly onto Gage's shoulder, pulling him in so Joey could whisper, "Follow the fuckin' rules for once."

"Sure, boss." Gage's smile didn't falter while his focus was trained on Layne.

When she got to where they both were, she saw Joey whispering to Gage. She was pretty sure it was some threat having to do with keeping her out of harm's way. After releasing Gage, Joey turned to her, his expression softening partially, but a sternness remained present in his eyes that reminded her of pools of melted chocolate.

"You. Behave." A simple instruction. His hand reached behind her neck and pulled her in close. While upstairs, he had been brief with his affections; he took his damn sweet time now - whether it be for show or not. His other hand dropped down to grab a handful of her sweet ass, possessively squeezing it in his hand.

The way Joey's lips claimed her own had her gasping for breath, only for his tongue to glide into her mouth, where it wrestled with her tongue. He didn't want that moment to end, so he soaked up as much of her taste as he could in the few seconds he had to spare.

Once he released his hold on her, Joey smiled gently. "I mean it, Layne."

Layne crisscrossed her finger over her heart with a grin. "Stop worrying so damn much."

After gathering his jacket and a duffel, Joey was out the door to take care of some contract business matters forty-five minutes away in the next state over. It left Layne and Gage standing there in the foyer of her home, staring at one another.

"So, princess, what's on your schedule for the day?" He didn't make an effort to move, waiting for her to feel like she was the one in charge. Gage had all day to figure out all her inner workings, and he was looking forward to it.

Before she had even come downstairs, she knew this day was going to go one of two ways. One or both of them were going to choose violence, and with him calling her 'princess,' it seemed he was intent on sealing his fate.

Recalling Joey's words to her to behave, she slowly filled her lungs with more oxygen to find some sort of inner peace or some bullshit like that. Layne exhaled the worst of her temper and settled on providing him a bitchy look.

"I have a few stops to make to check in with a few of my family's most loyal clients. You should be able to hang back and keep your space." She dug into her jacket pocket a moment before she tossed her car keys at him. "You're driving."

Gage caught the keys with one hand without missing a beat. He examined the blue and white luxury logo on the key fob before dropping it into the safety of his pants.

The moment Layne went to walk past him, he jutted an arm out in front of her, blocking her path. "You're going to have to do better than that."

Her feet stopped short, so she didn't walk right into his massive arm. "Excuse me?" She notched up a brow along with her attitude.

"I'm going to need names and places. I may be the new guy on the block, but this isn't my first gig. Joey may have his rules, but so do I." His tone was assertive, but it still had a pleasantness to it. It was irritating as hell.

Gage's past experiences in dealing with seedy busi-nessmen weren't just limited to cash transactions. During the infancy of Cassidy's Cave, he couldn't afford bouncers and had the pleasure of removing rowdy patrons himself and keeping his girls safe. Even outside of that scope, he had a few stints watching some spoiled brats with pervy stalkers—and fucking a few of them, too. The spoiled brats, that was.

Layne rolled her eyes; these De Lucas and their goddamn rules. She crossed her arms in front of her chest. "How do I make this easy enough for you to understand? I am not a wilting flower that some underboss has hired you to follow around while she gets her nails done. I am the fuckin' be-all and end-all of my damn business. You don't make the rules here, I do."

It took a hell of a lot of restraint on his behalf to suppress the laugh that was tugging inside his ribs. From his perspective, Joey had no problem setting rules for her. He wondered how well she followed them. She had a damn firestorm of an attitude that stirred excitement in his pants at the challenge it presented. "You this bossy in bed, too?" He gave a devil's grin at her.

Today was going to be a long one if he kept this up. "Too bad you'll never find out."

"Are you sure about that? You seemed to be quite content when I had you in my arms at the Cave." He leaned in, making his words softer, "Admit that you enjoyed being so close."

Refusing to admit to anything, her arms dropped down from her chest, and her hand shoved his arm out of her way. It didn't take much effort; Gage allowed her to make a path for herself. "McGregor's is first on the list." This man was going to drive her insane before the day was over. She led the way to the garage where her car was parked.

Gage smugly smiled to himself as he trailed behind her. It seemed little Miss Be-All, and End-All could submit when led down the correct path.

CHAPTER FOURTEEN

The office that stored all the administrative crap for the Irish pub, McGregor's, was located directly above the bar on the second floor. It could barely be called an office, though, it was merely a cramped room the size of a walk-in closet with hardly enough room for one person, let alone two. It had a vintage wooden desk with rickety drawers underneath it, a miniature window to allow a small rectangle of light inside, a short stool that often remained tucked under the desk, and creative storage solutions cluttering the area.

Now that O'Reilly Enterprises had a decent amount of workers, she could have left the more menial tasks like checking books to some of the guys further down the chain. However, there were a few long-time supporters whom Layne liked to keep the relationship strong with. McGregor's and its owner, Sean, was one of those VIPs.

Layne stood in front of the worn desk. Her finger flipped to the next page of the book that contained all the cash records. Slowly, she ran her finger over the line of each transaction, mentally calculating the incoming and outgoing cash flows for the past month. Nearly every transaction was appropriately labeled.

At her back, Gage was squeezed in behind her. He was close enough that she could feel each breath he exhaled while he hovered over her. The scent wafting off of him, spicy and warm vanilla notes, suffocated her senses so that she no longer noticed the musty smell of the ancient building that was strongest there on the second floor.

Not taking her eyes off the numbers written on the page, she spoke up, "You could stand right outside the door instead of hovering over me like an assassin is going to pop out from one of these drawers." She shifted uncomfortably as she tried to find herself more space.

Sure, he could have given her the extra two feet of space, but where was the fun in that? He grinned as he watched over her shoulder as she continued her financial examination. "Can never be too cautious, ya know? I gave my word that I would protect every part of your body from suffering any harm." The deep register of his voice quieted as he spoke slower, "Every. Last. Inch."

She slapped her palm down on the current page of the accounting records she had been reviewing and turned her head to glare at him. "Can you not?"

His lips curved into a smirk that suited his face, drawing his mouth up in a way that she was sure had girls everywhere ruining panties. "Just doing my job. You're all mine to watch over today."

Layne gave an exasperated sigh as she spun around to

face him fully, doing her best to still leave a little room for the grace of God. "You can do your job damn well while not invading my space. Just because you may have a history of playing nicely in the sandbox with Joey doesn't mean it automatically makes you entitled."

His face shifted to one of delightful surprise. "So, he finally told you about Rose?"

As Gage leaned toward her, his hands planted themselves on the edge of the desk on either side of her. Layne did her best to keep her back rigid while holding her ground as her eyes stubbornly stared at him. "We talked about it." She prayed that the sound of her racing heart couldn't be heard.

"That sounds promising." He nodded to himself, seemingly impressed at this new development.

She scoffed at his ability to feel so full of certainty. "Get over yourself."

Finally, her hand made contact with his chest. As her hand applied pressure to try and give herself some space, she could feel the strength of the muscles tensing just beneath his shirt. When her thoughts strayed to pondering what his broad chest looked like without his shirt, her hand immediately recoiled like she had been burned by a lump of hot coal.

The sudden jerk of her hand off his chest had him casting a quizzical look at her before it faded back to the amusement of her reactions to him. His hand captured hers and placed it back on his chest, dragging her palm down between his pec muscles. He didn't stop there; he moved her touch further down over his rippling abs.

With her breath caught somewhere between her throat and her heart, at the last moment, she jerked her hand back before it made it down to his belt buckle.

Quickly, she spat out, "I don't have time for this. Please, get the hell out of my way." Layne was now impatiently waiting for him to decide if he was going to take his foot off the gas pedal of flirtations.

Gage held his stance there before her for another heartbeat before he took two steps back, dropping his arms down at his sides. "Sure thing, lucky charm." He could still feel the ghost of her touch along the center of his body, and it sank even lower to his cock.

He still managed to grate on her nerves with his snarky little nicknames for her despite complying with her request. Layne knew she needed to get some space to douse the flames he had stoked inside her with some water instead of pouring more kerosene on it.

Before heading back downstairs, where Sean was restocking the bar, Layne grabbed this month's accounting records off the desk. When she arrived on the main floor with the book in hand, she dropped it on the bar top in front of him. "The numbers are off."

For as long as Sean had owned the Irish pub, she had never known his books to show as much as a penny difference. However, this month, his books were reflecting a discrepancy of precisely six-hundred and eleven dollars and twenty-four cents. The entry in the book had her initials, 'L.O.,' next to it in the accounts payable column with no detailed description.

Thankfully, McGregor's wasn't even open to the public

yet for another hour and a half, so there were no prying ears to overhear this rather sensitive topic. Sean ran his hand over the back of his neck, trying to look ignorant of the oversight.

Gage had followed Layne downstairs, resting against the edge of the bar with his elbow. Still thinking about their moment upstairs, he wondered about the current state of her panties. He could see the appeal his brother had in her. She was a strong little spitfire who didn't take any shit. In this line of work, it was rare to find a woman able to hold her own.

"Is there?" was the only acknowledgment of the accounting error Sean gave.

Layne frowned at him. "Sean…" her voice lost some of its edge as she stared at the man who wore his age poorly. The crows' feet at the corners of his eyes were more pronounced, his hair donning a little more white, and the restlessness in his soul, as seen through his eyes, was heavier.

"Sean," she repeated herself. "You're off by over six hundred dollars. Where did it go? There's nothing here in the books, and I sure as hell didn't sign off on it."

Using a bar rag, Sean wiped his fingers off before wringing the towel between his weathered hands. "Must have been these old eyes and rattled brain." The lie on his tongue caused Layne more distress than it should have. He quickly followed up on his excuse, "Let me double-check the entries tonight after closing."

She reached over and laid her hand on top of both of Sean's. "If it's anything but your eyes, I need to know.

You've been a great asset to my family since I was a little girl."

Layne recalled the way she used to carelessly run through the pub while her father checked the books or held private meetings. Often, she had gotten underfoot and received a scolding from her father. A much younger Sean had been there to soften the stern tone of Scott O'Reilly and made a Shirley Temple with extra cherries to help lift her spirits. Now, even as an adult, when she was aggressively hungover, it was something she craved.

Sean gave a half-smile at her before pulling his hands away so he could remove the book from the top of the bar. "Layne, you've been like a daughter that I never had. I have always respected and honored your family."

His words rang true with sincerity and honesty, but there was something about the way he looked at her that reflected a soul in despair. Layne withdrew her hands and nodded, hoping that after closing, she could sit down with him to figure out these numbers.

"I will be back by tonight after closing." She watched Sean secure the spiral-bound book containing the financials behind the bar. Layne looked over at Gage and nodded toward the door. He straightened up, pushing away from the edge of the bar, and joined her after she said her goodbye to Sean.

After they got back to her silver BMW, she placed her hand on the passenger door's handle. Before pulling on it to open the door, Gage was there with his hand on top of hers. The sunlight illuminated the intricate linework of the blossomed rose on the back of his left hand.

"Allow me." The soothing tone of his voice was like silk against her soul.

From an outsider's perspective, it appeared to be a chivalrous gesture. From Layne's perspective? It felt like an excuse to encroach on her space again. Her emerald orbs looked up at him, trying not to allow her breath to get caught in her throat again.

Layne slithered her hand out from underneath his palm, allowing him to swing the door open for her. Once she was settled in her seat, he closed the door for her before getting in on the driver's side.

She pulled out her phone and noticed a few messages from Joey, a smile immediately spread over her face.

JOEY

How are things going?

I may be a little later than I thought tonight.

I would rather be there with you than waiting on these assholes.

LAYNE

I haven't strangled him…yet.

Be careful and don't do anything stupid. I love you.

JOEY

Always and forever.

When Gage got in the car, he was watching as Layne's fingers tapped across her phone and the way her guard came down as her smile indicated she was likely texting with Joey. It was a glimpse past the hard exterior that she usually had wrapped around herself.

Layne looked up to see Gage sitting there watching her. The protective exterior snapped back in place as she shoved her phone into her pocket. "What?"

He sat up straight in his seat with his head held high. "Where to, your Highness?"

She shook her head. "Will you stop with the damn cutesy names?"

Gage relaxed his posture and smirked at her, hearing the irritation in her voice. "Just trying to see what fits you."

"Just fucking drive. 15 East 7th Street." Her hand waved him on, and when he complied, turning his attention to the road ahead of him, she couldn't help but allow her eyes to linger over his profile.

Casually, he was sitting back in the seat with one hand on top of the steering wheel, the rest of him appearing at ease as he navigated each street on the way to the next location. His right elbow was on the center armrest as he hung his arm over the edge of it. The tattooed word on the back of his hand was in plain sight: WRATH.

"Wrath? Who the hell gets that tattooed on their hand?" It seemed a pretty interesting message to make part of your-self forever.

Gage smirked to himself as he shifted in his seat. "You'd be amazed at what types of tattoos I've gotten over the years. This particular one just happens to be a promise I've made."

Growing more curious, Layne's eyes roamed over his

body while he drove. What other tattoos were hidden underneath all those clothes? "What type of promise?"

His voice grew more solemn. "To repay anyone who ever takes something from me again." In particular, to whoever had a hand in plucking his precious Rose from this lifetime.

All this time, he felt her eyes roaming over him, and he suppressed the urge to look over at her and acknowledge it. The one thing he couldn't suppress was the way his cock twitched between his legs, knowing he had her attention.

It didn't take much for the day to get away from them after several more stops checking in on a few establishments. There had been a variety of places on Layne's agenda, including a convenience store, a commercial real estate office, and the Brass Mirror.

After receiving several updates from Joey, it was clear that he was going to be lucky to wrap things up before the next morning's daybreak. Gage was far too happy to hear that his duties were still required well past the time frame he had expected.

Since it was beyond closing time at McGregor's, Layne figured she might as well get this awkward discussion out of the way with Sean to see if he was able to track down the accounting error she had discovered in his books.

Standing outside of the pub, she stopped and looked at Gage. "What are the chances of you staying out here so I can have this talk with Sean privately?"

He seemed to take a moment to mull over the response before he flatly responded. "None." Gage grinned as he leaned in with his hand on the small of her back. "But, after this, I will take you home, and you can tell me how close you want me." The innuendo was poorly hidden as the words held a husky purr to them.

"Keep dreaming." She stepped away from him and pulled on the front door to McGregor's. It didn't budge, the deadbolt already being turned. It was unusual for Sean to lock things up, knowing she was stopping by. Fortunately, she had a copy of the key.

Flipping through each of her keys, she found the correct one and twisted it in the deadbolt. Letting herself inside, the place was cast in an unsettling pitch black. Sean had known she was coming, why would he have closed things up and left? Her hand reached over and flipped on the light switch that she knew was just to the left of the entrance.

The bar area lit up and exposed a horrific site before her. Bar stools were broken and cast aside, tables on their sides, glasses shattered, all the photos on the walls destroyed, and ultimate destruction had left no part of the front room of the pub untouched. Aggressive and angry red spray paint stained the back wall where the iconic McGregor's handmade sign and logo were still proudly on display.

Sprawled in all caps was a very clear message: BACK OFF BITCH. YOU'RE NEXT. Layne had a sick feeling expanding in the pit of her stomach. She carefully stepped over the trash scattered across the floor. "What the fuck?" Her words were barely audible, even to herself.

Gage's head was on a swivel as he took in the devastating state of affairs in the same bar he had been in just earlier that day. "Layne, I don't like this." He kept close to her.

She chose to ignore him as she called out, "Sean? Sean, are you here?!"

When she made it to the back of the main area where the back room began, she reached a hand out to flip the switch to turn on that section of lights. Gage saw it before her brain registered the grotesque sight awaiting her discovery.

Despite his iron-like grasp snagging her backward and turning her into him, it was too late. The horror had already been captured by her vision. Sean's body hung from a blood-stained rope in the center of the backroom where her family had conducted so many meetings and negotiations over the years.

Adding insult to injury, Sean hadn't only been hanged but vertically ripped open, leaving a sickening display of gore and guts pouring down the front of his body. Layne's brain had trouble reconciling the terrifying and grisly image, but once it did, all she could hear was her scream ripping through the air. It couldn't have been Sean, it couldn't have been real, and it sure as hell couldn't have been a random and meaningless act of horrendous violence.

"Fuck." Gage's hand clasped to the back of her head, making sure she didn't turn back to see any more than she already had. He had seen some sick shit before, but even with his iron stomach, this was one for the top of the charts leaving even him queasy.

Layne's scream against his chest made him ache to take

away what she had just seen, wishing he could erase this memory for her. She may have been one hell of a badass woman, but she still had a soul deep inside of her that could hurt.

When her voice couldn't find any more sound to expel, her body began to tremble in his arms. Her form felt like it suddenly had no bones to support it, and Gage's strength was the only thing to prevent her from collapsing onto the floor.

"We need to get the fuck out of here." His arms easily supported her as he tried to walk her back to the front door. When he noticed her feet were unable to coordinate her movements, Gage leaned down and scooped her up with her legs draped over one arm and his other supporting her across her back. "I got you. Up you go, baby."

His hold was steadfast as he quickly navigated the destruction and got them both the hell out of there. If he could have driven without releasing his secure hold on her, he sure as shit would have done it. Instead, he managed to slide her into the front seat before taking up his spot behind the wheel.

Layne doubled over in her seat, trying to fight through her heavy breaths as her face got buried in her hands. She had no doubts that the threatening note had been meant for her. The problem was figuring out who she was pissing off badly enough for them to send the type of message that was now burnt deep into her brain.

CHAPTER FIFTEEN

She found herself sitting on the edge of her king-sized bed in the master bedroom, staring into a glass half-filled with straight Irish whiskey courtesy of Gage. The amber tones were muted by the darkness of the room, save for the one small lamp lit up on one of the nightstands.

Gage had driven her back home, stopping at least once so she could wretch up the contents of her stomach. He had stopped being the aggressive flirt long enough to hold her hair back away from her face despite her protests that she wasn't inept. After getting her back to O'Reilly Manor and settled upstairs, he kept a watchful eye over her.

Layne watched the drink's small ripples in her unsteady hands as her brain tried to eliminate the grotesque imagery of not just the hanging of someone she knew but the exposure of his insides as well. Victims who found the end of the rope were nothing like how movies portrayed it. It was a far more disturbing sight, with eyes bulging from their sockets and darkened by all the broken blood vessels. This is why she preferred simple shootings; they were quick, to the point, and not messy. What she had seen tonight probably had Eric Ellis beaming with pride in whatever circle of hell he was in.

Sean's death felt not just tactical but deeply personal, and she had no doubts that whoever was responsible had wanted to make sure Layne also felt the pain. They had accomplished their goal. This attack, combined with the night at the warehouse where the cops had been tipped off during her interrogation of the loose-lipped lowlife, she was certain someone was determined to keep a target aimed at her back.

Having heard the front door slam shut downstairs, Gage stepped out of the room, softly shutting the door behind him. The sound of heavy boots running up the steps at a fast clip suggested that Joey had just made it back from Newark in record time after Gage had reached out.

There was some hushed conversation right outside the door. Layne could hear bits and pieces as Gage filled Joey in on what had happened during his first day on protective duty.

"It was a literal bloody shitshow, man," Gage explained to Joey. "I got her out of there as quickly as I could, and she's holding up, but…" The words trailed off before the door opened up, and Joey walked in first.

With Joey's face full of concern, he approached her quickly, dropping down to both knees before her. His hands reached up to take hold of her face. "Layney, I'm sorry I wasn't there, but I'm here now." When his lips met with hers, she felt the love in them, but she couldn't summon the energy to return the gesture.

Gage stepped into the room, quietly bringing the door to a close as he gave them space. He was unwilling to leave his post, knowing first-hand what Layne had seen and the intentions behind it.

Her eyes hurt, dry from the tears that had already depleted any moisture from them. She continued looking into her glass like it was going to provide some answers or, even better, induce selective amnesia.

Joey used the firm hold on her face to try and shift her face so her eyes would fall on him. "Layne, look at me." His voice tried to hold a firmness but fell too soft. He could have tried to use his standard line on her to try and get her to do as he asked, but it would do no good in the state she was in.

He dropped his hands to rest on her thighs, rubbing them reassuringly. "We will find out who did this, and it will get handled. I can't do anything until I know you're still here with me." Joey was met with silence from Layne. That's when Gage came up next to Joey.

"Here." Gage's hand guided Layne's hands, holding the glass of whiskey up to her mouth. "Open up." His words demanded compliance from her. Joey may not have wanted to push her, but he was going to try things his way.

However, when she still failed to react to the edge of the glass pressing against her lower lip, Gage took it a step further. His hand slid up the back of her neck, grabbing a handful of her silky locks and tilting her head back slightly.

"What did I tell you? I told you to open those pretty lips and drink for me."

The order finally sank in past the volume of her thoughts, and her lips parted while Gage guided the angle of the glass to spill the heat-filled booze into her mouth. Once a generous amount was given to her, he eased the glass from her hands. "That's better," he murmured.

Layne swallowed the mouthful down, and only then did Gage release his hold on her richly colored chestnut hair. As the warmth filled her body from the mouth down through her chest and into her core, she finally was able to see past her recollections of the evening and into Joey's eyes.

"I don't understand…" Her voice cracked as it tried to fend off the emotions placing pressure on it.

Joey's forehead pressed to hers as he showered her with several more kisses. Despite how terrible it was, he was thankful that Layne hadn't been there when the attack had transpired. "We will figure it out after you get some sleep, let's just get you to bed." He looked over at Gage with an earnest display of grateful fortitude in his eyes, speaking all the thanks that was needed. "I will call you tomorrow."

Whatever remained in the glass Layne had been holding was immediately slung back and swallowed down by Gage. He shook his head stubbornly. "I'm not leaving her side. Not after tonight." It wasn't about how Layne fired up a desire in him, but the compulsion to make sure that both she and his big brother got through this fucker of a storm.

Both sets of similarly shaded brown eyes stared at one another, neither of the guys saying anything as something silently passed between them before Joey turned back to Layne. "C'mon. It's late," he said as he took note of the time on the clock on his side of the bed. It was half past four in the morning, and sunrise would be here all too soon.

Joey selected a set of pajamas for Layne to change into, one of his favorite things to do for her when she was having a rough day. It was a simple pair of pink cotton shorts she owned in the softest material he had ever felt and a corresponding cropped cami with a lace trim neckline.

While she was changing in the bathroom for privacy and while Gage was bound and determined to spend the night, Joey stripped down to nothing but his boxer briefs. Layne emerged from the bathroom in her sleepwear; her hair swept up into a high mound of a messy bun on top of her head.

Joey's arm wrapped around her shoulders and guided her into the bed, making sure the covers were pulled up to her waist as he joined her. She laid on her side to face Joey, immediately curling into his chest. The warmth of his body and his familiar scent eased the heaviness tugging on her soul while her eyes closed.

Sunrise came, and late morning arrived. Layne stretched out in her bed, having felt an immense sensation of safety and security throughout the hours she had allowed herself to sleep. The invasion of multiple scents wrapped around her senses: sage and leather with the essence of warmth from a spiced vanilla.

Her head rested in the crook of one large arm, a large hand rested on top of her hip while she lay there on her side, and another hand curled around the dip of her waist. When her vibrant green eyes fluttered open, still weary from sleep, she saw Joey's slumbering face before her. Her head was nestled into the bend of his arm, and his painted hand planted securely on the swell of her hip.

As she stirred, she felt the other arm draped over her waist, drawing tighter. She rolled onto her back and glanced to the side opposite of Joey to find Gage on her right and his arm steadfastly around her midsection. He lay there shirtless with the bulk of his upper body fully visible and only adorned with the silver chain around his neck that carried the round SPQR medallion he always wore. The white sheets shielded the lower half of him.

Gage's chest had fewer pieces of inked artwork than Joey's, with most of his designs creeping up from his hands onto his shoulders. There were roses of various styles scattered between the designs of many sharp-edged instruments ranging from daggers, swords, javelins, and others. Between the two of them, it was a delicious sight to wake up to and easily one she could get used to.

Feeling Layne's movement there in bed, Joey lifted his head from the pillow with half-open eyes. Joey's hand moved up to her jaw, turning her face to look at him. He greeted her with an adoring kiss; his lips massaged over her own until she forgot all about the other man sharing the bed with them.

The kiss grew deeper as Joey pressed himself up against her, letting her feel his excitement quickly growing against her lower stomach. Her leg draped over Joey's hip as desire grew more intense between her legs.

Feeling a shifting of movement behind her, it brought her back into reality. Layne pulled back from Joey's mouth, though he was reluctant to let her break the connection between them.

"Don't stop on my account." Gage chuckled, his arm giving Layne a squeeze at her waist.

Noticing the conflict in Layne's eyes, Joey glanced over at Gage, trying to warn him to tread carefully before he looked back at the woman he had fallen so deeply in love with. "Your call if you want him to stay, Layne." All she had to do was say the word, and he would shove his brother's ass to the curb with or without clothes.

With the choice being hers, she couldn't help but let her thoughts wander back to what had transpired after hours at McGregor's. Wincing at the scenes locked into her memories, the only part of the recollection that eased it was the way Gage had taken care of her and gotten her home. Layne needed something to get her past the fresh hell of those thoughts, and after hearing Joey talk about the way he and Gage shared a bed with Rosie, she was excited at the potential.

Gage scooted closer to her, making himself flush against her back as he whispered into her ear. "Better choose wisely, kitten. I am not for the faint of heart." The press of his erection was already prodding against her ass.

Layne swallowed hard as she tried to think past the arousal soaking her pajama shorts, having foregone any panties. Feeling two cocks already pressed against her body was sending it into a heated overdrive. She glanced back over her shoulder at Gage, who was still leaning in close, and then she looked at Joey, who maintained a neutral expression to avoid swaying her decision.

With a little smile full of mischief, she gave her response, "He can stay." The moment she gave her decision, Joey was ready to lean in and devour the taste of her mouth, but her hand on his bare chest right below his shamrock tattoo put an end to that. "I have conditions, though."

Immediately, Gage's eyes darkened with lust, and his smile twisted in amusement. "Lay 'em on me."

Layne rolled onto her back, squeezed between them both as she looked over at Gage. "Joey comes first. It stops when I say it stops. The second the two of you start bitching or fighting with one another, it's done. I'm not going to be caught up in some masculine tug of war."

He raised both brows as he shot a look at Joey. "She's adorable when she thinks she's going to be in charge." Gage traced his fingers along her arm until he found the engagement ring on her finger. There was a moment of admiration for the piece of jewelry wrapped around her before his fingers traced back up along the length of her arm.

His hand drifted over her shoulder before curling around her throat, his thumb stroking along the side of her neck. "Don't worry, you can keep wearing his ring on your finger. I just want you wearing my collar around your neck." Gage's dirty little smirk crossed his face.

CHAPTER SIXTEEN

Layne's legs pressed together as she felt the immense amount of excitement building between them as Gage's hand labeled with the word 'WRATH' wrapped around her throat. Her eyes felt heavy with lust while her chest rose and fell with a quicker tempo. The thin material of her cami allowed the stiff peaks of her nipples to be visible and straining against the fabric.

Gage bowed his head so his lips barely brushed against the side of her face while he whispered to her. His hand slid up along the length of her throat until his fingers firmly took hold of her jaw to keep her head still. "But first, I want to watch how you fuck my brother."

As if on cue, Joey's hand eased Gage's hand from Layne's face, replacing it with more of a loving touch as he cradled her face between his palms and leaned down to lock his lips onto hers.

She wondered if all of this was truly happening or if this was all some sort of intense sexual fantasy playing out in a dream. The only thing she knew for sure was she didn't want to wake up if that was the case. Her arms wrapped around Joey's neck as her hands ran over his upper back. The movement of her lips against his started off heated but only grew more scorching as he hungrily delved his tongue into her mouth.

Joey's arm slid underneath her, pulling her upright with him until they were both on their knees there in the middle of the oversized bed with Layne's back to Gage. Both his hands explored her toned body paying particular attention to the well-rounded ass he loved so much. He grabbed a handful of each cheek as he moved his mouth down to her bare shoulder, planting several tender kisses against her skin.

"You ready for me, Layney?" Joey murmured against her shoulder while his hands kneaded each globe of her ass.

"Mmm…" Her hands moved down over the chiseled strength of his upper body, her fingertips tracing over the images on display before her. First, the raven wings that led up onto the side of his neck. Then, the blood-stained sham-rock over his heart. The final one being graced by her touch was the 'Chaos Addict' words along his side.

She gave a playful smirk at him. "Maybe." Her hand slid between his body and the waistband of his underwear, immediately, she felt his hard cock straining in the confines of the boxer briefs while her hand wrapped around it. "It seems you're ready for me, though."

Gage laid back, tucking an arm behind his head as he watched the two of them engage one another. An intrigued smile never faltered from his face. His hand dug into his boxers, finding his throbbing erection, and began to give himself slow and long strokes. From this view, Layne's ass had the most delectable heart shape to it, even in those tiny shorts she wore.

Joey groaned as Layne grabbed a hold of his cock. His need for her grew more frantic as his hands came to the bottom of her cami and pulled it up. She was forced to release his dick as she lifted her arms to be stripped of the shirt. Her ample breasts were revealed as the camisole was pitched onto the floor. Before he continued, he quickly shoved his boxer briefs down to reveal each magnificent inch of his length. The precum glistened at the head. The sole article of his clothing fell to the floor, where it joined her top.

During her distraction with Joey, she recalled that Gage was still there in bed with them. She looked over her shoulder, her glistening green eyes admiring the sight of him laid out with his hand inside his shorts, very clearly working over himself. His eyes focused on her while he did so.

A hand came to her chin, turning her focus back to Joey as he grinned at her. "Didn't he tell you to do something?"

In response, she bit her lower lip as a smile tugged at the corners of her mouth. Layne pushed her hands against Joey until he lay on his back. She hooked her thumbs onto the sides of her tiny cotton shorts and worked them down over her hips. After wiggling them off her legs, she climbed on top of Joey, leaning over to engage him in a fiery kiss.

Teasingly, she rubbed her center against Joey's cock, letting him feel just how much her body wanted this. The slick arousal that had been worked up left a trail over his skin.

He groaned against her mouth as his hands massaged over her thighs. "Fuck, Layney, you're so goddamn wet." Joey's hips pushed up against her pussy, hoping to quench the thirst of his dick.

Layne reached between her legs and guided him to her entrance before slowly lowering herself onto him. Her wet desire provided a smooth entry as she moaned out, his size began to stretch her inner walls. "God, Joey, why do you always feel so good inside me?" She took a moment to adjust to his size before teasing him; her hips moved in a slow grind.

She had been so focused on Joey that she failed to realize that Gage had gotten up out of bed. It wasn't until she felt movement behind her and a pair of hands grabbing onto her hips that she was aware he had found another angle to watch the show from.

Behind her on his knees, Gage gave a low hum of approval as he looked over her backside while his hands took control of her hips. The heat of his mouth, when it made contact with the back of her shoulder with a single kiss, made her core melt even more. "I need to hear more of those beautiful moans coming out of your mouth."

As Gage knelt close behind her, she could feel his excitement prodding at her back, indicating he had ditched his boxers before coming over there. Her body felt full of electrical sparks, with Joey buried deep inside of her while Gage had only given the softest of kisses. It was inundating her senses.

With Gage's tight grasp of her hips, he forced her hips to ride Joey's cock. He took ultimate control of each movement right down to the speed and pressure. Layne's hands braced against the cut abs of Joey's stomach as she immediately was crying out in pleasure at the sensation mounting to a quick new height.

Joey's fingers dug into Layne's thighs as his gravelly voice groaned out. "Fuck. That's a good girl, Layney." His breathing turned into soft pants as he watched Gage put his hands on Layne from behind to manipulate her body on top of him.

Layne began tensing up with her nails scratching against Joey's stomach and her hips involuntarily fighting against the rhythm Gage was setting for her. Before she could hit her climax, he abruptly stilled her body. She exhaled a breathless whimper.

"What was one of your conditions?" Gage smirked, knowing damn well that he had Layne on the very edge of a sexual explosion. Yet, here he was, playing the sexual puppet master and orchestrating each part of her performance.

She whimpered again as she tried to catch her breath, her orgasm that had been so close began to slip out of reach. "J-Joey comes first."

"That's right. That means I don't want you to come until he fills your pussy, do you understand me?" Gage left another kiss on the back of her other shoulder, this time while he waited for her to answer him.

She furrowed her brows together. "That's not what—"

The man at her back took a handful of her messy bun

and tilted her head back so he could see her face. "Do you understand?" Gage's words were sterner this time as he cut off her words.

Layne gave a breathy response as she briefly looked into Gage's eyes, which looked like saucers of steaming coffee. "Yes." His hold on her hair released, and his hand returned to her hip, where he drove the movement once more.

Joey had always been dominant with her, but Gage was on a whole new level, and Layne couldn't help but find herself falling hard for it. Joey's hips thrust up into her as he felt how tight her pussy was squeezing around him. He moaned out, "Mm, you like taking my cock like this, don't you Layney?"

All she could do was nod between each of her gasps for air between her moans, struggling to adhere to Gage's instructions.

To push the limits even further, Gage slid one hand off her hip and down to the front of her, where his fingers found her swollen clit. "You better remember what I told you, baby girl." His fingers rubbed quick circles over the sensitive bundle of nerves, nearly sending Layne careening off the highest cliff.

She shrieked out as her body shook with the effort not to be overcome with the immense amount of pleasure that seemingly filled each vein inside of her. Her hands squeezed tightly onto Joey's sides while she shut her eyes tightly, trying to maintain anything resembling control.

With the intensity raging inside of Layne's body as she

fought against giving in to her release, Joey yelled out as her slick walls squeezed so tightly around him that he wasn't sure her body would ever let go. "Jesus fucking Christ, you got her choking my goddamn cock!" He gritted his teeth as the pressure of her body caused the build-up of pleasure to speed up towards its ultimate goal.

Hanging by a damn thread, she desperately looked at Joey. "P-please… I need you to come." Each of her words strained as she begged between heavy pants while Gage's assault on her clit continued.

Seeing Layne's face overcome with a losing battle of control and hearing her beg to fill her with his cum, Joey tipped over the edge as he shoved his hips up. The full length of his cock was as deep as it would go inside of her. He roared out as his orgasm tore through him, and he shot a massive load of his hot seed up into her.

Gage smirked, and he continued to use his one hand to direct Layne's hips to work over Joey's cock as it continued to empty into the depths of her cunt. His thumb and fore-finger gave a hard pinch to Layne's clit. As he predicted, she completely unraveled.

The peak of her pleasure came to its breaking point as it pitched her into utter ecstasy, leaving her feeling nearly blind or somewhere beyond this realm. Her moans devolved into screams and curses of the purest pleasure. Gage slowed the movements of her body against Joey but didn't halt them so she could ride out her orgasm fully.

Each moment that passed while the high of her climax took its toll on her had her body releasing all the tension that had built up. Gradually, the intense sensations began to fade.

Hearing just how hard her orgasm struck her, Gage's cock was leaking precum down his thick shaft. His own needs caused it to throb and ache, nearly painfully so. He relinquished his hold on Layne, and she immediately slumped forward on top of Joey, where they were both a sweaty and panting mess together. A few barely there kisses were shared between them.

Layne was pretty sure she wasn't even alive any longer, she would have bet money on it. It wasn't too long after she started to recover that Gage pulled her back upright. His hands pulled her off Joey and dropped her onto her back. With how loose the entirety of her body felt, she moved with the ease of a ragdoll.

"You know what happens when you follow directions?" Gage's eyes brimming with tremendous need and desire as he took in the sight of Layne's naked body splayed out before him. Damn, her body hit all the right marks from her perky and round breasts, the flatness of her stomach, the way her hips curved, and how fucking hot her swollen pussy looked as Joey's cum slowly leaked from it.

Getting her first sight of Gage without anything but his necklace around his neck and a few rings still adorning his fingers, she gasped slightly as her eyes trailed down over the bulk of his muscles. When her eyes lowered to drink in the sight of his lower half, she was greeted by one hell of a surprise.

He had a tattoo on his lower stomach that began right as

the V of his body ended. A branch of laurel followed the cut of his V at the front of each of his hips. The red plume of an ancient Roman soldier's helmet began a few inches below his navel. The bold design of the profiled helmet continued south until a wooden plaque with the Roman Legion initials 'SPQR' was etched right at the base of where his cock protruded from his body. Much to Layne's shock and intrigue, the tattoo continued to cover every delicious inch of his dick with a design of three broadswords intersected with one another on the top and sides of his shaft and the two branches of laurel appearing to twist and follow down along the underside of it.

Gage positioned himself to kneel between her legs and gave her a few moments to take a full look at the artwork decorating his body. It was a guilty pleasure of his, watching initial reactions to the location and design of the tattoo he wielded on his lower half.

Once he had given her sufficient time to get a good look at him, he lowered his body down on top of her. His face was intimately close to her own.

Layne slightly turned her head to snag a look over at Joey, who was watching with a grin as he was still trying to recover from his round with her.

"He had his turn with you," Gage spoke to her gently as his hand turned her head back so he could stare into those enchanting green hues of hers. "Now, I want you looking at me."

He had intentionally avoided kissing her up until this point, wanting to reward her for behaving for him. Gage took his time memorizing the features of her face while the backs of his fingers caressed over her cheek. "Damn…" The beauty of the woman lying underneath him had him trying to remember how to fucking breathe.

"What?" Layne asked in a whisper.

"You're gorgeous." Gage pressed a kiss to her mouth, slowly acquainting himself with the delicious taste that greeted him.

At first, Layne was reserved and hesitant, but that quickly all dissipated as she got lost in his lips, passionately returning the gesture as her hand held onto the back of his neck. When he drew back, he grinned at her. "I need to hear you tell me, Layne."

Looking up at Gage, it took a moment to register what he wanted from her. She sweetly smiled at him. "Gage, I want to watch you fuck me with those swords drawn on your cock." Her legs spread wider for him to get easier access, solidifying her words that granted him permission to take claim of her body.

Gage gave her another firm kiss before he supported himself above her enough that she could see his hard cock pressing up against her entrance. Layne peered down to see the tips of the swords begin to figuratively pierce into her as he gave a slow push inside her body.

Layne's hands held onto his bulky biceps, and she moaned out as her body accepted his thick member. Everything at her core was already so sensitive, feeling him enter her was quick to stir up intense feelings of pleasure.

He pushed himself deep into Layne until the tattooed swords completely disappeared inside her pussy. He groaned at the tightness of her slick walls, appreciating what Joey had likely been feeling when he had control over Layne's movements earlier.

Watching his little brother slide himself between Layne's legs and hearing the sweet song of her moans, Joey found himself swiftly growing hard again. He rolled over closer to them, lying on his side as his hand grabbed his dick.

Fully seated inside of Layne, Gage bent down and gave her an electrifying kiss. He drew his cock back out to the tip before pumping it into her again. He swallowed her moan with his mouth while his tongue pushed past her parted lips.

He created a rhythm of thrusting into her, getting rewarded each time with the sounds she made. She squirmed below him, writhing as her body's desire escalated quickly. Her legs wrapped around his waist to draw him deeper into her.

"God, yes!" Layne's hips found a rhythm matching Gage's as he continued to ram himself into her. The speed of each thrust increased in tandem with the carnal pleasure they were both experiencing.

She began to feel the head of his cock pounding against that sweet spot deep within her body. Her hands squeezed tighter on Gage's arms while she tried to fight the growing swells of the orgasm hovering on the horizon. She shook her head as she looked up at him. "I c-can't, I can't hold it back."

Knowing she was so damn close, Gage grinned at her. "I don't want you to, baby. You go ahead and come all over my dick while I keep fucking this cum-filled pussy of yours."

Joey fisted his cock, pumping it while he saw how Layne was being such a good girl for them both. Keeping one hand stroking his length, he leaned over and took a mouthful of her bouncing titty that was just calling out to him.

With Joey suddenly sucking on one of her stiff nipples, his tongue relentlessly swirling over the peak, she fell into her release hard. "Ah! Fuck, yes!" Her pussy clenched down onto Gage, clinging to his cock with profound need as her walls pulsed with her orgasm.

Despite how her body tried to still his thrusts, Gage pushed on in pursuit of his release. "Fuck, baby, that's it." He clenched his jaw after a few more shoves into her before groaning out loudly as he gave one final hard move-ment into her body, shooting off ropes of cum into her.

Gage remained in her to the hilt as he tried to catch his breath. Looking down at Layne, he saw her slowly melting into a puddle, her legs releasing from his waist down onto the bed, and on her left breast was Joey giving one final tug of her nipple with his teeth before releasing it.

Joey's hand worked his erection harder and faster, seeing Layne was fading quickly from her orgasm, he was going to get himself in her one more time. He shifted so he was sitting by her head. His hand eased her face to the side. "Layney, open up and be my good girl. I want to see you take a third shot of cum and swallow it down. Are you going to do that for me?"

She wasn't sure what was beyond cloud nine in terms

of hazy feelings, but she was pretty sure she was there. With Joey turning her head, she saw his hand quickly jacking himself off right beside her.

In response to his question, she opened up her mouth for him. Joey growled in excitement as he shifted himself so he could work himself into her mouth. "That's my fuckin' girl." It was only a few moments before Joey hit his second release, and he came into her mouth.

Layne swallowed the hot seed down despite fighting the exhaustion wearing on her. Joey pulled out of her with a sigh of satisfaction. Having her take his cock and watching her take Gage's afterward had brought his fantasy to reality. He never wanted to lose his memory of this. God willing, this wouldn't be the last time Layne was shared between them.

Gage withdrew himself from the sticky mess of fluids leaking out of Layne's used pussy, proud of his contributions to that amazing sight between her legs. It looked like a damn masterpiece that deserved to be framed and hung up in his bedroom.

While Gage temporarily disappeared to the bathroom, Joey laid down and drew Layne into his arms. He kissed her temple several times while squeezing her tightly in his arms. "I love you so damn much."

When Gage returned, he placed a glass of water and a bottle of ibuprofen on the nightstand. "For later." He had no doubts that Layne would be feeling the resulting soreness from the activities within a few hours.

He joined Joey and Layne in bed, placing a hand on her

hip to let her know he was right there while his older brother cradled her.

Besides feeling thoroughly worn out and feelings of satisfaction beyond anything she had ever experienced, Layne was pretty sure that she would never want to be without either of these men in her bed.

CHAPTER SEVENTEEN

Truth be told, Layne could have slept another hour or two if it hadn't been the grumbling of her stomach demanding she feed it. When she opened her eyes and lifted her head from the pillow, her bed was completely empty. Zero De Lucas to be found.

She lay there a minute longer, a smile forming on her lips as she thought back to what had transpired. Her toes curled against the sheets as she recalled how intense her feelings had taken her hostage.

Finally, she decided that tracking down some food was going to be priority number one after she hopped in the shower to wash away all the dried bodily fluids smeared between her thighs.

Layne scooted to the edge of the bed, and the movement gave a small protest of soreness between her legs. She saw the water and the ibuprofen that Gage had left for her before they all passed the hell out. Deciding it wasn't a half-bad idea, she went ahead and swallowed a single dose down.

After a shower that left her feeling refreshed, she left her hair down in dark and damp waves around her shoulders. Layne pulled on a pair of black joggers to go with a distressed tee that had a wide-scooped neckline, causing it to slip down off one shoulder.

While the guys had been the perfect distraction, her thoughts began to come back to her as to the sight she and Gage had stumbled upon at McGregor's. The erratic letters spray-painted on the wall communicated the message in no uncertain terms. Sean's body with a large and gaping wound while dangling there from the rope was meant to drive home the point of how serious the threat was.

When she got downstairs, she heard two familiar voices as she approached the kitchen. Entering the spacious area designed for someone with far better cooking skills than she possessed, Joey and Gage both turned to look at her. Each of them displayed their own unique signature smile. Gage's had a rugged yet boyish charm to it, while Joey's smile always seemed to have an edge of mischief tugging at the corners of his mouth.

Joey had on a pair of his navy sweats and a white tank clinging to the trim muscles of his torso. As usual, each of Joey's tattoos flexed with his movements, creating a show that she could watch for the rest of her days and intended to. As for Gage, while he had on a pair of jeans, he was missing a shirt. The cut of each of Gage's large muscles was on full display, while the necklace he always wore hung down in the center of his chest.

The sight of them both made her mouth water, and her mouth wasn't the only thing getting wet. It was a quick reprieve from the more serious thoughts floating around in her mind seconds ago.

"There you are." Joey approached her, one hand resting on her hip while his other slid into the soft chestnut locks of her hair. He greeted her with a kiss that had a fiercely possessive love behind it.

After he pulled away, he stepped away to rummage through the fridge. That's when Gage stepped up to her next. His hands came up to her face, and before he made a connection with her lips, he spoke in a low voice to her. "Did you take the ibuprofen I left for you?"

Layne nodded her head. "Yes."

Gage smiled in approval, but he still hovered his mouth over hers. "You forgot something."

When her eyebrows shifted in confusion while her emerald pools stared up at his face, looking for an indication of what he meant.

He brought his mouth to her ear while he whispered, "'Yes, Sir.'" The emphasis on the way he added the title to it sent a heat barreling deep to her core. Gage drew back to face her again. "Try again, lucky charm. Did you take the meds I left for you?" If she wanted him in on this little arrangement, he was going to make his expectations known.

The way his eyes felt like they were watching the burn of lust warming her soul had her willing to say any goddamn thing he wanted. "Yes… Sir."

After addressing him the way he demanded, Gage gave

her the kiss he had been withholding from her. His mouth gently caressed her lips as the expanse of his hands cradled her face just underneath her jaw.

Gage grinned happily after he eased away from the kiss. "Just had to make sure you'd be as much of a good girl as Joey said you would."

That earned a snort from Joey, who pulled out a sub from the fridge and began laying it out on a plate for Layne. "I said she's a good girl when I want her to be. I never fuckin' said that you'd get the same treatment."

"Hm, seems she's a quick learner." Gage flashed a wink at her before he walked back over to where there was an open bag of chips on the counter. He leaned back against the counter and dug into the crinkly bag for a handful of the salty snack.

With both of them talking about her, she shot them a sassy look. "If you both keep talking about me like I'm not here, I'm not going to be anybody's good girl."

That earned her a chuckle from Gage. "Oh, I'll be looking forward to that." He enjoyed dishing out punishments to bratty bad girls.

Layne walked over to where Joey was pulling the last of the paper from her sandwich. "Tell me that's for me. I'm starving."

Joey nodded at her and kissed her cheek as he pushed the plate towards her, not before giving a smack to her ass for her smart-ass comment, though.

After both of them watched her devour the roast beef sandwich in record time, Joey was the first to bring up the sensitive topic of what happened at McGregor's. "Layne, we should talk about what happened at the pub."

She raised a glass of water to her mouth, washing down the last of her sandwich. "I agree." Both Gage and Joey blinked at her unexpected response. Layne brushed off her hands over the now empty plate and continued, "I'm pissed —no, I'm fucking livid. When I find out who is responsible, they're going to learn real damn quick. If they want to fuck with me thinking I'm going to be scared off, they have another thing coming. This is one bitch that is going to come out, play the damn game, and win."

Layne was tired of people being ripped from her life, one tragedy after another. One of the other factions had to be at play here, and she was bound and determined to find out which one thought they were going to fuck with this O'Reilly. Her father, Scott O'Reilly, would have never tolerated this type of attack, and Layne wasn't going to either.

Her eyes looked at both of them, "I'm going to meet with the head of every damn faction in the city myself. Someone is going to give me answers." Layne's voice was firm but surprisingly calm.

Gage popped one last chip in his mouth, chomping down on the crunchy round quickly. "I like this plan. Let's do it."

It was Joey who gave an irritated sigh at Gage's enthusiastic response to what seemed like a reckless plan. He tried to be the voice of reason for all their sakes. "We've got an unhinged psychopath here. Before we shake up a hornet's nest even further, let me try to see what information I can shake out of a few sources."

She wasn't swayed off course by Joey's attempt to dissuade her. "I've already texted Jonathan, telling him to start setting up the meetings. I'm not backing off just because some coward wants to make a move behind my back." Russ was at the top of her list of suspects, and she was willing to put money on it that he was involved one way or another.

Gage had to take off shortly after their discussion with Layne. It was one of the most popular nights at Cassidy's, Eat Me, Greet Me night. All of the girls got candy necklaces, and with every purchase of a lap dance, each patron received one as well. The concept was devilishly simple: the candy could be eaten off of its elastic string wherever the necklace was placed on the other person.

Layne was doing what she did best, burying herself in work to avoid letting her mind wander too far into the darker depths of her soul. She had been holed up in her office all afternoon, making back-to-back phone calls to faction heads.

She sat in the office chair, her feet propped up on the edge of the desk as she leaned back with her phone to her ear, listening to the thick Russian accent of Alexei Kuznetsov.

"Pchelka," he sighed as he called her 'little bee' in his native tongue. "I am a very busy man."

Her fingers were buried into the hair on the top of her head, growing tired of political dances through minefields of oversized egos.

"And I'm a very busy woman, Alexei. In fact, I'm going to be even busier once I find out which of your men took shots at me several months ago." Layne's voice grew heated with irritation.

There was a long pause before he responded to her. "I told you, none of my men had any involvement. Was big misunderstanding."

She sat up in her chair, dropping her feet back down to the floor. "*Misunderstanding*?" Her harsh laugh at his minimization of the incident cut through the air. "If you want to avoid any *misunderstandings* when it comes to who feeds the hand of your vodka distributor, I would highly suggest that you find fucking time in the next week to make room for some drinks with me."

It sounded like Alexei pulled the phone away from his mouth as he yelled at someone in Russian. With the very limited knowledge she had of the Russian language, Layne only caught a word here or there—both swear words. As he returned to his conversation with her, he had a much softer tone. "Alright, pchelka. We shall talk, yeah?"

Feeling a sense of relief wash over her, she finally cracked a smile. She wrapped up the details with him before hanging up and tossing her phone onto her desk in front of her. There were knots embedded in her muscles all over her body, knowing the uphill battles she was fighting daily in the criminal underworld. This entire situation surrounding Sean and McGregor's added to the already heavy load.

The door to her office creaked open, and Joey popped his head in, no longer hearing or seeing her on the phone, he fully stepped inside. "Hey."

She lifted her gaze off the phone lying there on her desk to see him walking over to her. He came to her chair, turning it to face him so he could take her hands and urge her out of her seat.

Layne smiled sweetly at him. "Hey."

Joey could see the stress locked tightly into her shoulders. He released her hands and began to knead his fingers into the compactly coiled muscles around the base of her neck. "I wanted to talk."

She groaned and closed her eyes, giving in to the nearly painful manipulation of the stubborn knots his hands were trying to work out. "Mm, I already told you my plan. If it makes you feel better, I will let you or Gage come to the meetings with me."

"Let?" He raised a brow at her choice of words. Joey's fingers stopped their massage, and his fingers grabbed ahold of her chin. When she opened her brightly colored eyes at the interruption of his hands' work, she saw him with a heated gaze.

His face came in closer to her own as he spoke with his voice on the edge of a growl. "Make no mistake, Layney, one or both of us will be there whether you allow it or not."

The way he slowly spoke the words to her had her heart beating a little quicker inside her chest.

Joey wasn't going to fuck around with her safety. In a perfect world, she should have been perfectly safe having talks with the other faction heads as the head of her own criminal enterprise. However, he didn't trust any of those fuckers, not after they all had basically left her for dead when Liam was fucking shit up. "Do you understand me?" The seriousness weighed hard on his words.

Layne gave a small nod. "Yeah."

"Good." His mouth closed the gap between them, stealing a kiss from her to reassure her that he was still going to be her shadow whether she liked it or not.

After he pulled back, he gave her shoulders a squeeze. "That's not what I came to talk to you about, though."

His hands trailed down her arms. "I need to make sure you're good with how things are between us and Gage."

She glanced down, feeling the spread of the heat on her face at the way both the guys had taken care of her upstairs. Layne licked her lips before biting into her sheepish smile. "Joey…" Finally, she looked up at him. "I'm good. I'm a little surprised, but I'm good with all of it."

He dropped his hands onto her hips and grinned. "Surprised?"

She gave a soft chuckle. "I didn't expect you to be okay with any of it. You beat the shit out of a guy for dancing with me at a club, or did you forget about that?"

He grumbled, remembering the way the little punk had been putting his hands on Layne. The ass-beating had been justified. "That was different." Joey pulled her in closer by her hips.

Layne didn't look very convinced, so he further explained himself.

"I never want another man laying a hand on you. No other man deserves to hear how it sounds when you come. I never want to hear you screaming out any other name but mine."

She tilted her head as his words seemed to contradict everything that had transpired upstairs between them and Gage. Before she could question it, he raised a finger and pressed it to her lips to prevent her from speaking.

"The only exception is Gage. He is the only one who ever gets the privilege. Whatever the two of you do together is up to you. At the end of the day, you're still going to be all mine." Joey had shared all his favorite things with his little brother growing up, why should this be any different? Especially when Layne was able to get double the pleasure from it. Anything she wanted, he wanted to be able to provide it for her.

Joey removed his finger from those sultry lips of hers. Layne's hands ran up the front of his chest, her fingers enjoying the feel of hard muscle underneath them. She smiled lovingly at him.

"I will always be yours, Joey. But, two De Lucas?" She grinned. "You're both going to keep me a very busy girl."

A devious grin spread across his face. His hands roamed past her hips and gripped tightly onto her ass. "Just wait until I make you my wife, Layney. Gage is gonna have to fight for his turn with you."

He suddenly lifted her, tossing her over his shoulder. It caused a shriek from her as she was grasping onto the back of his shirt while staring down at his ass. "Ah! Joey!" After the unexpected change in her position, she giggled while he walked out of the office with her, carrying her up the stairs, planning on giving her a taste of what was to come after they said, 'I do.'

Gage looked at himself in the mirror, running a hand down over the light beard he was growing in. Fuck, he was a handsome bastard. His hands came down to the midnight blue suit jacket, straightening it out on his large frame. He left the top few buttons of his white dress shirt undone. Underneath the jacket, he had two handguns holstered. Two were better than one, right?

He reached into the pocket of his matching blue dress pants and retrieved his keys. Layne would pitch a fit if he was late, and Joey would throw punches if he was. Leaving his condo in Hudson Yards, he arrived at O'Reilly Manor about twenty minutes later.

Before he stepped up to the front door, it opened, and Layne emerged. He gave a large smile, seeing her all dressed up for her meeting with Kuznetsov. She had on a pair of smokin' hot black boots that stopped right above her knees. The black dress she had on nearly looked painted onto her athletically fit body and all of its delicious curves. The long sleeves had cutouts exposing the tops of her shoulders. His cock was already beginning to stir to life, especially when he saw the decorative chain around her waist that was useless in serving its purpose as a belt. Fuck, he was going to have fun with that later.

Joey stepped out behind her wearing his black tactical pants and shirt, indicating he was on his way out to take care of his more violent business dealings for the evening. He leaned over and drew Layne into a deep kiss, thoroughly enjoying the taste of her mouth before he pulled back. "Try not to piss off anybody too much tonight." His eyes darted over at Gage, silently expressing the same sentiment towards his younger brother. The last thing he wanted to find out was that the two of them both lost their tempers.

Layne smirked. "Never." Her hands dropped down to his firm ass giving it an appreciative squeeze. The way his pants hugged his behind was something she wished she could stare at all day long. "I would like you to come back in one piece. So, be careful and don't go getting yourself killed, okay?"

He grinned. "Never gonna happen." Joey looked over at Gage and gave him a nod. "She's all yours." They clasped hands and gave a brief hug with a hand patting each other's back.

After Joey left in his Challenger, Gage gave her another appreciative once over with his light brown eyes before walking her to his vehicle. Layne abruptly stopped as he led her to the doorless, busted-up army-green TJ

Jeep Wrangler with a tan hard top. "Are you kidding me?"

He hopped into the driver's seat and smiled at her. "What? It's a classic."

"It looks like a death trap." She was pretty sure that it was stubbornly clinging to the last moments of its life as she heard Gage turn the key, and the engine rumbled and sputtered.

"Put your ass in the seat, Layne."

She shook her head and climbed in, adjusting her dress to keep it secure around her thighs. Layne made sure her seatbelt was strapped securely around her body. They put doors on cars for a reason, and here she was, tempting fate in the open vehicle.

He reached over and grabbed the seatbelt, and gave it a firm yank with a bit of mischief in his eyes.

"Gotta make sure you're tied down."

In what seemed like such an innocent gesture of double-checking the seatbelt, his words sank deep to her core, imagining a series of intense scenarios, all leaving her aching between her thighs.

Seeing a tint of pink appearing on her cheeks, he chuckled to himself before sitting back in his seat and pulling away from the curb.

When they arrived at the agreed-upon nightclub, Alexei had his favorite table reserved for the occasion. Layne and Gage were escorted through the maze of tables tucked at the back of the establishment. The man guiding them was of average height, had a shiny bald dome of a head, and the personality of a paperclip.

He led them both to a table in the back corner where Kuznetsov rose from his seat, having a guard flanked at either side of him. Alexei may have been a small player in the game, but there was plenty of potential to turn him into a useful ally.

The man standing to greet her looked every bit his age and was approaching his golden retirement years. His goatee was showing the grey, overwhelming the light brown, and the same mixture of the two colors occurred on his shortly cropped hair. The lines around his eyes and across his face spoke to the toll the hard years had taken on him.

Alexei's suit was grey but almost looked silver with the sheen of its material. He gave her a polite smile as he opened up his arms. "Pchelka, so nice to see you." He leaned in to wrap his arms around her while pressing a brief kiss to both of her cheeks.

Gage visibly stiffened in his stance as he watched Alexei's every move. Polite greeting or not, he didn't like watching another man touch even breathing on her.

Layne returned the greeting, not looking to offend the man she hoped to get information from. "It has been a while, hasn't it?" She gave him a light smile.

The Russian gestured for her to take a seat as he took his own across from her. "Last I recall, you were just barely a woman, and now look at you. You are like a beautiful blossomed flower." He grinned at the sight of a matured

Layne in comparison to what he remembered her as when she was a young lady still trying to grow into all her curves.

He motioned with two fingers for the man on his right to pour a drink for Layne from the open bottle of premium vodka sitting on the table.

Layne sat in the chair, crossing one slender thigh over the other, not bothering to glance behind her to ensure Gage was nearby. The scent of his delectable spiced vanilla cologne gave his presence away and provided her reassurance. Her hand reached out and took the glass full of vodka and raised it slightly in Alexei's direction, "Vyp'yem."

He did the same in return, echoing her toast in his native language before drinking from his glass. Layne sipped the vodka, which by far had to be one of her least favorite drinks of choice.

"I appreciate you taking the time to meet with me," she began, "I don't think it's any secret what I want to discuss with you. I'm sure you've already heard about what happened at my favorite little watering hole."

With his glass still hanging from his fingers, he extended his hand to one of his men, and with a snap, there was a cigar being handed to him. After getting it lit, he sat back and let his mind ponder over his carefully worded response. "Yes. Word travels quickly. You know who is responsible for such a disrespectful act?"

She gave a small shrug. "I have my suspicions. I was hoping that maybe you'd help to confirm them." Her eyes stared at him to reflect the serious nature of her inquiry.

He laughed before taking another puff from his cigar, blowing the smoke up into the air above the table. "Me?"

He smiled in amusement. "Pchelka, you must think me a fool. If I knew, I would be wise to keep my mouth shut, just as you would be wise to heed such a stern warning."

Layne drew another sip of the vodka into her mouth. "Alexei, don't fucking play games with me. Your little weasels have their hands in a little bit of everything; I'm sure somebody knows something." That earned her an irritated grunt from one of Kuznetsov's guards apparently, he didn't like being called a weasel.

Still donning his smile, he shifted his gaze over her body. "I might know a thing or two. For a price." He ran his tongue over his lips like a wolf eyeing up a lamb.

She could feel his eyes trying to burn a hole through her clothing and what lay underneath. Now, it was her turn to laugh. "Oh, who is playing who for a fool, now?"

He shrugged casually. "Everyone must pay for something, yes?"

While he wasn't wrong, but Layne wasn't about to earn a reputation for fucking every faction head in the city anytime she needed something. She stood, causing not just Alexei's guards to shift into a state of readiness but Gage tensed up in his stance.

Layne stepped over to the Russian, bending over at her waist while leaning down to bring her face up close to his. Her words melted into a sultry whisper. "Oh, Alexei." She drank down the rest of her vodka and placed the glass between his legs on the seat of his chair.

It took everything Gage had not to intervene and tell Layne to stop playing with goddamn fire. She was toying with a very dangerous man and teasing another—him. The way she was bent over, the hem of her dress was threatening to reveal what lay underneath, forcing Gage to swallow down a groan. He mentally reminded himself what his purpose was here, and it sure as hell wasn't sinking his cock into her in the middle of the club.

She pressed the side of the glass forward between Kuznetsov's legs, bringing it up against the package bulging against the crotch of his pants. Layne's lips found his ear, where she whispered something only meant for his ears. It prompted Alexei to visibly shift in his seat.

Layne straightened up, leaving the glass where it was on his seat. "I want a name." She stared down at the man seated before her.

He cleared his throat. "I once told your father that you would make a nice printsessa for one of my sons. I misjudged. You are more like your father than I realized. I think you will find the answers you are looking for over at a little souvenir shop across from the Empire State Building." He placed his serving of vodka down on the table.

Her look turned dark as she got the answer she was looking for. "Thank you."

As she stepped away from him, his hand suddenly grabbed her wrist. Layne looked down at his tight hold on her, his grasp engulfing the narrowest part of her arm. She flexed her arm, pulling on his hold as she looked up to see his eyes.

"Be sure of your actions, pchelka. You do not want to lay judgment on the tiger only to be bitten by the snake." He released his hand from her.

She sat there thinking about his words and nodded. "Of

course." Layne wasn't quite sure what he meant by the cryptic saying, but she wasn't going to let anyone in this city destroy her—tiger or snake.

Leaving the nightclub, she approached Gage's Jeep with determination in her steps. Before she could climb in, his hand grabbed her arm to turn her to face him. "What did you say to him in there that made him change his mind?"

Layne smirked. "That I knew his interests didn't lie in bedding the O'Reilly in front of him, that he would need to take a trip to visit Liam in Rikers Island to get his fix." Her devious little smirk grew before she added, "And that if he didn't give me what I wanted, I would cut his balls out, place them in a glass, pour his shitty fucking vodka over them, and make him drink it all."

"That's fucked up." Gage stared at her, knowing he should have been shocked, but found himself even more turned on knowing how she could hold her own in the big leagues.

"I know." She slid her arm out of his hold and got into the Wrangler.

After Gage joined her in the vehicle, he took a look at his phone and sent a text before tucking it back into his jacket pocket. He drove them back to his condo just south of Hell's Kitchen.

"What are we doing here?" She lifted a brow as he parked in the underground garage of a newly constructed building that laid residence to condos that were larger in square footage than the average American home. "Joey said he would meet us back at Cassidy's after he was done."

Gage didn't say anything when he hopped out of his

seat and came over to her side. He reached over and pushed the release of her seatbelt, easing it off of her. "I told him there was a change of plans."

Her words held both irritation and suspicion. "What change in plans?" She hadn't been made aware of any changes, and she didn't like she was kept out of the loop. Layne got out of the Jeep and stared him down intently.

He took her jaw into his hand possessively. "Told him you were being a goddamn tease, and you were going to learn what happens when you shake your ass at me like that." His words were firm and laced with lust-ridden intentions.

CHAPTER NINETEEN

When they arrived upstairs at Gage's 24th-floor condominium unit, Layne was shocked to discover it was far different from the apartment Joey used to have. This was downright fancy as hell.

There were floor-to-ceiling windows in the primary living area upon entry that she imagined provided an impressive amount of natural light during the day. The furniture appeared to be high-end pieces, with a large cream sofa with navy throw pillows, a round coffee table in front of it, and an impressively large television mounted on the wall.

Gage slid out of his suit jacket, exposing the dual shoulder holster holding twin nine-millimeter semi-automatics. He tossed the jacket over the back of the couch before taking a seat. He leaned back as his eyes followed every movement Layne made.

"Layne," his voice husky and laced with need. "Come stand in front of me."

Maybe she was still riding her attitude and sass from her earlier conversation with Kuznetsov because she smirked at him. "Trying to be bossy now?" However, she still complied and walked over to stand in front of him, her hands perched on her hips.

His eyes narrowed at her, but he didn't respond to the question. Instead, he gave another order to her. "Turn around and bend over."

Oh, so he did think he was going to be the boss now, didn't he? She grinned as she felt excitement travel down her spine until it reached between her legs. After dropping her hands from her hips, she slowly spun around until her back was to him. Layne bent over halfway before looking back at him. "Satisfied?" The back of the dress still kept her body tastefully covered, barely.

"Not even close, baby. I want you touching your toes. Let me see that perfect ass of yours that you were so quick to taunt me with earlier."

She drew her bottom lip between her teeth, lightly biting it before continuing to fully bend down. The back of her dress crept up her backside until most of her ass was entirely exposed to him.

With his cock reacting to the sight of her holding that position, he contemplated plunging himself into her right then and there. He convinced himself to hold off; he wanted to teach her bratty side a lesson. "You realize how much I wanted to toss you down on that table tonight and spread your legs, not giving a fuck who saw? I would have drunk shots of vodka off your pussy before shoving my dick in you."

Layne had heard her fair share of dirty talk, but Gage's mouth was in a league of its own. The thin strip of her thong was very quickly getting soaked from her arousal as his vivid description had her aching from her core.

"Now, take off those panties and come sit on my lap." His palms rubbed down the length of his muscular thighs. Gage focused on keeping his hands to himself so he didn't get hasty and grab hold of her. There would be plenty of time for him to have her whenever it suited him, but tonight he had other intentions.

Her fingers hooked onto the sides of her thong, tugging them down her legs, and stepped out of them. After she straightened up, she brushed some of her dark locks of hair away from her face. Her face was flushed from all the blood that had rushed to it from being bent over for him.

She walked up to him, taking her spot and straddling his hips as her dress rode up past her hips to reveal what lay underneath. As she sat down on him, she could feel his cock trapped in his pants, begging to be freed.

"Mmm, you're doing such a good job listening. That's what I want from a good little submissive." Resting his hands on top of her thighs, he shifted his hips under her weight that rested on top of his erection. He didn't need to glance down to know her arousal was leaving its mark on his pants. She fucking wanted his cock in her as much as he needed to give it to her. "I want to see what else is mine underneath this dress." Gage ran his tongue over his lips, his hunger for her increasing.

Layne unhooked the decorative chain from around her waist first, dropping it onto the cushion next to them. Then, she pulled at the bottom of her dress, sliding it up until it was fully stripped from her body. Her fingers found the hooks of her bra and popped them free, letting that last piece of her clothing fall to the floor. The only thing remaining on her body were those over-the-knee boots she had been wearing all night.

Gage stared at the sensual buffet in front of him; he forced his arms back to rest along the back of the couch as he sat there. If he continued to lay his hands on her body, he knew there would be no stopping himself.

"Are you always this demanding?" She playfully asked him while her hands rubbed up the front of his chest, enjoying the feel of the solid wall of muscle under his shirt.

Allowing her hands to explore his body, he grinned at her question. "You haven't seen demanding yet. After the way you behaved tonight, taunting me with your ass, you're going to fucking find out. Consider yourself lucky I've shown as much restraint as I have."

"Oh, poor Daddy Gage, couldn't handle a little tease?" Layne playfully chided him with a fake pout. The attitude with this one was strong tonight.

His hand immediately found its place on her throat, pulling her face towards his own. "Don't. Play. With. Me." Gage's breaths were burdened with his desires as he fiercely stared at her. God help him with this woman that was driving him and his cock wild. With his hand on her throat, his imagination was drifting towards what his cock would feel like deep inside of it. How would her gags sound? Would her stunning eyes tear up?

Layne's gasp was nearly tainted by a moan when his strength took hold of her. Softly, she spoke, "Whatcha going to do about it?" Her hips rolled against the bulge of his pants to add a little extra tease behind her provocation.

His hand dropped from her neck, and he growled in response to her body grinding up against his already throbbing dick that wanted to find its way deep inside her. Wrapping an arm around her waist, he stood with her, walking over to one of the many windows that overlooked Midtown.

Gage put her down on her feet. He spun her around and bent her over so that she was revealing herself to the skyline of the city just on the other side of the massive window. "Don't move."

Layne gave a cheeky little smile but obeyed him, holding her position there.

He took off his shoulder holster, laying the equipment down on the coffee table next to them. His fingers yanked his shirt from his pants before undoing each button down the front until he could slip it off from his body.

Stepping up to her side, he ran his hand down her back and over the curve of her ass, enjoying the softness of the skin underneath his fingers. "You're going to count for me."

Her eyes tracked his movements, admiring the sight of him shirtless. "Count what?"

Smack!

A harsh sting of his hand coming down on one of her ass cheeks had her jolt from the sudden impact.

Gage smiled as the red outline of his hand graced her flesh. "If you want to show this hot ass off, you can do it for all of New York to see." His hand rubbed over where he had smacked, easing some of the heat of the strike. "But, you're gonna do it with my handprints all over it, so there is no mistaking who this ass belongs to. Do you understand me?"

The warmth of the smack against the curve of her behind wasn't the only heat in her body; her core was growing hotter with desire for his touch over more of her body. She nodded. "Yes, Sir."

He gave a grin filled with satisfaction at her response. "Now, fuckin' count until I've decided you have earned my cock." On the same spot he had just swatted her, his hand came down on it again.

Layne squeaked out, "One."

Gage brought down several more spanks on the beautifully fair skin, watching as it glowed an angry red with his large handprints. He waited between each one for her counts, and about halfway through, he switched to her other side. A total of six on each cheek plus one extra for all her sass.

He leaned over and pressed a kiss to the beautifully marked skin when he was finished. "You did so well, baby."

She was still bent over, breathing heavily, caught between the line of pain and lust each time his hand made contact with her.

Gage pulled her upright to face him. With gentler hands, he drew her face in to kiss her affectionately. Layne melted into the kiss, her hands landing on top of his chest to explore each cut and line of the strength of his body.

As the kiss grew deeper, Gage walked her back to the elongated chaise section of the sofa, refusing to break their connection as he did so. His hands quickly unlatched his belt and opened up his pants to drop them down to the floor.

With an increasing need for her reward from him, she pulled away from his mouth and laid herself back on the large section of the sofa. Layne smiled as she parted her legs for him, letting him see just how worked up he had her. The light pink folds between her legs soaked with her arousal.

Her eyes sparkled as she watched him dispose of the rest of his clothes. The grand reveal of the swords tattooed on his swollen cock had her hand dropping down between her legs, her fingers finding her sensitive clit and beginning to circle it. A moan slipped from between her lips. "I need you to take my pussy, Gage."

He didn't think his dick could grow even harder than it was, but when he saw Layne begin to play with herself, he damn near exploded. Smiling, he knelt on the cushion between her legs, positioning them against his shoulders.

His hand pulled her fingers away from her nub and slowly sucked the taste of her body from them before letting her go. "You better ask nicer if you want me stretching out your tight cunt with my dick."

Gage's hand went down the length of her boot until he

found the zipper and slowly eased it off her foot. Doing the same with the other as he admired Layne's body laid out for him, waiting and begging to take him inside her.

She squirmed as she saw him hovering closer to her entrance. "Please, Sir, fuck me with your cock."

"Much better," he grinned and grabbed ahold of her legs up against the front of his chest. He placed a few soft kisses on each of her legs, making her wait just a little longer. "I could stare at your body all night long, watch as you stay wet with anticipation of having me shove myself balls-deep inside of you."

Layne whimpered as he continued to deny her of the thing that she yearned desperately for. Her legs pulled against his hands, which held them still. She was pretty sure she would lose her sanity if he didn't get inside of her soon.

As much as he was enjoying watching her ache for him, he had his own hard need for her. Gage rubbed the tip of his cock over her clit, relishing in how Layne cried out at the brief contact. Before she could beg for him, he lined up and pushed inside of her, making those swords disappear in her body.

Immediately, he groaned out in pleasure in unison with Layne's loud moan as he filled the tight space of her primed and ready cunt. At that point, he couldn't hold himself back as he leaned over, forcing her legs over his shoulders, and he began to drill into her roughly. Watching as his movements had her beautiful breasts bouncing, he groaned out appreciatively.

The sensation of him shoving inside of her sent her into

a tailspin. Ecstasy began pulsing through her veins, and her voice, saturated with pleasure, filled the room. Her hand squeezed onto one of his that was braced on the cushion while her other found the back of his neck.

Gage showered kisses all over her body, starting at her shoulder and working his way up her throat until he found her mouth. Each time she moaned against his lips, he felt his dick fiercely ache with more desire inside her.

"Ah! Gage! Yes!" Her already tight walls began to squeeze even more around him as the peak of her pleasure built up to its breaking point. With stars floating across her vision, she cursed out, calling Gage's name as she came.

"Baby, that's fuckin' it, come for your Daddy," he growled into her ear. As Layne got lost in the depths of her pleasure, Gage couldn't fight his own anymore, and he gave a final thrust into her as his cum shot out like a damn bottle rocket.

Panting and resting his face up against the side of her neck, he gave tiny kisses. Despite having asserted his dominance over her and having her submit to him, deep down, he knew that very quickly he was the one becoming a slave to her. He was damn sure that no matter what Layne asked for, he would give it.

CHAPTER TWENTY

She balanced on the chair as she reached up to hang yet another framed picture on the wall of McGregor's. It was one of what felt like hundreds of photos she had reframed after the pub had been trashed the night Sean's body was discovered. So many of the framed images had been broken and scattered. Some of the actual photographs hadn't been salvageable, but she had saved what she could.

The walls had always been covered in snapshots of patrons from across the many years, and she sure as hell wasn't going to allow this incident to dishonor that part of Sean's heart and soul.

"Layne, we can have someone else do this." Joey chimed in from behind her. He watched as she stubbornly stood on her tiptoes to stretch to reach the nail on the wall just a few inches out of reach.

"No. I need to do this. They're holding Sean's wake here tomorrow, and hell, if I'm going to let this place look anything except as it should. Besides, I want to send a message to whoever did this." She grunted as she cursed her short legs.

Not waiting to watch her fall and break her neck, Gage wrapped his arms around her legs and lifted her so she could make the next few inches to hang the frame from the nail. Once the frame was secured, he softly dropped her onto her feet while keeping his arms around her.

"You're not going to send much of a message if you fall off a chair and break yourself." Gage gave her a gentle scolding before patting her on the ass and letting go of her.

She sighed quietly, knowing that he had a point. "That was the last one anyway."

Joey came up to her, turning her to face him. "It looks great." He leaned down and gave her a loving kiss.

While moving the wooden chair she had been using back to the table it had come from; Gage glanced over at the two of them. "How did the rest of the meetings go with the other families?" With things at his strip club picking up thanks to some porn convention in town, he had been unable to accompany Layne to several of the meetings she had with the other faction heads. Joey had happily stepped in to play the big, bad, masked man at her side.

Layne shrugged. "A few of them feigned ignorance. Two of them outright didn't want to get involved, which leads me to believe they're in Russell's pocket. Kuznetsov seemed to be the most willing to help. The rest of them seemed supportive, but who knows when push comes to shove where they'll land."

"What time is your meeting with Russ tonight?" Joey

checked his watch, wanting to ensure they would have enough time to prepare.

"Ten o'clock. He said he'd text the location to me an hour ahead of time." Layne readjusted her hair, pulling it back into a loose ponytail at the back of her head.

"Gage, be ready to go by eight." Joey didn't want to run the risk of a last-minute time change when the ball was in Russell's court. "I trust this fucker as much as I'd trust the devil himself," Joey muttered.

Gage gave a nod back to Joey in acknowledgment. "For this? My schedule is wide open." Already hearing of the history between Layne and Russ, hell, if he was going to pass on the opportunity to be there.

She stared at both of them. "It's a courtesy meeting, not a beatdown. So, both of your asses need to settle down." Layne had no intentions of confronting Russ Spencer tonight if he was behind her troubles. She preferred to let him think she didn't know better while she gathered her resources behind the scenes.

That earned her a look from both the guys. Joey was the first to step in close to her, his hands cupping her face. Within seconds, Gage was at her back, and his hands grabbed a firm hold on her hips. The combination of their two scents mixing around her while she stood in the middle of a mouthwatering De Luca sandwich was fucking intoxicating.

Gage's voice whispered in her ear, "We have to keep our lucky charm safe, so you better settle *your* ass down." The hum of his words prompted goosebumps to rise over her skin and her lips to part slightly.

Joey smirked as he watched Gage get the subtle reaction out of her. He pressed his forehead to hers so that she would be forced to stare into his eyes, which could have commanded the stars in the sky to rearrange themselves. "You want to rephrase that, Layney? It almost sounded like you were trying to tell us what to do."

She was frozen between them, disarmed by the proximity of their bodies to hers and held captive by their words. Layne swallowed down any smartass comments. Despite her independent nature, she hoped these men would never relinquish their protective hold on her.

That evening, Layne received the text at precisely nine p.m.

RUSS

Bethesda Fountain

LAYNE

We will be there.

RUSS

Bringing your lap dog?

She gritted her teeth at Russ's snide comment, making a jab at Joey. Her fingers typed a response that initially had some colorful language before she decided to delete it. Instead, she took the high road.

LAYNE

Can never be too safe.

See you soon.

"He wants to meet at Bethesda Fountain in the middle of Central Park. It's a public spot, but at this time of night, it's pretty isolated." That was the nicest way of saying that anyone who had a care for their safety avoided Central Park when the sun disappeared, and the fountain was no exception.

Joey finished tightening his belt around his waist. "How romantic," he sarcastically responded to the divulged location of choice. He made sure he had his skull mask in his pocket.

Stepping out of the bathroom, Layne noticed Gage had chosen to mirror his brother in choice of outfit. Both of them had on all black, from the boots to the utility pants and black shirts.

Seeing the expression on Layne's face, Gage gave a goofy grin. "If I had known that dressing like this would get that look out of you, I would have ditched the expensive suit from the get-go."

Joey smirked and tossed a second mask over at Gage. "Wait until you see her face when you put this on."

Catching the mask out of midair, Gage looked over the design and chuckled, "Nice."

She was beginning to feel naked without her mask to round out the trio, but Layne reminded herself tonight wasn't about kicking asses and getting herself in trouble. It was all about having diplomatic discussions. It was the whole reason why she was dressed in a dark-washed set of jeans and an ivory blouse underneath a black jacket. Her chestnut hair was half pulled back, so it stayed out of her face.

Call her skeptical, but she wasn't showing up without a firearm tucked in the back of her jeans. Joey had said it best earlier; it would be easier to trust the devil than it would be to trust Russell Spencer.

Since they were using the Challenger, Joey demanded he drive. He had seen the condition of Gage's Jeep and Layne's lack of parallel parking skills. Upon arrival, he ended up parking a short distance from the terrace that overlooked the fountain. Both the guys stretched their respective masks across their faces, concealing their handsome features.

Gage's mask didn't mirror the toothy grin of Joey's skull design. Instead, his artwork resembled a demonic smile with splashes of red, misshapen teeth, and canines that were far too long and curved to be human. Joey had been right, the look on Layne's face when he put on the mask had been one of a woman about to pounce on a mate. He noticed the way she tried to hide her body's subtle reactions, her thighs pressed together firmly, and her hands grasped onto her arms tightly while her tongue wet her suddenly dry lips.

Reminding herself this was like any other discussion she had over the past few weeks, Layne drew in a deep breath to prepare to switch to the woman who both deserved and commanded respect while standing tall at the top of her empire's ranks.

Both masked De Lucas fell in line behind her as they walked across the terrace to the large circular fountain with amber lights barely keeping it illuminated. There waiting for her at the north side of the fountain was one cocky-looking Russell Spencer. He had three men of his own keeping him company.

He smirked as he took note of the masked guards behind Layne. "Two lap dogs?"

She didn't need to hear the light rumble from Joey to know he was irritated at the dig, the prickling heat of his anger perking up could be felt in the air.

"I wouldn't worry about them. It's the bitch who bites." If Russ wanted to draw parallels, she would be more than happy to fire verbal shots right back at him.

Russ chuckled as he approached her. "I quite remember that spirited bark of yours, Layne. Tell me, is that why we're here tonight? Our interactions in the past would have me believing you're returning to yap at me. Have you come here to disrespect my livelihood?" He tilted his head curiously at her.

"Depends, have you been disrespecting mine?" Her eyes stared threatening daggers at him.

A mild smirk pulled at his mouth. "Let's take a walk." Seeing the uneasy shift Gage made, he held a hand up in his direction while looking at Layne. "Tell your pack to stay; I would prefer we be out of earshot for such sensitive discussions. One can't be too careful these days."

Layne looked back at the two masked men at her back and gave a small gesture for them to hang back for now. Turning her attention back to Russ, she gave him the all-clear, "Lead the way."

He gestured to the other side of the large fountain where the spilling of water into its base pool made sure that no one could overhear their conversation. She walked with him to his chosen spot, still within sight of both their sets of security detail.

"You must think I don't have ears on the streets, Russ. You haven't been particularly quiet about whatever problems you have with my family." She got straight to the point.

Russ nodded in agreement. "Liam couldn't pick up the slack, and this isn't the line of work where a woman should be left in charge."

"Someone stepped foot in my territory and left me with a hell of a threat, Russ." Her eyes assessed every movement he made, from how often he drew a breath to how he blinked his eyes.

"I'd tread very carefully, Layne. It almost sounds like you're insinuating I had something to do with it. That would be in poor taste to come here and start hinting at something that could start a war."

She gave an indifferent shrug. "From the tone of your voice, it sounds like you wouldn't mind if there was one."

Russ grinned and reached out to touch her arm. She drew it back from him, not caring for him to so much as trace a finger on her jacket. He got the hint and dropped his hand away from her. "I won't argue that I have had my eyes on your territory for some time, but don't be mistaken in believing I'm the only one."

They stood there talking for another twenty minutes before returning to their initial meeting spot. Most of the conversation was full of useless back and forth, with Russ trying to come off as innocently not having his hands in the pot of shit this time.

"Oh, Layne?" Russ called out to her before she turned to leave.

She turned to look at Russ. "Yeah?"

"This business is cruel and unforgiving. I wouldn't want to see you or anyone you care about end up beaten to near death and then dumped at the nearest animal clinic in hopes of quick euthanizing."

Gage had been prepared to leave, but as Russ gave his parting advice, he was immediately triggered by memories of the past. He stepped forward. "What the fuck did you just say?" His blood was boiling in his veins and turning his vision red with rage.

Russ was unfazed as one-half of Layne's security seemed to take issue with his comments. "I said I would hate to see her treated like a stray, beaten and discarded like an unwanted animal."

Both Layne and Joey had been prepared to leave when Gage suddenly broke rank with them. Not initially picking up on Russ's comments, Joey was taken off guard by his brother's sudden shift.

After Russ repeated himself, it sank in for Joey. *Rose.* Her poor, battered, and tortured body and the way it had been dumped at the veterinary office. "Fuck," he uttered before bolting for Gage.

"You sick fuck! I will fucking rip you apart!" Gage lunged at Russ. Joey managed to grab hold of him, yanking him back from making a deadly mistake. It seemed he was just in time as each of Spencer's men were already reaching for their weapons. Joey's strength struggled to contain the threat of Gage's wrath getting loose.

Layne knew that if this outburst got the best of Gage, this meeting would end up poorly for them all. She ran over to put herself right in front of him, her hands coming to his chest to try and capture his attention. "Hey! Look at me!"

He continued shouting over Layne's head. "You destroyed her! I will send you straight to fucking hell after what you did!"

With her hands balled up in his shirt while Joey grunted to restrain his little brother, she yelled at him. "HEY! Not here! NOT HERE!" Her eyes filled with concern seeing how quickly this could go tits up if Gage's recklessness got the better of them all.

Finally noticing Layne's boldly colored eyes wide with panic, he stopped trying to charge at Russ. "You watch your goddamn back! I will end you!" He allowed Joey to pull him back, stumbling a few steps until he voluntarily turned around. He shoved Joey's hands off him as he headed back toward the car with Joey close on his heels.

Layne looked back at Russ, who appeared riddled with entertainment as he spoke up, "Better keep those dogs on a leash, Layne."

"You just worry about your damn self, Russ." She glared at him briefly before quickly jogging to catch up with the guys who were already halfway back to the car.

CHAPTER TWENTY-ONE

Layne squeezed into the backseat behind Joey, who slid in after her to take his seat at the wheel and start up the engine.

Scooting over to the center seat so she could look at both of them, she primarily focused on Gage, who was already sitting in the front passenger seat. "What the fuck was that?!" She shouted at him.

Gage was shaking his head, seething as the anger rolled off of him in waves. His fist punched the dash several times. His other hand yanked down his mask as he glared at Joey. "He fucking had a hand in it! You're just going to let him walk away?! That motherfucker deserves a one-way ticket straight to hell!"

Joey removed his mask, tossing it down forcefully into the cupholder between the front seats. His hands rubbed over his face, trying to think past Gage's yelling in his ear.

She did her best to get Gage to bring it down a notch as she leaned forward and reached a hand out to touch his cheek and turn him to look at her. Layne wasn't sure what the hell had Gage ready to go on a goddamn bender, but she needed to find out.

It took a lot of coaxing from her to get him to take his eyes off Joey while his breathing remained heavy from the aggression flexing all over his body. "You need to calm down." Her words were stern.

Dropping his hands down onto the wheel, Joey put the Challenger in drive and began to head back to O'Reilly Manor. "Layne, put your seatbelt on." His eyes glanced back at her in the rearview. He wasn't driving particularly aggressively, but hell if he wasn't going to make sure that she was safely secured in the event of an unforeseen accident. As far as Joey was concerned, Layne was the most precious piece of cargo in the vehicle.

Ignoring him, she kept her eyes on Gage as the softness of her fingers stroked over the coarse hairs of his short and dark blonde beard. "Gage, look—"

In unison, both De Lucas cut off her words while shooting demanding looks at her. "Put it on!" It seemed that Gage also had a vested interest in her safety.

She sighed and sat back in the seat, dropping her hand away from Gage's face. After she drew the belt across her body, latching it in, she wanted nothing more than to stick her tongue out at them both childishly.

Keeping his eyes on the road, Joey finally gathered enough of his thoughts. "We don't know it was Russell."

"The fuck we don't. Who the hell makes that type of comparison except someone who has first-hand knowledge of some incredibly dark shit?" Gage sat back in his seat, trying his best not to assault the dashboard again. "Did you see the smug look on his face?"

"He always has a smug look on his face; it's a permanent affliction." She chimed in from the backseat. "The two of you need to fill me in on what the hell is going on." If Russ was potentially involved in something more than conspiring against her becoming a force to be reckoned with in this city, she needed to factor that into her next move.

She was met with silence.

"Oh, for fucks sake. Pull over."

When Joey didn't immediately make a move to pull the car off the road, she slammed her hand on the back of his seat, giving it a good jostle. "I SAID PULL THE FUCK OVER!"

Her temper and intolerance reached new peaks that must have surprised even Joey, who didn't hesitate to pull over to the side of the road. Layne released her seatbelt and cursed this godforsaken two-door vehicle. If she could have easily climbed out, she may have done just that and walked her ass the rest of the way home.

Instead, she leaned forward over the center console and looked at them both. "Both of you listen to me very clearly. I'm tired of the damn looks you keep giving one another while you decide to keep shit to yourselves. You both signed up for this, so I'm going to need you to respect that I have a business to run that requires me to have all the cards laid out in front of me. If you don't want to do that, then I will get out of this damn car right now."

With both sets of eyes staring back at her, shocked expressions plastered over their faces.

"Well? Are you going to fill me in or not?"

Out of the corner of her eye, she saw Gage's hand adjusting himself in his pants, clearly thinking about filling her up instead. Then, she glanced down at Joey, who hadn't even bothered to hide his erection, creating a tent between his legs.

Exasperated, she murmured, "Jesus, help me." Layne was sure that trying to get through to both of them was going to require her to come up with more creative ways so their brains didn't immediately drop into their dicks.

"I don't think Jesus is your type," Gage smirked. It was the first indication that his vengeful mood had simmered down a little. Joey stifled a laugh in response with his hand, trying to subtly hide his grin at his brother's comment. He didn't want Layne murdering him in his car, which was his pride and joy.

Sombering up a little, Gage turned more in his seat so he could fully face Layne. "You're right, baby, but I'm not talking about it here. Let's get home first 'cause I'm going to need a damn drink for this." He leaned over and heatedly captured her mouth with his, trying to ease away her frustrations.

Joey's hand reached over and eased her face away from Gage's so he could also apologetically share a loving kiss with her. "Layney, we will share what we know, okay?" He didn't want to jump to conclusions about Russ's statements, but Gage's instincts very well could have been on the right path this time.

She straightened herself up, still riled up from the way they had always been dancing around some giant elephant in the room while she was around. "Thank you."

After getting settled back in her seat, safely belted in, Joey drove the rest of the way back to their home.

Once inside, they all got more comfortably dressed and gathered in the living room. Layne sat down on the sofa in a set of midnight blue shorts with a matching white and navy zip-up hoodie. Joey took a seat next to her, drawing her into his lap while he wore a pair of basketball shorts and nothing else.

Gage entered the room wearing a pair of grey sweats borrowed from Joey and his tightly fitted black tank. The sweatpants were Layne's favorite pair Joey owned, and seeing them on Gage, she could agree that they were, without a doubt, the world's best sweatpants.

In Gage's hands, he showed he came bearing gifts, three glasses, each filled with bourbon poured over a large sphere-shaped piece of ice. He handed off a beverage to both Layne and Joey before easing himself down onto the sofa. His hand pulled Layne's feet into his lap. Both men felt more at ease having a physical connection with her.

There was a moment while she sat there that she wondered if this was how she could envision a random weeknight with both of them. Something as mundane as lounging on the couch together, simply enjoying one anoth- er's presence without worrying about what was going on outside their little world. It was a bittersweet fantasy, some- thing that she wasn't sure would become a reality given all the risks they all took on the daily.

It took a few sips of the mahogany-colored liquor before Gage finally eased into the topic at hand. "You already know about our relationship with Rosie, but I don't think we've been clear about the details of what happened."

Layne sank back against Joey's chest, his arms squeezing around her like she was his security blanket to clutch onto.

Gage continued to talk, trying to keep his voice even as all the memories of the past came to the forefront of his mind. "She wasn't just beaten, but the men who took her chained her to a pole and treated her like they were breeding a fighting dog." He strained to get the words out loud enough.

His fingers ran through his hair at the difficulty in revealing what had been the most painful twenty-four hours of his life. "The medical reports said she had trace amounts of pentobarbital in her system—the same drug they use to euthanize animals. Between that and the beatings, she never had a chance of waking up."

Joey nuzzled his face into the back of Layne's neck, inhaling deeply the scent of her soap still clinging to her skin. He quietly chimed in, "They sent pictures of what they did to her."

She sat there, not realizing how tightly she was holding onto her untouched glass of bourbon. It was clear that what had happened to Rosie ended up deeply scarring both of them. Her heart ached that they both had to endure such a horrific nightmare. It pissed her off that anyone had so viciously not only inflicted this pain on them but had accomplished it by taking it out on an innocent soul in the process.

Raising his glass to quickly consume the rest of his drink, Gage looked over at them. "I know Russ had his hand in it. I don't know how, but my gut is telling me that fucker knows something at a minimum."

If all of this was true, it made Russ an even bigger target on her list than he already was. She tried to sort out everything she knew about Russ's business affairs, his interest in keeping her from coming into her own power base, and what she had learned from several other criminal underlords throughout the city.

"Joey said that all of this was all over a bad business deal? Who was it with?" She hoped maybe that would lead them to get answers if Russell was involved or not.

Joey tensed at her back, not giving her much comfort in whatever answer she was about to get. "I know what you're thinking, Layne. That maybe we can use them as leverage, but it's a dead end."

She looked back over her shoulder at him. "Tell me who." Her voice lowered slightly with the weight of her demand on her tongue. Dread filled her chest, making her question if she truly wanted to know the answer.

Recalling how they had agreed to tell her all the details they hadn't yet revealed, he held himself to his word. "Eric Ellis."

Her eyes damn near fell out of her head. "What?!" She pulled her feet out of Gage's lap and shifted around to stare at Joey in disbelief. "Why wouldn't you tell me that?!"

After placing his glass on a side table, Joey's hands

rubbed over her arms. "Because it doesn't matter. He's gone, and there's not much to learn from a rotting corpse, Layne." Not to mention he hated bringing up the asshole's name.

Gage sat forward, resting his elbows on his knees. "I asked him not to. When Joey told me about your experience with him, it was clear the history I had with Eric had nothing to do with your encounters. At the time when this all happened, Eric was still working the small deals in Jersey City, nothing like the type of shit he got into by the time he moved here."

She frowned, still not liking that they both had kept this from her, even with her best interests at heart. "So, why do you think Russ is involved if the deal was with Eric?" Layne looked over at Gage, hoping he would fill in the gap.

He answered, "Eric had already left the state, and he didn't have the manpower, he had to contract it out to somebody."

She considered his response and thought it through. "So, you think that he had Russ doing his dirty work for him?"

Gage nodded.

She sat there thinking over everything she had learned about Eric. Were there any ties to Russell that would support Gage's theory?

Her mind drifted back to the audio recording where the pervy Andrew Correlli had been speaking with Eric.

"Good. Now, make sure that you go make good on our arrangement and go make friends with Russell for me."

Eric hadn't just been playing Layne, but he had been

playing Andrew and Russell both. It could have all started with hiring Russell to take the hit on Rosie years earlier on Eric's behalf. Then, in a play to manipulate Layne, Eric sends Andrew as the pawn to a known associate—Russ Spencer. If Layne had lashed out at Russ, there would have been no skin off Eric's back at the end of the day. Instead, he had her dispose of the middleman linking these two assholes together.

The fucking manipulative bastard was juggling back-stabbing everybody and anybody. Even from the goddamn grave, he was still fucking with her life.

CHAPTER TWENTY-TWO

Joey knocked on Rebecca's door with one hand tucked in the front pocket of his jeans before dropping the other down to slide it in the other. Layne was stuck getting all her hired hands to dig into more information surrounding Russell and his connections. How deep had Eric's influence sunk into the dark underworld of New York's criminal organizations?

The door swung open, and Rebecca gave a welcoming smile. "Hey, you made it just in time, I just got back." She had been out watching the children for the family she nannied for while the parents had a brunch date together. Layne had always said that punctuality had always been Joey's thing. She wasn't kidding. Rebecca stepped back, opening the door wider to let him step inside her apartment.

"Thanks. You said you had some stuff for Layne to look at for the wedding?" He shut the door behind him. His eyes surveyed the inside of her apartment that she always managed to keep clutter-free, except for all the various wedding-related items she held onto for Layne.

Rebecca nodded as she walked over to a stack of boxes she kept in the corner of her quaint living room. Each box was meticulously labeled and organized. Samples, favors, flowers, music selections, brochures, and color swatches. "Yeah, she still needs to decide whether she wants the Kelly Green or the Hunter Green for the chair sashes."

He lifted a brow. "Aren't they both just green?"

She rolled her eyes and shook her head. "No! You see, Kelly Green has a little more—you know what? Never mind. She just needs to pick one. Tell her that I think the Hunter Green is more aesthetically pleasing, but the Kelly Green fabric feels nicer." Rebecca dug into one of the boxes, pulling out a small plastic bag containing two fabric swatches.

Joey smirked. "You know she's going to close her eyes and pick one at random, right?"

She hated to admit it, but she knew he was likely right. Rebecca groaned at how difficult of a bride Layne was turning out to be. "Don't tell me if she does."

As she extended the samples over to Joey, her facial expression changed slightly. One that Joey was having a hard time deciphering. He may have been able to read Layne in an instant, but he hadn't yet been able to interpret the many expressions of her best friend.

He pocketed the samples she handed over. "Is there anything else?"

Rebecca stood there quietly, debating with herself

before deciding that it was a topic of conversation worth bringing up. "Do you have a few minutes so we can talk?"

Joey shrugged. "Sure."

Rebecca headed over to her kitchen table and pulled a chair out for herself. Joey followed behind but remained standing, unclear of whatever was weighing on her mind. If something was bothering Layne's bestie enough to bring it to his attention, he was interested in hearing it.

Fidgeting with her fingers in her lap, she looked at him. "I know I occasionally give you a hard time." She grinned at her choice of words. "Maybe more than occasionally."

He grinned knowingly. "I wouldn't expect anything less."

She nodded. "It's just… Layne has been my best friend since we were in elementary school. I always knew her family was different - that she was different. She has never been one to back down from a fight. I remember she beat the crap out of the first guy who ever broke my heart."

Rebecca softly laughed at the memory. Poor Kevin had been on the receiving end of Layne's anger in front of the entire high school in the auditorium. "She got suspended from school for a week, but she had said it had been worth it to see the regret and embarrassment on his face after getting his ass handed to him by a girl."

Joey smiled, imagining a scrappy teenage Layne putting some kid in his place. "Sounds like her." Part of him wished he had known Layne in both of their younger years; it would have allowed both of them to spend even more of their lives together.

Sitting back in her chair, her pale blue eyes looked over

him. "You know how much she has been through. I don't think I've ever seen her as happy as she is when she's with you or even just hears your name."

Joey did his best to keep Layne happy, even with her challenging personality that matched his equally challenging temperament. "I'm sensing there's a 'but' coming."

She gently smiled at his accurate prediction. "*But*, I still worry about her. I don't pretend to understand what she's involved in, and she has never been one to allow me in so that I can understand it. All I know is that it carries a lot of risk. The whole thing with Eric was…eye-opening." That was putting it mildly. It was the first time that she got a front-row seat into just how much Layne stared danger in the eyes without fear.

He shifted in his stance, knowing that Layne had made it clear in no uncertain terms with him that she didn't want Rebecca to know more than necessary. After Eric had threatened Rebecca's well-being, he couldn't exactly blame her. Layne had tried to go as far as to entirely ghost her friend in the name of avoiding any other incidents. However, he knew that Layne needed Rebecca in her life. It had taken weeks of convincing on his part to persuade her that she needed the time with someone who wasn't in this line of work. Rebecca was the moral compass they all needed every once in a while.

Joey ran his hand over the back of his head, smoothing his dirty blonde hair down. "Look, Rebecca…"

She was quick to shake her head. "I'm not looking for the nitty gritty, Joey. I'm just pointing out what I do see." A concerned frown came over her face. "I'm just scared. I worry that one day…" Tears began to form in her eyes as her chin quivered. Quickly, her fingers swiped away the first two tears that escaped her blue hues. "I'm just scared I'm going to wake up one day to the news that my favorite person in the world is no longer in it."

Legitimate fear filled her face despite trying to push back the emotions tugging on her soul. She glanced down and shook her head. "Sorry, I-I just can't imagine not having her to call up any time something stupid comes up, like the hot mailman smiling at me or that I had a great day or even a shitty one." Rebecca sniffled and attempted not to break down entirely. "I would rather be helping plan this wedding than planning a funeral."

Joey furrowed his brows and walked over to where she was seated. He squatted in front of her so he could look at her face. Taking her hands into his, he gave them a firm squeeze. "I don't want you to be sorry."

His voice was gentle as he began to realize in his own way he shared the very same fears. "There isn't a single moment of my day that I don't worry about her. Even when I'm sleeping, keeping her safe is all I dream about." Taking a deep breath, he prepared to share with Rebecca some of his most vulnerable feelings. "I promise I will always do what I can to keep her safe and mostly happy."

Rebecca raised a brow at him at the last part. "*Mostly* happy?" She was ready to lash out at him for not wanting to keep her one-hundred-fucking-percent happy.

He gave her a knowing grin. "Have you met your best

friend? She can be a real stubborn pain in the ass that doesn't even know what is good for herself some days."

She laughed out loud, knowing that he was spot on. Layne really could be her own worst enemy at times.

His hand patted hers. "I love Layne more than I could ever tell you or anyone else. There is nothing I wouldn't do for her. I can't tell you that her life will ever be without very real risk and danger. All I can do is promise you that for the rest of her life, she will never go a single day without all the happiness I can give her."

Rebecca full-on burst into tears after hearing his words. She pulled her hands from his so she could toss herself at him and wrap her arms around Joey's neck in a massive hug. She nearly knocked him over while he was balanced on the balls of his feet while in his squat.

"Oof!" His hand had to grab onto the table for a moment so he didn't lose his balance. He wrapped his other arm around her, squeezing in a hug full of reassurance.

She pulled back and eased herself back from him, her hands hastily wiping off the tears from her cheeks. "You tell her I went all mushy like this, I will kill you." Rebecca joked as she smiled at him.

Joey pushed his hands against his knees as he stood back up. "Your secret is safe with me." He winked at her.

Now that she had gotten all of that off her chest, she finally was able to move the conversation to something a little more lighthearted. She grabbed a tissue to dab underneath her eyes at the last couple of tears that hadn't dried.

"Layne still hasn't told me if you guys are going on a honeymoon. She keeps telling me it all depends on work."

Based on the expression on Rebecca's face, she was none too happy with that response.

He smirked. "Don't worry, I will steal her away from the city for a little bit, even if she kicks and yells the entire way."

They sat and chatted with one another for another twenty minutes, going over a few minor details about the day of the wedding. Most of it related to things he could give an opinion on, like the freely flowing booze.

When he finally left Rebecca's place, he began jogging down the stairs of the apartment building while checking his phone for any new calls or messages.

There was one in particular that caught his attention. It was a text from Layne. When he opened it up, he was greeted by a selfie of her scantily clad body and her flirtatious smile. It looked like she had found the black lace piece of lingerie he had bought for her and had been hiding as a surprise. Underneath the picture, she had sent him another text.

LAYNE

Finders keepers.

You need better hiding spots.

Joey had to grab onto the handrail to prevent himself from tripping over his feet at the delicious distraction displayed on his phone. He quickly texted her back.

JOEY

Funny, that's what I always say about you.

I will be home in ten, you better be ready
for me.

He had found the one woman in this world who could make him want for nothing and planned to always keep her.

CHAPTER TWENTY-THREE

It was the end of yet another successful night at Cassidy's Cave. Gage sat in his office, leaning back in his chair with a sigh as he rested his eyes. It was nearly two in the damn morning. He wasn't thinking about sleep, though. Instead, he had one particular image in his mind. The way Layne looked up at him while on her knees through her dark lashes, how her body moved while taking him in, and the sight of his handprints being left behind on her curvy ass cheeks.

His dick was quickly twitching in his jeans, growing harder with each thought of Layne and all the things he still wanted to do to her. Gage wanted to see her tiny hands bound together while laid out on his bed, begging to be taken any way he pleased. He pictured how his collar would look around her slender neck. All these thoughts had his dick raging with need. His hand drifted down to undo his belt and pants. Sliding his hand inside his pants, he took hold of himself.

Quietly, he whispered to himself, "That's it, baby. Beg for your Daddy." He groaned, imagining Layne's response in his head.

It wasn't long before his fantasy was chased away as he was rudely interrupted by a knock on his office door. Before he could call out to acknowledge the knock, Danielle poked her head in. "You have a second?"

Pulling his hand from his pants, Gage opened up his eyes and leaned forward in his chair, forcing her a smile like he wasn't just about to jack himself off. He scooted his chair in while he discreetly and single-handedly closed his pants back up.

"Yeah, what's up?" He shifted in his seat, trying to ignore the throbbing of his cock.

Ever since the night that Layne had come into the private room and interrupted Danielle's weekly gig for Italo and his guys, she had been picking up extra shifts to make up for the generous tips she was now missing out on. Gage had to admit, she was working extra hard around here. If half the girls would put in a fraction of that effort, he would be making bank on even their slowest nights.

Danielle walked in, wearing a pair of black hot shorts that left most of her ass hanging out and a white Cassidy's Cave crop top that barely fit over her fake tits. Like most of the girls he hired, she was extremely attractive and held up the strip club's reputation for having some of the best adult entertainment.

"Before I leave for the night, I was wondering if you need anything." She flipped the extensions of her long, bleached hair back over her shoulder. Her eyes drifted down towards his waist.

He stared at her and shook his head. "If you've already closed out all your tabs and helped clean up the tables, you're free to go." Gage wasn't an idiot; he knew that some of the girls had their sights on him. When they all walked around nearly naked, he had seen his share of wet panties and sexy innuendos directed at him. As a good business practice, he didn't lay a finger on any of them. After meeting Layne, he didn't even want to.

She tried to mask her disappointment that he hadn't even thought twice before responding to her. "If you need anything in here taken care of, I can help out." Her eyes glanced down to his lap again as she started to lean forward over his desk.

Another intrusion into his office followed before he could dismiss Danielle's advances, this time, it was a much more welcomed one. Layne walked in, stopping short as she had expected him to be alone.

Layne had on a pair of tight and heavily distressed jeans with strategic rips and tears across her thighs. Under the forest green jacket, she was wearing what looked like the top half of some lingerie. The black lace was flush against her skin and pushed up those nicely sized breasts of hers that she flaunted so perfectly.

Right behind her was Joey, who seemed equally as surprised at Danielle's presence. He wore a black leather jacket with a faded graphic tee underneath it. His jeans had a few minor spots of old motor oil, indicating he was likely working on his car while wearing them at some point.

Straightening up from her bent-over posture, Danielle glanced back at the two party crashers in disappointment. "Just give me a ring if you change your mind." She turned from Gage, walked up to Layne, and wrapped her arms around her neck in a hug.

Layne stood there awkwardly, unsure if she should hug the girl back. She opted for a light pat on her back as she looked over at Gage with a confused expression on her face. Secretly, she had hoped that one of them would save her from the bizarrely random gesture. Had this girl just gone from flirting with Gage to suddenly hugging her? And for what?

Danielle smiled at Layne after releasing her hold. "I wanted to thank you."

One of Layne's eyebrows perked up. "For what?"

"Oh!" She gave the fakest of giggles as she realized that it was unclear to Layne. "Ever since Italo and his gang stopped coming here, it has been such a blessing. They were a bunch of creeps. Honestly, they were shitty tippers with even smaller dicks. After you came that one night, they haven't bothered showing their faces again."

The twist of confusion on Layne's face increased as she tilted her head at the statement. Sure, she had interrupted Danielle's private party in that room, but she had been wearing her mask.

"Um. You're... welcome? I don't know why you think..." Layne shot looks over at Joey at her side and Gage across the room.

Danielle gave her a wink. "I would know these curves anywhere." Her hand slapped Layne's ass. It came so unexpectedly that Layne nearly jumped out of her boots as her eyes widened slightly.

The guys seemed to find humor in Layne's surprised reaction as they stifled their laughter. Danielle walked out of Gage's office, and Joey shut the door after she was gone. "It seems we're not the only ones that appreciate how fuckin' hot you are," he said as he moved over to the chair in front of his brother's desk and took a seat.

Layne was still a little weirded out by the entire encounter. Sure, Rebecca had given her ass a smack or three, but it had always been during drunken shenanigans. She shook her head, trying to reset her focus on why she and Joey were both here.

She approached Gage's desk, partially taking a seat by perching half her ass on it so she could look at both of them. "I heard back from Brandon." Or, as he preferred to be called by his hacker name, Cowboy. He had been a great asset to Layne after Joey had introduced them during their initial investigation into Eric's dirty work.

"He said that technology has changed so much over the last ten years there wasn't much to work with to confirm if Russell had a hand in what happened with Rosie. As for Eric," she swallowed down the nausea churning in her stomach at even saying his name. "His operations were still in their infancy, making them far more difficult to trace. He could have contacted Russ, but there's no way to be sure."

Joey's eyes still held a little bit of rage, knowing that Eric was still stirring up shit postmortem. He shifted his look to Gage. "Also, since Sean hated anything that left a trail, we don't have anything like cameras to rely on."

Despite repeated requests from patrons to at least put a television in McGregor's, Sean had been a hardheaded son of a bitch and refused any bit of technology.

Gage ran his fingers through the shortly-cut blonde hair on his head as he tried to think of other avenues. "What about street cameras?"

Layne shook her head. "That area is jam-packed with people coming and going. It would be impossible to tell who may have been inside at any given time. We'd be pulling from an entire city's worth of straws."

"Fuck," Gage sighed. This wasn't the news he was hoping for. He really wished that Joey and Layne had just let him shove a gun down Russ's mouth that night at Bethesda Fountain. It would have solved a shit ton of his problems, or at the very least, would have made him feel better.

Joey propped his feet up on the edge of the desk, crossing his ankles. "The best we've got is what all of the city's top-tier criminal leaders have had to say." Which wasn't much.

The cocoa-colored hues belonging to Gage reflected a moment of realization of a new approach. "What about your brother?"

She wrinkled up her forehead. "What about him?"

"Would he have insight or something that could be a lead that we haven't already considered?" Gage looked so hopeful that maybe this was the key to it all.

It made Layne snort. "Liam wouldn't know good intel from his own ass."

"Is he still at Rikers?" Joey curiously asked since he hadn't heard Layne griping about her brother recently.

Layne shrugged, the lack of fucks obvious from how she did so. "Probably, I guess? I haven't talked to him. I know he didn't make bail at his arraignment, and that was the last shit I had to give about it. Let him pay the piper."

"Alright, then back to square one. We keep digging." Gage still was sure that Russ had involvement in all of this. He sure as hell wasn't going to let history repeat itself and allow Layne to suffer the fate that Rosie had. He knew they were two very different women, but he never wanted to see Layne endure anything less than what a goddamn goddess deserved. A fuckin' dangerous goddess that deserved the gods of chaos and wrath at her side.

They all sat around and chatted a little longer, talking out some other unturned stones that perhaps they could turn over. Finally, Layne had decided all the iced coffee she had ingested earlier needed an outlet. She left Gage's office to see herself to the ladies' room.

Once Gage was sure that Layne was out of earshot, he looked over at Joey. "She's stressed. I don't like it." Layne would never admit it, but she would carry the weight of her world on her shoulders even though she had a hell of a support system to share the load.

Joey nodded in agreement. "Until this all gets resolved, I don't think it's going to get any better. She was talking earlier about postponing the wedding just until everything settles."

With an immediate opinion on that issue, Gage shook his head. "You didn't agree to that, did you?"

Dropping his feet back down to the floor, he could only shrug. "It doesn't matter if I agreed to it or not, Gage. She's hellbent and set on it. Rebecca even got involved, threatening to wear some hideous pumpkin gown if Layne didn't change her mind."

Nodding his head as he soaked this all in, Gage let the gears in his head spin. He suddenly smirked, thinking back to earlier when he had been alone with his thoughts. "You know what I think she needs?"

Scoffing, Joey was sure Layne needed a lot of things, but he didn't initially follow the mischievous look on his brother's face. He glanced over at Gage, who appeared to settle on a devious course of action. Finally catching on, Joey grinned. "You mean…?"

Gage nodded slowly, giving a large smile. "I do. I'm game if you are. Everything should be shut down up front, and everyone gone for the night."

"Fuck, yes." Joey's excitement was already building up. "Let's go get her."

Gage's hand dug into his desk drawer, retrieving something that just might come in handy. Shoving the item into his pocket, he stood from his chair, ready to give their girl the time of her life.

CHAPTER TWENTY-FOUR

When Layne came out of the ladies' room, she expected to cross through the main area of the club, where all the stages were spread out, and head back past the bar to Gage's office.

Instead, what she found when she approached the center stage was not what she had expected. Sitting on the edge of the circular platform with their legs dangling off the side were both Joey and Gage seemingly waiting for her.

The two of them looked at her with a hungry gaze. She slowed her steps as her heart began to beat a little heavier, and her breaths became a little lighter. "What's going on?" The suspicion tainted her voice.

"Be a good girl and come over here," Joey begged her closer with the gesture of his finger. He gave a devilish grin at her, knowing damn well his words would have her getting weak in the knees.

She walked over to the stage that was raised a few feet

from the ground. It was a large circle with a silver pole in the middle, and the platform itself was painted black. The only thing that marred its coloring was the glitter that would likely be forever adhered to it no matter how much it got scrubbed and cleaned.

Layne stood before the two of them. "I thought we were wrapping up to go home."

Gage hopped down from the edge of the stage, landing on his feet with a gentle thud. He circled 'round her until he was at her back. His hand got wrapped up in a fistful of her silky brunette locks, and tugged her head back. "Not yet, baby." His hand slid down over the front of her jeans and possessively grabbed between her legs.

Despite the thick material of her pants, her breath caught in her throat as her eyes filled with need when she saw Joey still seated there across from her, with desire thick in the air between them.

"Gage, she's looking a little flushed. It might be a little warm in here for all that clothing." Joey was down on his feet quickly after that and came to stand before her. He ran his hands over the top of her chest, sliding them underneath her open jacket. Slowly, he pushed the fabric away from her shoulders until it was falling down the length of her slender arms.

While Joey worked on removing her jacket, Gage kept his hand securely wrapped up in her hair while his mouth began to drag kisses along the side of her neck. He glanced down at the tops of the curves of her breasts that were now straining against the material of her lacy top with her excited breaths.

Layne moaned quietly, feeling the stiff bulge of Gage's cock pressing up against her ass while his lips caressed over the most sensitive spots of her neck. "You both are going to be the death of me."

Joey smirked as his hand rested on the side of her face. "No, Layney. We're going to make sure you've never felt so alive." His mouth possessively claimed hers while his hand slid onto the back of her neck to secure his hold on her.

With Joey's hand grasping onto Layne, Gage relinquished his grasp on her hair and brought both his hands down to her jeans, where he undid the button and zipper. He pulled her pants by the belt loops until they were down around her ankles.

Gage tapped her left shin. "Foot." When Layne shifted her weight off of her left foot, Gage was able to extract it from her shoe and shove her pant leg off. He repeated the gesture for the other foot until she was finally left in nothing but that revealing black top and a black g-string that kept her fine ass on full display.

As Gage rose up behind her, he found the round cheek of her ass too tempting not to indulge. He gave it a couple of delicate kisses before giving a playful bite to its fullness. After, he fully stood and began to strip himself down.

Feeling Gage's teeth bite into her, she gasped into the kiss that Joey was still assaulting her mouth with. Her tongue was fighting for dominance with his and very quickly losing the battle. Finally, Joey broke the connection between their mouths. His hands grabbed her by the shoulders and turned her to face Gage.

Standing there only wearing his excited smile and a thick erection on full display, Gage didn't hesitate to take his turn, pulling Layne up against him as he shared a ravishing kiss with her. His dick pushed up against her lower stomach. She barely had enough time to catch her breath as she went from one De Luca to the other.

Behind her, she could hear Joey stripping down and clothes hitting the floor after being tossed. When he came up behind her, it was skin-to-skin contact as his hard cock pressed up against the line of her ass teasingly. His hand firmly grabbed her hip while the other slid between her thighs.

His fingers easily pushed past the string of her underwear until they stroked along her crease. Joey groaned out as her arousal quickly coated his fingers. "We're only getting started, and you're already fuckin' soaked. This wet pussy of yours is going to be put to good use, Layney."

Gage swallowed up her moan as Joey's hand teased along her sex. His grin spread into the way he kissed her before he drew back and stared at the beauty of her face, flushed with desire.

She was slightly panting from the quick and sinful turn of events that left her body full of intense need. Layne pressed her hips back against Joey's hand, wanting his touch where it mattered most. However, when his touch was removed from her body, she was left with a pout.

Taking her by the chin, Gage's thumb ran across her lips as playful darkness filled his deep brown eyes. "You're going to work for both of our cocks tonight, baby. Then, you're going to thank us for every orgasm we give you. If you do as you're told, we will leave you full of our cum. Do you understand?"

Layne's lips got distracted by the way the tip of his thumb traced over them. She opened up her mouth to draw his thumb in, lightly sucking on it.

From behind her, Joey's hand curled around her throat, lightly squeezing. He growled into her ear with a heated command. "I didn't hear you tell him 'Yes, Sir'."

She was already full of lust that needed to be released, her thoughts running on fumes as all her blood was rushing to other seemingly more important parts of her body. Layne's mouth let go of Gage's thumb. "Yes, Sir."

"Go get up on stage." Gage nodded at the one they had been seated on earlier. "Let us watch as you give us a show."

Both of the guys took their seats in chairs placed front and center. Layne smiled at them as she was more than ready to give them what they wanted, and maybe even more. She stepped up onto the stage, and fuck if she didn't need any more inspiration than what she saw before her.

Joey and Gage sat there, both completely naked and looking like a feast worth devouring for eternity. Both of their bodies were covered in their hard muscles, the intricate artwork canvased over their flesh, and two sets of chocolatey brown eyes watching her every move.

With the sensual music still playing over the speakers even after hours, it wasn't hard to find a rhythm as her hand grasped onto the metal pole. Her hips swayed as she engaged in a hell of a strip show for them. Her fingers coaxed the lacy top from her body. It was discarded by being flung at Gage's face.

Gage had his hand firmly wrapped around his thick cock while watching her body tease them both. Thank God she never became a stripper working at Cassidy's, he would have broken his no-touching rule a thousand times over. His hand caught her top, taking a moment to inhale the scent of her from it before tossing it to the floor.

Layne's breasts had now joined the show, her nipples in stiff peaks, showing how her body was enjoying this as much as they were. She suggestively grinded up against the pole with a come-hither look in her eyes.

Seeing Joey's hand also working over his large length, she worked her tiny bit of underwear down her legs. Using her foot, she flicked it over at Joey, managing to make the shot of a lifetime as it landed right around his cock.

Joey's face lit up like he had just won the damn lottery, and he was getting antsy in his seat, barely able to sit back and watch her much longer.

She saw the slipping self-control and decided to push both their buttons a little more. Layne got on her hands and knees, crawling to the edge of the stage. Her emerald eyes shimmered with the heat of several suns as she reached between her legs. Her finger found her clit, slick with her body's desires, and began to circle over it.

The first moan she let out had both men clamoring to join her on the stage. Gage barely made it there first as he pushed himself onto her, rolling her onto her back. His hands gripped each of her wrists, pinning them above her head. "Who said you could touch this needy little cunt of yours?" He smirked, looking down into her eyes.

"Seems like you need a reminder of who is responsible for all your pleasure, Layney." Joey stepped up onto the stage. "Give Gage a taste of that delicious pussy."

Changing positions, Gage laid on his back, already licking his lips in anticipation of the meal that awaited him between her thighs. "Sit and ride my face, baby. Show me how much you want to fill me up with your taste."

She was lucky she could feel her legs at all the way they both had her on the edge. Layne got herself on her knees, hovering her center over Gage's face.

"Goddamn, you smell delicious," he murmured before he pulled her the last few inches down to his mouth. Gage's hands quickly captured her hands behind her back, holding them tightly together. It forced her back to arch slightly, thrusting her breasts forward more.

Layne cried out as Gage didn't waste a moment in drawing his tongue along her folds and capturing the flavor of her need. Hungrily, he sucked on her throbbing clit like it was his last meal. Her body squirmed under the intense sensations, only encouraging him to continue.

Joey wasn't going to sit back and be excluded from the fun. Layne's mouth looked like it needed something other than the moans it was forcing into the air. He grinned and stepped in front of her, his hands grabbing her head. It forced her attention to him, her green hues staring up at him while heavy breaths pulled at her chest.

"Beg for my cock like a good girl. I want to hear how you want your mouth fucked while you get eaten out."

Joey's eyes soaked in the sight of her with her hands restrained behind her while she had his brother tasting the sweet nectar of her body.

Gage's tongue was relentless in its pursuit as her hips drove against his face. The coarseness of his beard only intensified the sensations as it brushed against her most intimate parts.

With Joey's dick right there in front of her, pre-cum glistening over its head, she was quickly being launched towards her release. Her strained words made it very clear that she was approaching the slippery slope. "F-fuck my mouth, Joey… Feed your cock to me." Her words were saturated with the need to have both of them touching her at the same time.

On her next moan, Joey pushed himself past her parted lips. Her mouth opened up wider to take him while he kept control over her head.

Gage's tongue snaked up into her entrance, feeling the tight opening already quivering. The muffled cry above him made his cock painfully hard, knowing that she must have had a mouthful of De Luca. Squeezing onto her wrists tighter, his teeth scraped over her sensitive bud as he continued to use his mouth to leave no part of her hot core untasted.

Feeling the back of Layne's throat squeezing onto his tip, Joey groaned out. With her moans vibrating against him more frequently, he began to thrust into her, letting the feelings send his cock into a frenzy. "That's my fuckin' good girl. Suck my cock and leave a mess on Gage's face." He released a moan, "God…"

As Layne's body began to quiver, Gage took the opportunity to release both her hands so he could slide two fingers up inside her while he sucked hard on her little bundle of nerves. His fingers reaching deep up into her pussy and curling to press against the magical spot.

The second she felt her walls having to accommodate the new intrusion into her body, she got slammed with her climax. She screamed out in pleasure, but it got lost as Joey shoved his length deeper, pushing past her gag reflex at the back of her throat. It prompted her eyes to water, but she hardly noticed as wave after wave of her body's release overcame her.

Gage continued to push against that spot deep inside of her while she rode out her orgasm. When she came with such force, he got exactly what he had wanted from her as a stream of liquid filled his mouth.

Joey pulled out of Layne; his fingers wiped the leftover saliva on her chin. She gasped for air as her release began to slowly fade.

Layne was quickly shifted around as Gage moved her by her hips off his face. She was slid down the front of his body so her head could rest on his chest, which was also rising and falling after his oral efforts. She gave a sigh of satisfaction at the delightful high that had overcome her and had her head swimming.

Gage affectionately rubbed the back of her head to give her those few seconds to recover.

She stuttered out. "T-Thank you..." Her words barely above a whisper.

Gage kissed the top of her head. "You're welcome, but

we're not done with you yet, lucky charm." His hands moved her again, this time so his still-aching dick was between her legs, rubbing against her slit.

His hands came up on either side of her neck while he kissed her passionately several times, letting her taste the remnants of her cum on his lips. "Go ahead and sit back on my swords," Gage smirked at her as his tattooed cock wanted nothing more than to be deep inside of her while she rode him, but this time not on his face.

While Layne was getting a brief reprieve from their affections, Joey stepped away to retrieve a small bottle of slippery and clear liquid from Gage's pants. The item Gage had retrieved from his desk drawer in anticipation of their dual conquest over Layne's body tonight.

Once Joey returned, he positioned himself on his knees between Gage's legs while he admired the view of Layne's ass facing him. His hand slid up along her back, making sure she remained laid on top of Gage so he had just the right angle.

Gage's hands ran over the sides of her slender body, feeling each curve along the way until his hands grabbed her ass and spread it wide for Joey's viewing pleasure. Layne pushed back onto Gage's cock, her tight entrance stretching around each inch while she sank onto him.

Layne moaned out as she got one of her holes filled up with one of her guys and another hole being prepared to take the other.

Joey took the lube and prepped not just himself but Layne as well. He knew that what was already going to be a constricted entry was going to be more so with Gage buried inside her cunt. "Layney, are you ready to have us both? I'm not going to be able to fucking hold back the second I'm in your tight ass." God knew it was one of his favorite places to take her, and she had taken him so well there many times before.

"Yes," her voice breathy with half a moan as she pushed her hips back, aching for them both.

"Good girl." He grinned and took his cock up to the entrance of her ass, and eased the first inch inside. Immediately, he could feel the difference in the amount of effort it was going to take and groaned. His hands grabbed her waist tightly to use her body as leverage as he shoved himself into her. Layne's gasps had a tingling sensation of pleasure at the base of his spine.

It wasn't just Joey who groaned out from the pleasure of having her while she was so full, but Gage did as well, as having Joey in her ass placed more pressure on his cock buried inside her pussy.

Layne heard them both, and her body was already trembling, something fierce as she cried out from being so full of De Luca cock. As promised, Joey didn't hold himself back as his feral side began to take over.

Working in tandem, Gage's hips drove up into her and helped her ride him hard while Joey kept his rhythm, ramming himself into her ass.

"Fuck!" All her moans drowned out the music playing in the background. Her hands clutched onto Gage's chest, his silver SPQR necklace getting tangled in her fingers and pulling against the back of his neck. His face painted in his own pleasure, struggling to maintain control of it.

Between his own pleasure-laden breaths, Gage looked up at her. "You're taking your two Daddies so well, baby." He groaned out the words.

Joey grunted as his hips smacked against her ass, his hands squeezing onto her waist tighter with each movement. "How's it feel to have two fuckin' cocks, Layney?"

Stars. That was it. Just stars and blinding light danced across Layne's vision. She had no clue if she even answered either of them as her body was taken elsewhere to another galaxy as her release smashed into her. She had never come so hard, even in her dirtiest fantasies.

As her body was wracked with ecstasy, she tensed up from her fingers down to the curl of her toes. It created a chain reaction as Gage's fingers dug into her thighs as he yelled out, and his seed shot out of him like a missile. Joey's hips shuddered as he gave one more harsh thrust into her ass, his cock spasming as he also tumbled over the ledge of his release.

With heavy pants from all of them, Joey collapsed into the pile of tangled limbs with Layne and Gage. Both guys wrapped arms around her, showering her with kisses anywhere they could find a spot on her damp skin.

She closed her eyes, not wanting to move so much as a toe while she lay there in their embrace. Quietly, she mustered enough energy to whisper, "Thank you."

Gage chuckled and kissed her forehead. "Anything for you, lucky charm."

Nuzzling his face into the side of her neck, Joey brushed some hair away from her face. "I love you more than life itself."

Right outside of Cassidy's Cave, someone sat in the darkness of their vehicle waiting. How long were the two men and the O'Reilly girl inside going to stay there? What the fuck were they doing?

Just as the person's impatience was hitting an all-time high, the establishment's front door opened up, and all three of them emerged from the strip club. Layne on Joey's back, legs around his waist, and her arms wrapped around his neck for support as he carried her out into the parking lot. Gage fell behind for a second while he locked up the door before jogging to catch up to the other two.

They all walked to a black Challenger parked next to Gage's shoddy-looking Jeep. Staying glued to the older brother's back, Layne leaned over and engaged in a sultry kiss with the younger De Luca like the whore she was.

Fuck her and fuck them all.

CHAPTER TWENTY-FIVE

The three of them headed back to Hudson Yards since it was only less than a mile away, and the sun would be rising sooner rather than later. Exhaustion overcame them all, and they crashed right into Gage's bed together.

Layne had never slept so hard in her life. With Gage on one side of her and Joey on the other, she felt entirely at ease. All the stressors of her life took a backseat as she allowed herself to succumb to a state of utter relaxation. After several hours of slumber, when she began to wake up, Joey was still in bed with her. His hand was securely attached to her bare breast underneath the t-shirt that Gage had given her to sleep in.

She giggled quietly as she leaned over and laid a sweet kiss on his mouth while the growth of his facial hair tickled her skin. He must not have been sleeping as soundly as she thought because he suddenly gave a growl and yanked her closer to him while kissing her neck and nipping at her throat playfully.

Layne outright squealed and fell into a fit of laughter while squirming in his hands. "Ah! Joey!"

He rolled on top of her, pinning her down with his body with a sparkle in his rich brown eyes. "Good morning…" Joey's hips suggestively rolled against her, with his cock already beginning to harden in his boxer briefs.

Gage walked into the room with a smirk. "If you both are going for round two, I'm going to need more coffee first." He stopped at the side of the bed, wearing just his black silk boxers.

She cupped Joey's face in her hands and lovingly kissed him. "Maybe later. I am supposed to meet up with Thomas today for an update on what the pulse is across the city's factions. If something is being stirred up, there are going to be whispers, and I want to make sure I hear them first."

Joey squeezed her tightly with his arms before rolling off of her and onto his back. Tucking his arm behind his head, he sprawled out there amongst the charcoal sheets, with the sunshine filling the room and lighting up the lines of his collection of tattoos on his bare chest.

As for Gage, he smiled at her and leaned over, scooping her up into his arms. "You're not doing anything until I get you in the tub so you can recover a little more before you start your day."

Her hand held onto the back of his neck as she found herself quickly laying across his arms as he began carrying her to his master bathroom, where he had already prepared a bath for her. "I think I can handle a little soreness."

"Are you arguing with me?" Gage grinned teasingly and set her feet down on the tiled floor of the extravagant bathroom. It had a massive floor-to-ceiling window with a view of the Hudson River that allowed the bathroom to be drenched in natural lighting. A dark granite tub was inset into a rectangular base right next to the window.

"No, Sir." Layne smiled as she found herself in awe of the beauty of not just the design of the oversized bathroom but the view it would give her while she soaked.

His fingers lifted the edge of his tee from her body until it was completely removed. "Good. Go get in the tub, and I will bring you some coffee and your phone so you don't bitch you're not able to get any work done." He patted her ass lightly as encouragement.

She stepped into the warm water and gradually lowered herself down into it. "How well you know me," Layne smirked. Gage seemed to take to heart that despite how much he got enjoyment out of bossing her around between the sheets, he ultimately wanted nothing more than to spoil and take care of her afterward.

It was a few minutes later that she was alone in the bathroom, her mug filled with freshly brewed coffee in one hand and scrolling through her phone in the other. Gage had been right, the warmth of the water with a mixture of scented salts was gradually melting the soreness away from her body.

She sent a message to Thomas informing him that she needed to push back their meeting by at least an hour. After setting both her caffeine and her cell to the side on a dry ledge, she leaned back and got cozy. Her eyes couldn't have been shut for more than five minutes before her zen-like state was interrupted.

Gage was heard yelling from the other end of his condo. She couldn't hear his words, but he sounded livid. She opened her eyes and sat up in the tub hesitantly as she strained to hear the words he was shouting.

Layne got out of the tub, drying herself off before wrapping the fluffy, bright white towel around her body and securing it under her arms. She left the bathroom and made her way to where Gage's voice was growing louder.

"What the fuck do you mean the damn alarm didn't go off?!" His voice thundered in the kitchen. Joey was standing there sipping from his cup of coffee, leaning against the counter, waiting to find out more information about this not-so-pleasant phone call his brother had received.

Gage punched one of the kitchen cabinets with his balled-up fist. "I set it myself! It was fucking ON!"

She stepped into the kitchen, staring at the both of them for a few minutes before Joey noticed her. Setting down his mug, he walked over to her and rubbed her arms gently. "Something happened at Cassidy's last night after we left," he explained quietly.

Pacing back and forth, Gage listened to one of his managers on the other end of the line. He grabbed a handful of his hair in frustration. "I will get down there when I can." His words were slightly calmer but still vibrating with anger. He hung up on the caller and tossed the phone down on the counter. "Motherfucker!"

Layne grew worried and stepped away from Joey to try

and ease Gage's fiery rage. Her hand rested against his tightly tensed bicep. "What happened?" Her eyes were full of concern as she peered up into his eyes.

Not wanting to misdirect his anger at Layne, he took several ragged breaths. "Someone broke into Cassidy's last night sometime after we left and before my manager came in to prep for opening later. The joint got completely ransacked."

Trying to think of a way to help, she rubbed his arm soothingly. "I'm sure if you pull the camera footage, it should at least show who it was, right?"

He swallowed hard, his jaw clenched as he was internally kicking his own ass. With a softer but still strained tone, he replied, "I turned them off before the three of us…" His words trailed off.

She frowned that the one thing that could have perhaps captured who was responsible was not available thanks to Gage's consideration and thoughtfulness of not evidencing their extracurricular activities together.

"I'm sorry, Gage. Look, we can go down there, assess the damage, and maybe try cleaning it up." She tried to share some of her optimism with him.

Joey placed a hand on Layne's shoulder with a gentle squeeze and patted Gage on the back supportively. "I agree with Layne. We will all go down there and take a look."

Layne nodded. "I will reschedule my meeting with Thomas for another day. I will see if I can get some of my men to come down and help once we know what level of damage there is. I just need to run home first and get a fresh change of clothes."

Gage tried to take a calming breath, his fury still simmering underneath the surface but remaining under control for now. "Alright. Joey, you take her home. I'm going to make some phone calls, and then I will meet you both over there in two hours." He leaned over and gave Layne a tender kiss. "Don't the two of you get into trouble when I'm not around to join in, okay?"

She chuckled. "I will make sure he behaves." Her emerald hues gave a playfully stern look at Joey.

After both she and Joey threw on their clothes from last night, they left to head back uptown. With both of them deciding that a shower wasn't optional, they got cleaned up and dressed, ready to do some potential dirty work that didn't involve exchanging bodily fluids.

Her fingers swept her long locks of hair up into a pony-tail as her thoughts plagued her mind. "It can't be a coinci-dence that Gage's club was targeted. He got involved in my life, and now…" The first signs of guilt weighing in on her conscience began to seep through the cracks of her strong façade.

Pulling his shirt down over his head, Joey immediately came over to her and forced her to turn and face him. "This is *not* your fault."

"But isn't it? I could have said 'no' to all of this. I could have slammed the door shut in his face. It could have just been you and I against all five boroughs. Now?" Layne shook her head. "He shouldn't have to be targeted and potentially end up like—"

"Sean?" Joey finished her thought.

Layne hung her head and tried to swallow down the

truths that clawed at the little bit of morality she had left. "Yeah."

Joey tilted her head back up with a finger under her chin. "We all chose this—together. We will get through this together. You already know how I feel about you, and I can tell you that Gage's feelings for you run just as deep. His stubborn ass may not know it, but I see it."

She swallowed past the swell of a lump in her throat, still struggling with allowing her emotions to get the best of her. "I don't want to see him or you get hurt because of me."

"Layney," he smiled and gave her several small kisses. "I wish you could see what I see right now."

Layne wrinkled up her nose. "What's *that* supposed to mean?"

Chuckling, he wrapped his arms around her shoulders and drew her into a tight hug. "Nothing you won't figure out eventually." Joey ran his hand over the top of her head, his fingers trailing along the length of her ponytail before kissing her forehead. "We need to get going if we're going to make it back over to Hell's Kitchen. God knows one of us is going to need to prevent Gage from lashing out at any fucker that looks remotely guilty."

She nodded in agreement. There was no reason to have Gage dealing with this on his own. Just as she was dedicated to being at Joey's side, Layne needed to make sure that Gage knew she wasn't going anywhere. She was just as much his as she was Joey's.

CHAPTER TWENTY-SIX

When they pulled up to Cassidy's Cave, the pathway to destruction was clear. Spray paint marred the exterior in senseless patterns, and spiderwebs of cracked glass adorned the exterior windows. Trash was strewn about the sidewalk right out front.

Layne wanted to believe the outside of the building was the worst of it, but realistically, she knew that the inside had to be far worse. She spotted Gage's Jeep already parked outside, indicating he was likely inside assessing what had transpired during the early morning hours.

She and Joey entered the strip club, and the sight they were greeted with was far beyond even their wildest imaginations. The club wasn't just vandalized, but it had been thoroughly wrecked. Holes were in the walls, shattered glass everywhere, and broken furniture—the whole nine yards.

This wasn't just a small-time crime spree or random

strike. Everything about the sight laid out before them screamed intentional and deeply personal like a fit of rage. Flashbacks of what she had seen at McGregor's came rushing forth from her memory.

They weren't the only ones to show up. The bar manager, Rory, was cleaning behind the bar and disposing of busted liquor bottles. A couple of dancers were sweeping off the stages of scattered trash and debris. Even the dressing rooms had been struck by the looks of it as Danielle carried out a handful of colorful pieces of lingerie and dropped them into a large trash can.

Joey's hand came to the crook of her neck and squeezed affectionately to find comfort for them both. He stopped one of the girls on her way to take a bag of trash outside. "Where's Gage?"

The redhead gestured towards his office. "He said he'd be in his office making phone calls."

Layne didn't wait to head that way, stepping over piles of busted electronics and trash strewn about. The door to Gage's office was left partly ajar. Her hand slowly pushed it open wider so she could look inside. "Gage?"

His head shot up from its position on top of his desk. "Yeah, come in." He shook off the emotions that came with seeing the business he had poured so much time and energy into in such a state of disrepair.

With a frown partly filled with sympathy, she looked over at him while noticing the signs of distress in how he pushed his eyebrows up into his forehead. "It looks like you have a few hands to help out around here, at least."

Gage nodded and looked at both her and Joey. "This

place belongs to the girls just as much as it belongs to me. It gives them a home in a sense." His fingers pinched at the bridge of his nose, trying to rub the worst of his thoughts away.

Joey shook off his black leather jacket and draped it over one of the chairs. "Where do you want us to start?"

The offering of help gave Gage some relief and perhaps even a smidgen of hope that they could salvage this place. "Fuck, I don't know. Anywhere you can."

With that simple instruction, they got to work. The three of them began to tackle the harder projects like busted speakers and closing several of the bathroom stalls until replacement sinks, toilets, and plumbing could be installed to replace anything that had been smashed.

Layne walked to the back door to grab a few more contractor bags for the guys. Danielle followed behind her. "Layne?"

Hearing her name, she glanced back at the girl while looking for the next box of bags that Gage told her had been back there. "Yeah?"

"Do you mind helping me? I took some bags of trash out back earlier, and they were too heavy for me to lift into the dumpster. I could use another set of hands if you don't mind." She looked at Layne hopefully.

Stopping her search for the bags, she looked at the door next to her that led into the back alley where all the dumpsters were located. "Sure."

"Oh my God, thank you! The other girls just told me to get one of the guys to do it. I guess they didn't want to get their hands dirty or whatever." She shrugged and walked out the backdoor, holding it open for Layne to follow.

Quickly following Danielle out back, the door shut behind Layne. Danielle stopped and turned to Layne before they reached the dumpster. "You know… I expected better."

Layne scrunched up her face. "What?"

That's when, from behind her, a hand clamped down over her nose and mouth, muffling her immediate yells as it yanked her back into a massive body. When she felt a sharp jab into her thigh, she initially assumed it to be a pitiful excuse for a knife. Following the impact was a burning sensation of something being injected into her. The drug rushed through her veins from her adrenaline, pumping her blood fast and hard.

Each of her limbs, despite her will to keep them fighting, grew heavier. As pervasive as Layne's stubbornness was, she couldn't fight the dissociative anesthetic disarming her body's ability to remain under her control. While her vision grew blurry, one of the last things she saw was Danielle's sick smile as she stood there with her arms crossed in front of her chest.

After her vision blacked out entirely, her body went limp in the arms of the man who had administered the needleful of the heavy dose of an anesthetic. The burly man easily scooped her up and hoisted her over his shoulder.

Noticing Layne's phone sticking out of her back pocket, Danielle approached and plucked it from her jeans. She pitched it down at the concrete as hard as she could, ensuring the screen got all smashed up and rendered useless.

"Get her in the back of the van before anyone starts missing her." Danielle gestured toward the grungy-looking van with some electrician's faded logo on it.

The man Danielle had hired was a good little listener and brought Layne's unconscious body to the back of the vehicle, tossing her into it carelessly like she was nothing but a bag of garbage being tossed into a dumpster to be disposed of.

After the crony got into the driver's seat, Danielle joined him, and just like that, they were gone before Joey or Gage could intervene.

Joey finished unscrewing the bashed-in paper towel holder from the bathroom wall and looked at Gage, who was looking at one of the stall's doors, which was crookedly hanging on its hinges. "Layne said she was bringing back another box of bags, right?"

With a sigh, Gage gave up on trying to come up with a plan for the broken door. "Yeah, let me go see what's taking her so long. The box should have been right there by the back door." He wiped his hands on the thighs of his jeans and left the men's room.

When he got to the back, he saw no sign of Layne, and the box she was supposed to get was sitting right there in plain view. Gage's gut began to form a knot of apprehension as his instincts immediately began to swirl like a cyclone inside him. Trying to be rational, he took a step out back to see if maybe she was throwing out some garbage or grabbing some fresh air.

After realizing she was nowhere to be found outside, his worries began to escalate. Before walking back inside, he caught sight of something on the ground. He bent down and picked it up. The back of the phone case had the image of chains forming the shape of a shamrock on it. Upon recognition that it was Layne's phone, his thoughts spiraled out of control. "Layne?!" He yelled as he spun around, looking for any sign of her, and when he saw nothing to quell his fear, he ran back inside.

"LAYNE!" He frantically checked the other rooms inside the club despite knowing deep down he wouldn't find her there. He looked anywhere and everywhere, even places that were illogical for someone to be found.

Hearing Gage's voice booming out for their girl, Joey came out of the bathroom, nearly crashing into his brother. "What's wrong?"

Gage was filled with a storm of emotions, his jaw ticking with anger at some unknown person and at himself. The guilt and worry only added to it all. "She's gone."

Groggily, Layne lifted her head that had been slumped forward, causing an ache along the back of her neck right into the base of her skull. Her brains felt so goddamned scrambled. Trying to lift her hands to her face, she found them unable to move. As her green eyes fluttered open, she noticed several ropes wrapped around her forearms, keeping her stuck to the uncomfortable metal chair she was sitting in.

Part of her just wanted to vomit after coming out of the fog of the ketamine dosage. She groaned and closed her eyes again. It was unclear if she took another nap or another minute or so passed by, but her eyes gradually opened again when her head was forced back by a grip on her hair. Layne found herself looking at the blonde bitch that worked for Gage at Cassidy's.

"What…the…fuck?" Her mouth felt dry as shit, and of all people to see in front of her, Danielle wasn't who she expected.

Giving a painful tug on Layne's hair, Danielle smirked. "Did you have a good little nap?" Her words came off her tongue in a mocking tone.

Progressively getting a little bit more of her wits about her, she winced at the pain tugging at her scalp on top of the headache that was making itself more known by the second. Hoarsely she spat out, "Fuck you."

The next thing she felt was a harsh slap across her cheek. The pain helped Layne shake off a little more of the grogginess. It had been a lighter slap in comparison to the experience of a heavy smack of a man's hand, but it still left a stinging sensation and a red mark on her skin.

Looking around the room now that she was trying to piece everything together, she discovered that it couldn't have been a space bigger than a single-car garage. The concrete floor had dirt and stains, and it was lit up with a single lightbulb in the ceiling. There were no windows and nothing else other than the bitch standing in front of her.

"You know what your problem is, Layne?" Danielle began to pace in front of Layne.

In response, she couldn't hold back a scoff, Layne could make a list of things that were her problems. Danielle was very quickly making her way to the top of that list. "Why don't you tell me?"

Giving Layne a hard glare, Danielle continued her thoughts. "You don't know when to give it up."

"A character flaw, I know. I give it up to Gage just fine, though." Yes, Layne was feeling fucking sassy despite not being in a position to be sassing anyone. It helped keep her head focused to push buttons and assess just how much of a threat Danielle truly was.

Mission accomplished, blondie's face turned bright red with anger, and stalked over to her, getting up in Layne's face. "You're a fucking slut who slept her way into power! You'd be nothing but a sex toy like the rest of us if you didn't go around opening your legs for anything that resembled a dick with money and resources!"

Danielle drew back a fist and unleashed it on Layne. The small hand connected with the corner of her mouth, Layne's teeth cutting against the inside of her cheek and spilling the taste of copper inside. Layne spat out the blood toward the floor.

Layne's face remained unfazed even as she was verbally assaulted with false accusations and physically assaulted with a pitiful punch. "Is that what you think I did to get to where I am?" Her words were dangerously calm. This chick was walking a very fine line between injury and death once Layne figured a way out of the whole being tied to a chair situation.

She was curious as to what the hell Danielle was on and

who everyone was that she referred to. "I don't know what your game is here. If you're just pissed because some guy doesn't fawn over you or what. You clearly have some fucking mental issues, so why don't you clue me in as to why you're trying to take them out on me."

Danielle straightened back up and gave a broad smile. "I'm going to be the one that takes your place and snatches up all the power in this damn city. There's only room for one queen amongst all the kings."

Layne outright laughed; this girl was on some seriously good drugs with the lack of sense she was making. "Good luck with that. Who the hell is going to listen to some delusional stripper?"

Now, it was Danielle's turn to laugh. "You don't know? Oh, gee, this is awkward." Her voice made it clear that this girl didn't feel the least bit bad about any awkwardness.

She squatted down in front of Layne so she could watch her reaction. "I only took that job at Cassidy's, so I could keep tabs on Italo and his pathetic little crew. Then, you came along and disposed of him, and it was clear that it was worthwhile sticking around. You see, I have a vested interest in making sure Daddy gets his way if I'm ever going to rise to the top."

Layne had been good at controlling her face up until this point, but the more Danielle spoke, the more she realized this was far worse than a case of a psycho chick with jealousy issues.

With the confusion in Layne's eyes growing, Danielle smirked. "You didn't know my last name is Spencer, did you?"

That may as well have been the atomic bomb on Layne's brain. Everything began to snap into place as all the events that had transpired to this point were on rewind in her brain. The interest Danielle showed in Gage. Being present at all of Italo's meetings as the entertainment. Straight back to the day she had barged into the souvenir shop Russ owned to confront him about poaching Andrew Correlli.

Layne walked into the retail storefront, ignoring the girl at the cash register scrolling through her phone.

Even Alexei Kuznetsov had tried to warn her.

"I think you will find the answers you are looking for over at a little souvenir shop across from the Empire State Building."

She had thought he was referring to Russell's offices hidden in the back of that building. Not the girl who worked at the front counter. The very same girl that stood at the front of the store that day wasn't just someone looking to earn a few bucks; it had been Russell's daughter—Danielle. Fuck. This just went from being an inconvenience to being a goddamn crisis with potentially fatal conse-quences.

The realization left Layne speechless as she tried to sort through all the frantic thoughts in her brain. Even Alexei's cryptic words to her during their meeting were floating to the forefront of her mind.

"Be sure of your actions, pchelka. You do not want to lay judgment on the tiger only to be bitten by the snake."

She was snatched out of the things going on inside her head when the snake's hand grabbed her by the face. "Just wait until he gets here, he's going to be so proud to see what I have wrapped up in a slutty little package for him. I bet you'll even spread your legs and beg for him, too."

Layne didn't avert her eyes from Danielle's scornful face. "You have no idea what you've just done…" Her heart may have been beating faster than it should have, but she had never felt more sure of what needed to happen.

Danielle stood up, releasing her hold on Layne. Her eyes lit up with excitement. "Oo, is this where you tell me that your two boy toys are going to come save you? That they'll come here and save their damsel in distress?"

Layne shook her head. "No." She made direct eye contact with Danielle, a gaze filled with violent promises. "This is where I tell you that you've started a war. A war that I promised I would bring to your dad's front door if he crossed me ever again. A war he won't win."

It seemed that Danielle wasn't too concerned by the shrug she gave. The stupid girl was clueless about how the city's criminal politics were played. "In case you haven't noticed, you're not in a position to be doing much of anything. You would have been much smarter to start the war after I convinced my own boy toys to do a little redecorating at that little dive bar you love so much. I heard the owner put up a hell of a fight."

"You sick fuckin' bitch!" she screamed out. There was the temper flare that Layne was known so well for. She yanked at her arms bound by those ropes and thrashed in her seat, wanting to cover every inch of Danielle's face with the bottom of her boots.

Danielle cackled in amusement as she backed up

towards the door. "You don't know the half of it. Maybe I will send my boys in here to teach you a lesson or three, a lesson for each of your holes. See you in a bit!" She blew Layne a kiss before she left the room, slamming the door shut behind her and clicking the locks in place.

Layne yelled out in utter frustration as she pulled at her restraints despite the pain it caused. This bitch needed to die, and Layne decided that it would be her life's mission to end it in a spectacularly glorious fashion.

CHAPTER TWENTY-SEVEN

Layne sat in isolation, tied to that chair for what felt like hours. Her thoughts were jumping all over the place. She was worried, not for herself, but for her guys. They had to know she was missing by now, and they were likely ready to burn the city down just to find her. It hurt her heart even thinking about what they were going through. God, she hoped that they weren't doing anything stupid that put their lives at risk.

Then, there was the person who was responsible for putting her here. It seemed that little Miss Spencer wanted to follow in her daddy's footsteps, or maybe she was trying to compete with Layne. Either way, she was a poor imitation of what strength and strategy looked like in this line of work.

She couldn't be sure how much time she had before Danielle made good on any threats of sending in a bunch of cowards to torture or assault her. The ropes that kept her bound to the metal chair were creating burns against her skin from all the attempts to wiggle free from them. None-theless, she kept working at them.

As she heard voices approaching the door, she rushed her efforts along. It seemed not quick enough as the lock shifted and the door swung open. Danielle's shitty face with too many layers of cheap makeup was the first thing she saw, followed by three men. Well, this was going to be a goddamn rager of a party, wasn't it?

There was a brief thought in her mind reflecting some self-doubt. Layne shoved it back down into the place where she fed her temper. This bitch wanted to make good on her threats? Layne was going to make good on hers.

Danielle damn near skipped in and was so full of happiness. "Did you miss me? I brought some friends to keep you company."

It may have looked like Layne was sitting there refusing to speak out of defiance, but what she was doing was making calculations. Out of the three men, all wearing cheap ski masks, she did quick assessments of their heights and builds and how that would translate into who was the biggest potential threat. One had a gun on his hip, and she'd pay a fortune in blood to get her hands on it. Of all of them, Danielle was the weakest link; she'd die last just so Layne could get satisfaction out of it.

"Cat got your tongue, Layne?" Danielle stepped off to the corner of the room. Did she have intentions of watching this all unfold? Layne hoped so. "If you're worried about dying, don't. I'm sure my dad will want to have a few words with you after I tell him about everything I've accomplished without his help. Then, afterward, he can watch while I do the job myself."

One of the men came up behind her and began working on untying the ropes that held her down to the chair. The other two stood in front of her, perversion clouding their eyes as they stared at her. It seemed they were feeling confident that three fit men could handle one fired-up Layne. Oh, they were going to learn some things today.

"I'm just wondering if you've figured it out yet." Feeling the ropes gradually loosening up around her, the adrenaline began amping up in her body. She was going to have one chance at making this happen.

"Figured out what?" She looked perplexed at Layne's statement.

"That you'll never be me. You'll never have what it takes. I didn't get where I am by shaking my ass; I got here by getting my hands dirty, even when I was at rock bottom. I don't rely on a bunch of cowards to do it all for me." One more shift of rope was all she needed; it would be just enough to get out of this damn chair.

Danielle rolled her eyes. "Oh yeah? Look where it's gotten you."

Layne smirked. "Right where I want and deserve to be." Then, there was the last bit of slack in the rope that she required. Before the ropes were fully removed from her body, she was able to push up onto her feet. Her foot kicked the chair backward into the man behind her. It sent the metal piece of furniture into him for just enough time to catch him off guard.

It started a scene of complete chaos, with the other two

men lunging for her. She blocked a punch from the guy on her right before jabbing her elbow into his ribs, doubling him over. Layne immediately gave a front kick to the man on the left directly into his gut, forcing him to stumble back.

There was no hesitation for her to spin around, expecting the third guy to be coming at her from behind, which he was. She thrust her fist up under his chin, causing his head to sharply tilt back from the impact before she kicked him right in the balls, ensuring he was going down and staying down.

The arms of the man who had taken her elbow to his ribs locked his arms around her upper body. With the only other guy standing, mistakenly thinking she was being contained, he approached to strike out at her. He threw a punch that hit home right across her cheek. Now that he was close enough, Layne drew up both feet, kicking him in the chest and knocking the wind out of him. She pitched her head back, slamming it into her captor's face hard enough that he dropped her from his hold.

Layne spun around, and while the man was holding his face, she grabbed the gun from the holster on his hip.

Bang! Bang! Bang! Bang! Click.

Well, fuck her. The asshole hadn't kept his firearm fully loaded like a good little henchman.

She still managed to fire one shot to the chest of the guy who had brought it to the party, two at the man who was still writhing around holding his balls, and one at the last man. It was a fucking shame there hadn't been one bullet left for Danielle, who was standing there in the corner of the room, frozen by the obscene unfolding of events.

Already surrounded by three dead bodies, Layne breathed heavily, trying to catch her breath as she stared at Danielle. She tossed the now empty gun down on the ground. She spread her arms wide, welcoming Danielle to come at her. "Don't be shy now." Layne gave a winded chuckle with a hint of unhinged mental instability.

The slimy bitch made a run for the door. Layne grabbed the nearby metal chair and swung it at her, making contact right with her face with one of the legs. Danielle screamed out and fell back onto the floor from the momentum of the impact.

Layne tackled her the second Danielle tried to scramble back up onto her feet. They wrestled there on the floor, each of them trying to gain the upper hand with each punch that was thrown. Finally getting back on top, Layne grabbed a handful of over-processed blonde hair and put everything she had into smashing her fist right into Danielle's face. She didn't stop there; she followed up with at least four more until Danielle wasn't fighting back anymore.

Wearily, Layne stood up, her hand aching fiercely as blood dripped from her knuckles. "You wanted to start a damn war? Well, guess what, Danielle?!" Layne angrily yelled the question at her. "You started it with the wrong fucking family!" The sweet taste of blood pooled in her mouth. Layne spit out the blood from her mouth and down at Danielle. Hell, if she was going to be taken out by some fake bitch with a bad boob job.

Danielle groaned out in pain, barely finding it in herself to move, let alone respond with any more of her snarky comments.

Layne went over to where the rope was lying on the floor that had previously held her hostage. She picked it up and walked back to Danielle's battered body. When Danielle began to open her mouth to either beg or protest, Layne stepped on one of the bitch's hands before kicking her harshly in the jaw with her other foot. "Shut the fuck up."

All the feel-good and fuzzy emotions had left Layne the second she woke up in this room. Knowing all that Danielle was responsible for left Layne with nothing but the urge to inflict pain and death. Drawing enough length of rope, she leaned over and wrapped it around the girl's throat tightly before knotting it.

Layne dragged Danielle by that rope around her neck until they got to the door. The gagging and choking sounds fell on deaf ears. She took the other end of the rope and wrapped it around the door handle until Danielle was forced into a sitting position if she didn't want to strangle herself.

After securing the rope, Layne checked one of the corpses lying in a puddle of blood. She found a knife, and looking it over, she glanced back over at Danielle. "This'll have to do."

Feeling the weight of the knife in her hand, she looked at her target, who was now beginning to face the fear of death with wide eyes. Layne squatted down in front of her. Danielle didn't deserve any words of comfort or any parting one-liners before meeting her demise.

Grabbing the knife tightly, Layne slammed it into the hollow of Danielle's throat just below where the rope was wrapped tightly around her neck. The entirety of the blade sunk into her body, utterly destroying the esophagus and major arteries. It left Danielle choking on her own blood in her last moments until she all too quickly bled out.

Leaving the knife lodged in the throat of Russell's daughter, it was one of the few deaths Layne was more than happy to have on her hands. She pulled the door open, which took more effort than it should have, considering Danielle's body was still attached to the backside of it.

Now it was time to get the fuck out of here, wherever here was. Layne was quickly losing energy now that the rush of adrenaline was fading. Not knowing where she was or who else was there with her, she moved quickly and quietly. Navigating the only hallway that led her around a few corners, she ultimately came to an exit.

She stepped outside of the building, noticing how dark it was outside. It must have been considerably late because the only people she saw looked like they were working the street corners in search of a date.

Layne groaned when she didn't recognize the area. The building she had just come out of had signs saying 'Permanently Closed' plastered all over it. The original business logos had long been faded and almost entirely peeled away from the exterior.

Needing to be nowhere near this hellhole, she began walking. Exhaustion would have been welcomed by comparison to how she felt. Out of sheer desperation, she asked one of the hookers for her cell phone. The girl had been too quick to hand it over.

While dialing the only number she knew by heart, Layne caught a look at her reflection in a parked car's window. No wonder the girl hadn't argued, she had blood splattered across her face and clothes. Layne's split knuckles had stopped bleeding, but the stickiness of the dried blood remained. "Fuck…"

Layne listened to the other end ring only once before the gravelly voice answered on the other end, "Hello?" She collapsed down onto a bench, hearing the sound of heaven on earth.

"Joey?" She leaned over with her elbows resting on her knees as she sighed with relief. "Please come get me."

CHAPTER TWENTY-EIGHT

When she had spoken with Joey, he rapidly fired off what felt like a thousand questions. He asked her if she was okay, where she was, what happened, and more. Layne couldn't focus on answering any of them except the nearest intersection she was at. Everything was beginning to hurt, even her thoughts.

Within twenty minutes, both he and Gage had picked her up. The drive should have taken at least thirty, but Joey ignored just about every traffic law on the way. She was just over the New York State Line in New Jersey.

When they arrived, Joey nearly forgot to put the car in park before hopping out. The two of them smothered her with hugs and kisses despite the wreck she was. Gage had managed to stop Joey from hammering her with a million more questions. The important thing was that she was okay, and they weren't going to let her out of their sight until they had the full story of what transpired.

On the ride back to O'Reilly Manor, she laid across the back seat of the Challenger with her head in Gage's lap while his hand stroked over her head. For once, they hadn't harassed her about buckling up. Seeing the state she was in, they both didn't want to do anything more than allow her to find a little bit of comfort. Once they made it back to her house, they gave her the space she needed despite wanting to hover.

The guilt and fear had eaten away at Gage while she had been gone, and nobody knew where she was. If Layne hadn't been there helping clean up, she wouldn't have been in the wrong damn place at the wrong time. Conversely, Joey had simply been ready to start busting down every criminal syndicate's door and racking up body counts in search of her.

She stood in the shower for nearly forty-five minutes, washing all the filth and blood from herself as the hot water and soap stung the abrasions on her body. Afterward, she pulled on a pair of her favorite sleep shorts with a bralette. It was the only set of clothes she could get comfortable in with the way her body ached.

Now, she found herself sitting on the kitchen counter with both the guys staring at her. "I told you I'm fine, just tired." Her fingers pinched the bridge of her nose while trying to fend off the lingering headache.

Gage dabbed some antiseptic on her knuckles, eliciting a hiss of pain from her. "Sorry, I'm trying to be gentle, baby."

Joey frowned as his hand carefully turned her head so he could inspect what injuries she had now that the blood had been washed away. Every bruise, cut, and rope burn he saw notched up his anger one more tick. He knew that for each mark visible on her, she had to be hurting internally on top of it.

Taking a measured exhale, Joey turned her to look at him. "What happened?"

Layne shook her head. "I don't want to get into it. I just need my phone so I can call Thomas and—"

"Now is not the time to make me ask twice, Layne." Joey's voice grew heavier, and from the look of his brown eyes, they were ready to turn black with death.

She knew this was all going to go over like a damn lead balloon for both of them. Layne began to recount what happened, from being jumped in the back alley after Danielle lured her out there to waking up in the dingy room tied to a chair and Danielle's failed attempt to get her boys to do all her dirty work. All the while, Layne avoided telling the kicker of it all. If Joey and Gage both didn't already have all the reasons to lash out at Russell Spencer, this was going to be the breaking point.

Gage finished patching up her hand and laid a kiss lightly on top of the bandage. "Why? What the hell was her issue with you?"

"Besides being twisted in the head?" Layne paused, hating that they were at this point. She had both guys staring at her, looking for answers that would make all of this make sense.

The silence from Layne continued for a little while until Joey's agitation began to eat away at him. "I swear, Layne if you don't just spit it the hell out..." It may not have been the gentlest of prompts, but it was effective as he saw Layne's shoulders sink in forfeit.

She shook her head. "Her dad is Russell Spencer. She wanted to make him proud or some shit, I don't know."

"Motherfucker!" It was Joey who reacted first. Before he could storm off, Layne grabbed him by his belt and nearly slid off the counter if it hadn't been for Gage, who caught her before she did. He eased her down onto her feet while Layne refused to release her grasp on Joey.

"Dammit, Joey, wait!" She pleaded. "I don't think he knows, and I want it to stay that way. If shit is going down, I want plans in place. That's why I want to get Thomas on board so he can prepare the rest of the team."

He reluctantly turned back around. The desire to go visit Russ right now and destroy every bone in that fucker's body was right up there with, wishing he could resurrect Eric Ellis just to send him right back down to hell.

"Wait for what, Layne?! Wait, so another motherfucker can take a shot at you?!" All of Joey's pent-up frustrations and fears that had weighed on him during her disappearance were all getting unleashed. "I'm tired of waiting around! You could have died, and there was *nothing* I could have done to stop it. Do you even get that?!"

His words of anger were accompanied by a sense of misery in his eyes that he had been hurting, knowing that there had been the possibility of her life being ripped from him forever.

In response, her green hues began to glisten with unshed tears as she felt the pain in his words.

Gage interjected, speaking to his brother, "You're not

going to do shit without me." Then, he turned to look at Layne. "And you're not doing anything until you get some rest." He wasn't going to add to the already emotionally charged situation with what he was feeling.

Now it was her turn to be irritated, but with how much her body wanted to crash, she couldn't even raise an argument with him.

Joey sighed, realizing he probably shouldn't have gone off on her the way he did. It didn't make anything he said less true, but his fears had come uncomfortably close to fruition. "Look, it's been a fucker of a time for all of us. Go get in bed, and we'll be up in a minute to join you." He agreed with Gage's determination that Layne needed to sleep and allow herself to recover after everything she had been through.

Maybe it was the 'we' in that statement that convinced her to listen or the fact that she could hardly keep herself up on her feet, but Layne nodded. "I'll be upstairs, don't take too long."

After Layne left the kitchen and went up to the master bedroom, it was Gage's turn to lash out with all the emotions that had been locked away to prevent Layne from getting any more riled up. His hand smacked the bottle of antiseptic off the counter angrily, sending it flying across the kitchen. "Son of a bitch! I fuckin' *knew* Russell was bad news. He and his entire goddamn operation needs to die."

Joey looked over at Gage, filled with a calmer variation of his rage. "This isn't going to be pretty. If she makes this move against Spencer, she is either going to get torn apart by the other factions or have half the city by the balls."

Slowly nodding, Gage ran his fingers through his hair in frustration that they both had come too close to having history repeat itself. "Then let's make sure she gets her seat on the throne she deserves to be on."

<hr>

Layne thought she felt like shit when she had gotten back home last night, but when she woke up the next morning, all the aches and pains were tenfold. Her pride refused to voice the weight of her body's angry protests. She was moving much slower and fighting through it all on her own.

She curled up on the sofa, watching the morning news on the television with a cup of coffee held between her hands. Joey came up behind the sofa, leaning over and rubbing his hands over her shoulders lightly before kissing the top of her head. "You're up earlier than I expected."

"I couldn't sleep." She sipped from her piping hot morning routine in a mug.

He came around the end of the couch and took a seat next to her, resting his arm along the backrest behind her. "I have ways to help with that," Joey smirked at her playfully.

Lightly smiling, she leaned over into his side, soaking in the warmth and safety his presence provided. "Some of the best ways. Is Gage still upstairs sleeping?"

He shook his head. "He went out to take care of a few things. He promised he'd be back in a little while with food."

"Mm, I could use something to eat. I'm starving." Her stomach rumbled in agreement.

She leaned over to cement a kiss onto his mouth. Joey's hand wrapped around the back of her head to hold her in close for the kiss. Murmuring against her lips, he teased, "I got something for you to put in your mouth to hold you over."

She smiled against his mouth, and the kiss began to grow into something more passionate before getting interrupted.

The female news anchor spoke with a solemn voice, "Breaking news. This just in, several bodies have been discovered at an abandoned veterinary clinic in Jersey City. Police are investigating the incident and, at this time, say there are no leads. Maria is reporting live from the scene."

Layne pulled back from Joey to look at the screen, which showed the very building she had escaped. This time, it was surrounded by yellow crime scene tape, flashing lights, and an excessive amount of law enforcement.

The image of the reporter standing in front of the building had the same tone that all reporters seem to have, one which evokes seriousness with perfectly crafted sentences and a hint of suspense. "Thank you, Susan. I spoke with one of the officers earlier, and he said that there were four bodies discovered inside. Three of them died of apparent gunshot wounds. The fourth was of a woman who suffered in what was only described to me as a 'heinous act of disturbing violence.'"

Setting her coffee on the table in front of them with a groan, both of her stiff movements and a realization. "Fuck. I need to make a call."

"What is it?" Joey sat up, eyeing her.

Slowly, she eased herself up off the couch with a wince. She looked at Joey with eyes that reflected her anger at herself for making a stupid rookie mistake. "My fingerprints are all over the murder weapons, Joey."

He tried not to add to her worries with his own as he stood up. "We'll get it fixed. Your prints won't mean anything if there's nothing in the system to compare them to."

Layne stared at him, her face full of concern, not easing up any.

He raised both his brows. "When the hell did you get arrested?"

She gave a small smile, recalling the little she remembered about the incident. "Things got a little ridiculous on my twenty-first birthday. After the cops were called, the one Boy Scout in the group didn't like that I flashed my tits at him."

He smirked. "One lucky son of a bitch. I would have arrested your ass just so I could have you all to myself." Joey wrapped his arms around her and showered her with a few hungry kisses.

There was no fighting the smile and the way he could put her at ease. "Ok, ok! I have to call my contact at the crime lab to make sure that any prints that are lifted are determined to be inconclusive."

His hand rubbed over the curve of her ass. "One call, then you're mine for the rest of the morning until Gage gets back."

They both left the room, leaving the television on. The

image shifted to the studio news anchor again to transition to another news story. A familiar face appeared in the upper right part of the screen while the woman continued her news coverage.

"In Midtown, another young woman was found deceased. Kristill Hendricks, twenty-four years old, was discovered by her neighbor after noise complaints about Hendricks' Chihuahua continuing to bark for hours on end. Sources say that the young woman had a history of drug abuse and prostitution, but police aren't ruling out foul play. More to come."

CHAPTER TWENTY-NINE

A war had been brewing, and Layne was now ready to kick it off. She had been spending the last couple of weeks making plans with all her associates. Danielle may have been the most recent primary aggressor, but the Spencer name would spread like cancer if Layne didn't take action to put an end to it now.

Russ knew what games he was playing, trying to encroach on the O'Reilly territory, and hell, if she was going to let him get away with it any longer. She had been too nice in trying to play politics. The time for sweet talking was over. She was going to send a message loud and clear to any factions in the city that supported him that she wasn't going to tolerate his bullshit any longer.

Joey and Gage both had her back in this endeavor. It didn't hurt to know if they wiped Russell from the playing board, with a little bit of luck, they would also get to unleash their chaos and wrath on the man responsible for Rose's death.

Layne sat on the hood of her car in the middle of an empty parking lot, looking at her crew of men who had shown up for this evening's strategized power play. She was dressed in all black, from her boots up to her long-sleeved shirt, and in her hand was her skull mask with its orange and green laces. Her hair crisscrossed into a French braid with matching orange and green ribbons running through it.

"Ethan, you take your crew and see to it that Russell's little souvenir shop with his office gets a hot bath in some gasoline." She couldn't wait to see that retail storefront burn down to its foundation.

Layne pointed at the man standing next to Ethan. "Sammy, go see to it that Russell's right-hand man doesn't see the light of day tomorrow."

She smiled as she got to the last of her senior associates gathered there with them. "And Jonathan, pay a visit to his favorite butcher shop and let them know we will be taking over all the accounts. If they have a problem with it, they can expect Ethan to show up there next."

Jonathan nodded at her, understanding the assignment, but he had some hesitation. "Layne, there's a lot more business in Russ's territory, this is a drop in the bucket."

She crossed her arms in front of her chest and sighed. "I know, but it will have to be the starting point. We can keep pushing until everybody learns a damn lesson of who not to fuck with in this city."

Standing back a few feet from Layne's car were both De Luca brothers. Each wore tactical black pants and black hoodies, ready to assist Layne in her role in tonight's endeavors. Joey had on his mask with its smiling skull jaw on it, and Gage wore his hellish demon mask across his face.

"Actually…" Joey stepped up to Layne's right with a phone in his hand and showed it to Layne. A familiar face was on the video call, smirking at her.

"Pchelka, why did you not invite me to the party sooner, eh?" Alexei winked at her. "I have my men on their way to visit a few other of Mr. Spencer's top clients. Consider it an early wedding gift."

Her eyes stared at Kuznetsov in shock and then over at Joey, who, even with his mask on, seemed to be beaming with pride at this little surprise he presented her with. "Thank you." Layne meant it for both the Russian on the video call and the sneaky asshole who had coordinated with him.

Then, Gage came up on her left also with a video call on his phone. "That's not all, lucky charm."

Layne blinked a few times as she looked at Gage, and on his screen were several faces she didn't recognize at all.

"I called in a few favors from some old friends from my days in Jersey City. They're going to help us out wherever we need them tonight." Gage explained to her, and one of the guys on the phone spoke up with a heavy Jersey accent.

"Don't let him fool you, he's a conniving asshole." The man joked with a hearty laugh. "Anything you need tonight, we got you."

She smiled and looked at Gage, moved that he had also gone out of his way to seek out extra help. God, she loved him. She loved them both so much. Layne offered her words of appreciation for Gage's friends before hopping down onto her feet in front of her car.

"Let's go give Russell the news." She dismissed the crew present with her and then turned to see Joey and Gage now side by side, ready to accompany her.

Joey stepped up to her, took the mask from her hands, and placed it over her face. "No matter what happens, I've never been prouder, Layney."

"Me, too." Gage came up to her side, and the three of them came into an embrace.

She smiled and patted each of them on their sides. "Alright, let's go before I change my damn mind and beg you both to take me home instead."

Each of their hands gave a swat to a side of her ass, with Joey chuckling. "You can beg us later."

They piled into her car, and Layne took the seat behind the wheel. She drove them all to Russell's house, which was on the Upper West Side. Parking down the street from the Spencer residence, she sat in the driver's seat for a second, running down her checklist and patting herself down to ensure she had her weapons all in place.

She took one more deep breath and nodded to herself. "I'm ready." Pulling out her phone, she shot off a text to Ethan to give him the green light to proceed burning down Russell's base of operations.

Layne got out of the car and began heading towards Russ's house. If she was going to do this, she was going to bestow the news on him herself. Joey and Gage stuck close to her, keeping an eye out for anything that might become a threat.

It was quiet in the neighborhood, which she had counted on, being that it was half past midnight. She jogged up to Spencer's front door and waited off to the side, glancing at her watch. Layne was waiting on Russ getting the call that his shop was on fire, given the yelling she heard from coming inside the house, he had just received the unfortunate news.

A few more minutes passed, and she nodded to Joey and Gage, who were across from her on the other side of the door, as she heard footsteps approaching from inside the house.

The moment the door opened up and Russ was ready to rush out to deal with the situation at his store, Gage rushed him and pushed him right back inside. Layne followed next, and Joey filed in behind her, shutting the door.

Alarmed, Russ yelled out as Gage's hand had a grip on his shirt, shoving him back against a wall. "WHAT THE FU—" His exclamation was cut off by Gage's fist colliding into his face.

A huge smirk pulled at Gage's mouth underneath the mask, it had felt exceptionally fucking cathartic to hit this motherfucker. Russ was stunned by the strike and was now glaring at the three of them. "What do you want?"

Layne pulled down her mask away from her face. "Hi, Russ." Her smile at him was full of confidence and fake pleasantries. "Hope you don't mind the late-night visit. I was just in the neighborhood and thought I'd swing by."

Joey did a quick check to make sure that there wasn't anyone else in the house before coming back to standby while Layne had her conversation.

Russ shook his head. "You stupid little bitch! Didn't you learn anything from the last time you came barging onto my property?"

She pursed her lips in thought. "Hmm, it seems not. It also seems you didn't learn anything either." Layne stepped in front of him, her striking green eyes staring at him. "I promised you a war. The sad thing about war is that it comes with casualties. Your psycho-bitch daughter was the first of what I imagine will be many more to come."

He made a move to come at her, but Gage shoved him back against the wall, and Joey stepped up to assist in pinning him there. With one hand on Russ's shoulder, Joey dug the end of a handgun up underneath Russ's jaw. "Give me the tiniest excuse to blow your fuckin' brains out."

The ding of her phone went off in her pocket, followed by another one and another. She pulled her phone out and smiled to herself. "You see, Russ," her finger flipped through a few messages on her phone. "I have my men all over the city tonight taking over your assets one by one."

He scoffed at her. "You don't have the resources."

She gave an indifferent shrug. "No, you're right about that. However, I had quite a few friends step up to the plate to provide some assistance. While you were so busy focusing on picking off my assets one by one, I was having talks with other factions. It turns out you're not as much of a well-liked guy as you seem to think."

Russ scowled at her and tried to maintain his confidence that this was all one huge bluff. "They'll all turn on you the moment you close your eyes. Even if they don't, my employees will feed your corpse to a bunch of rabid dogs."

She placed a hand on her chest, feigning the hurt of his words. "Oh, wow. That hurts nearly enough to make me change my mind." Layne shook her head and smirked. "Tell me one thing, Russ, who's going to give the order to come at me if I don't let you walk out of here tonight?"

Layne pulled up a photo on her phone from a message that had just come in from Ethan. She showed it to Russ, and the way his face fell and the color drained from his face had been worth all the stress and sleepless nights the past few weeks. There on the screen was a photograph of his second-in-command, lying in bed with two fresh holes in his head.

She turned off her phone and slid it back into her pocket. "What happens next is up to you, Russ. I have some questions that I'm dying to know the answers to."

"Yeah, like what?" He struggled to get comfortable with both Joey and Gage tightly gripping onto him and the ever-present threat of the firearm lodged up against his neck.

Watching his face carefully to see how his expression would change, Layne spoke casually, like they were about to discuss who won last night's hockey game. "When did you first meet Eric Ellis?"

The question seemed to throw Russ, unclear of where she was heading with this. "What?"

Gage tightened his hold painfully. "The lady asked a goddamn question." He said through clenched teeth.

Russell seemed to take a moment to count back the

years. "It was well over ten years ago. Why the hell do you care about Ellis? He's fucking nothing but worm food now."

She pressed her lips together in a hard line, knowing the next question quite possibly had an answer that she didn't want any of them to hear. Not because she wanted to live in ignorant bliss but because she knew that it would be one that either confirmed years of pain and brought healing or left them at a loss with more unanswered questions.

"Did you take a job from him? One that involved taking an innocent woman and physically collecting a debt from her that left her for dead?" She swallowed hard as her chest tightened.

The reaction from him didn't satisfy Layne, and she stepped closer so her face was up near his. "Did you?"

"I tossed Eric a favor every now and again, so it's possible. If you're talking about some blonde cutie that my guys picked up, then yeah, she was easy money. Too bad she broke a little too easily, though, I had to ditch her to get her pussy sewn back up at the nearest vet." Each of his words lacked remorse.

Layne shook her head in disappointment and stepped back. "I am more than happy to let you walk out of here tonight, Russ. I want you to see how it's me taking all your assets from you and letting you get swallowed up by the rest of the scum in this city."

She looked at Joey and Gage, giving them both the look they had been waiting for. "But it's not about what I want. These two," she motioned to the masked men standing before him, "won't be allowing that to happen. They're going to be collecting a long overdue debt from you."

Joey shoved his pistol into his thigh holster so he could use two hands on Russ. They both yanked him away from the wall and dragged him through the house until they got to the kitchen.

Layne followed behind, watching as Russ cursed at all of them and attempted to wound them with insults. She leaned back against a wall and comfortably crossed her arms in front of her stomach. Her eyes were void of any empathy for the man who had scarred both her guys so many years ago.

What transpired next ended up being a kind ending to Russell Spencer's life in comparison to what he had put Rosie through. Both Joey and Gage took turns using him as a punching bag, allowing all their years of accumulated pain to be taken out on the man responsible for it. After that, things got a little more creative with the use of the garbage disposal, destroying each one of Russ's hands at a time. The heavy stainless steel fridge door was slammed against the man's head until the door itself broke.

Finally, just when Russ was losing consciousness from the brutal attacks, Gage tossed him to the floor and pinned him there underneath the weight of his boot. "Goodnight, motherfucker." He pulled out his semi-automatic and fired three shots into the back of Russ's skull.

Layne slowly released a breath as it all came to a bloody conclusion. Standing there witnessing them both avenge Rosie's murder filled her with a mixture of feelings. One of which had her understanding both the guys on a different level. Her panties were growing damp with desire and arousal as each of them unleashed their fury.

She hoped that tonight could help them both heal and find their peace. More importantly, she hoped that this would be a clear message to anyone who fucked with her or anyone that she loved that Chaos and Wrath would follow. If anyone found themselves in the presence of Luck, may it be her good side.

CHAPTER THIRTY

The night they sent Russell Spencer to his grave had gone off smoother than even Layne had expected. While she didn't have half the city's criminal factions at her back as she had promised Russ she would; she was slowly building up her rapport and gaining respect from the other families across all of New York. There was still going to be a long way to go before she elevated herself beyond her father's legacy, but she was confident it would happen someday.

Alexei had made good on his word, and as a token of her appreciation, she guaranteed him a portion of the income she was drawing in from Russell's assets she had seized.

Several of Gage's friends had agreed to sign on to her team, willing to help be extra manpower whenever she needed it. Gage had managed to get Cassidy's entirely renovated and remodeled. No longer known as Cassidy's Cave, it was renamed to Cassidy's Chains. It was now being dubbed as one of the hottest new nightclubs, with a sexy twist, of course.

Rebecca had been hounding Layne with last-minute wedding details, ensuring that Layne wasn't getting cold feet and constantly reminding her that the big event was only a week away. While Layne hadn't outright told her best friend about her involvement with Gage, it seemed Rebecca had already connected the dots without forcing Layne to have the awkward conversation about her unconventional relationships.

Joey had gradually eased out of his contract work to help Layne manage her growing team of enforcers. He took a job here and there, but now his primary focus was training each member of her crew. If Layne was going to be successful, all of her associates needed to be able to tackle problems with ease.

Layne had decided to get her very first tattoo. It wasn't much in terms of size, but it fit her to a T. Across the back of her neck, in a black feminine cursive, was a single word:

Luck

The bottom of the 'k' swirled below the rest of the letters and dropped down into an upside-down shamrock, representing both sides of the same coin. Luck was neither inherently good nor bad and was always to be found in the eye of the beholder.

Gage had been hopping between his place in Hudson Yards and O'Reilly Manor, depending on the day. Both he and Joey kept Layne busy in the bedroom and out. Date nights rotated between one-on-one time and then all three of them. All of it felt so easy with both the guys, making her one lucky bitch.

Getting home from a rambunctious night out with two De Lucas who had their eyes on her, Layne laughed as she ran over to the stairs, resting her hand on the railing. "You both were on terrible behavior all night!" She kicked off her silver heels, so she was standing barefoot on the step in her little dark green dress.

Joey smirked at her. "Can you blame us? You have been giving that look where you bite your lip, knowing it goes straight to my cock."

Shrugging off his jacket, Gage tossed it onto the mounted coat rack, not giving a shit if it actually landed on a hook or not. "Not to mention, you've been talking back to me all night. All I've been able to think about is bending you over my knee and smacking your ass." He grinned deviously at her.

Layne flashed them both an innocent smile. "Well, you know the rules, only one of you gets me tonight. Guess we'll see who catches me first."

Both of the guys paused to size one another up before attempting to shove the other one out of the way before they both chased after their girl. Layne let out a shriek and ran up the stairs.

Joey doubled up steps going up the stairs, but Gage was quick behind him. Once both men were at the top, Layne was already dashing down the hallway toward the master bedroom.

Gage pulled at Joey's shirt to yank him back to get the

lead. He ran like his life depended on it and quickly gained on Layne, an arm scooping her up around her waist and pulling her back against him. He growled into her ear. "Got you."

He got her into the bedroom, kicking the door shut behind him. "Sorry, man, you'll have to wait 'til tomorrow morning!" Gage yelled back at his brother as he released his arm from around Layne. His hands tugged the back of his shirt over his head as his eyes filled with lust and something else more mischievous.

"Dammit!" Joey sighed on the other side of the door. "You two better at least try to keep it down this time!" While disappointed, he also had taken a few liberties during dinner with his hand up Layne's dress and buried it between her thighs, taking advantage of her lack of panties. If Gage wanted to gloat, he intended to make him pay for it and watch as he fucked Layne on the kitchen table tomorrow morning during breakfast.

Layne giggled as she did that damn lip thing again. She backed up until she flopped down onto the edge of the bed, leaning back on her hands. "Going to come here and claim your prize?" Her eyes sparkled with excitement as she watched him reveal his bare chest.

He didn't make a move. Instead, he beckoned her over with his finger. "Get over here and get on your knees, baby."

Still feeling quite sassy, she smirked while crossing one leg over the other, showing she had no intentions of listening to his command.

"You've already racked up a good number of punishments for tonight, are you sure you want to add a few more?" His dick had been hard all night every time she taunted him, and she was only adding to the number of times he was going to have his payback for it. His mind came up with several ways to teach his bratty lucky charm that he was in charge when it concerned that pretty pink box between her legs.

She shrugged at him coyly. "You're dealing with one of New York's most dangerous women right now. How lucky are you feeling?"

Gage laughed and walked up to her, his hand coming under her chin and tilting it so she looked up at him. "Go ahead and try me."

Layne suddenly made a move to grab his arm to pull him off balance and take control of him. It hadn't been a full-out effort, but even if it had, she knew that Gage would have overpowered her any day of the week. He easily avoided her half-assed attack on him, grabbing hold of her and pushing her back onto the softness of the mattress. He flipped her over onto her stomach and pinned her down with one hand.

He got between her legs; his other hand came up underneath her, pulling her hips up so she was ass-in-air for him. Gage groaned as his fingers shoved the dress up her body until it was bunched up at her waist, revealing her bare ass being offered up to him. "What do you tell your Daddy when he's got you right where he wants you?"

Her hips pushed back against the front of his jeans, moaning as she felt his large cock begging to be freed. "I will take your cock wherever you want to bury it, Sir."

"Mm, that's right." His fingers traced down over her slit before pushing three deep inside her wet entrance. "Did you think I didn't notice how Joey fucked you with his fingers throughout dinner? I wanted nothing more than to pull you under the table so you could wrap your lips around my dick."

She squirmed and moaned out as the heat in her core began to pool when he inserted his fingers into her wanton pussy. The silver rings on his fingers rubbed at her opening for extra stimulation. "Please, yes!"

Gage pumped his fingers into her harder, luring her closer to her release. Just as she glided along the fine line of falling into a world of ecstasy, he removed his fingers with a grin. He took his time sucking the taste of her body from each finger while he began to open up his jeans with his other hand.

Layne whined as he left her hanging there on the edge of what had promised to be a hell of an orgasm.

He got up off the bed and shoved both his pants and boxers down, stepping out of the rest of his clothes. All of his tattoos spread across his body were on display, especially the Roman helmet and corresponding swords that were drawn over his length.

Layne took the opportunity to sit up so she could lift her dress over her head and fling it to the side. She crawled over the edge of the bed in front of Gage, sitting back on her ankles while she rested her hands on top of her thighs. Her beautiful doe-eyes looked up at him, full of need.

"You're going to get more than just my cock tonight."

He smiled at her and leaned over, taking her pouty lips hostage with a deeply held kiss.

Layne's hands reached up to hold onto both sides of his bearded face, moaning with a desire for him. She urged him to come down onto the bed with her, dropping a hand to wrap around his swords, stroking him encouragingly.

Gage moaned, feeling her hand working him from base to tip. Before they got too carried away, he pulled his mouth from her and leaned over to pull something out of the nightstand on the side of the bed he often slept on. "Turn around for me, Layne."

It was the way he said her name that grabbed her attention. She released her hand from his cock. Reluctantly, she moved her position so that she had her back to him while she sat back on her ankles again.

"Let me see your tattoo, baby." Another request came from him, and she complied, her fingers gathering up her length of chestnut tresses, holding them away from the back of her neck.

The bed shifted as Gage joined her on it. Soon, his hands were placing a cool strand of metal around her throat. The gold necklace fit comfortably around her neck. Hanging from the clasp at the back was an extra two inches of chain that had a small sword charm dangling from the end of it. After it was secured on her, he leaned over and laid several kisses across the nape of her neck.

Layne's fingertips drifted over the front of the piece of jewelry with a smile, having not expected a seemingly random gift from him. Her hand released her hair, letting it fall back down beyond her shoulders.

Gage's hands turned her around to face him, his face full of warmth as his light brown eyes filled with love for the woman he saw before him. "This is my collar for you. It's my promise that I will always be here to take care of you, no matter what. You will always be my lucky charm, worth protecting with my life. This isn't a symbol that you're mine but that I'm yours. I love you for all that you are, and I will be yours for as long as you'll have me. Just know that next week, when we're all in that church together, Joey may be saying the vows out loud, but I will be saying them with my heart."

She melted as she saw Gage lay out his feelings for her. Layne's heart swelled as his love for her filled it even more. "Gage De Luca, I couldn't possibly love you any more than I do right now. You make my life complete; you and Joey both make me the happiest woman to ever exist. I don't want to picture my future without either of you in it." Layne wrapped her arms around his neck and pressed herself up against him, passionately taking hold of his mouth with her lips.

He embraced her, laying her back until he was on top of her. His tongue slid into her mouth to greet hers, stroking over it in a sensual dance. His hands explored her body; his palms kneaded her breasts as her stiff nipples pressed into his touch. Gage's mouth left hers to travel down her throat; his teeth lightly tugged at the collar around her with a playfully possessive growl.

His hands held tightly onto the dip of her waist, ready to move her at the drop of a hat. The coarse hair of his short beard dragged against her skin while he continued to kiss down the length of her body, stopping partway to draw each nipple into his mouth and circle it with his tongue until the sound of her moans graced his ears.

"Where do you want my cock first, lucky charm?" He smirked as he looked up at her.

Layne lifted her head from the pillow to look down at him. "First?" She smiled excitedly, hoping she had heard right.

"There's no part of you that isn't going to feel me tonight, baby." He lowered his mouth down to her pussy that glistened with her arousal. "You're not going to come until you are begging me to take one of your tight as fuck holes. I want to hear how needy you can be." His tongue dragged over her sex, just barely flicking her clit, prompting her hips to twitch at the small shock of pleasure.

Gage made good on his promise, dragging her to the edge of pleasure time and time again. For every time she had run her bratty mouth at him that night, he was sure to taunt her body by always keeping her release just out of reach.

Finally, he turned her over with her ass raised for him to take as he saw fit. His hand slapped her ass harshly for the last bit of sass she had given him. Not waiting for her to acknowledge the heat of the smack, he plunged his rock-hard cock deep into her pussy.

She cried out in relief as he rammed himself inside her, filling her up. He pounded into her, his hips making contact with her with each thrust. "Fuck, baby, I've got your pussy a wet mess, and I'm nowhere near done with you yet." His hand reached down and grabbed a handful of her hair, pulling. "Now you can come like a good girl."

The words barely needed to be spoken; just feeling him stretching her tight walls had her knuckles turning white as she clutched onto the sheets of the bed. Layne screamed out as the intensity of her release tore through her body.

Gage spent the rest of the night making sure that he had her in that constant state of utter satisfaction until he couldn't hold back from spilling his cum into her.

Once all the noises coming from the bedroom upstairs quieted, Joey silently crept up to the second floor. Pushing the door open to their room, he looked inside and saw Layne and Gage there in bed, passed out in each other's arms. He joined them, bringing his chest to Layne's back so that he could be lulled to sleep by the natural scent of her body's arousal mixed with her perfume of rain-kissed daisies.

He never would have thought that anything would be so perfect as the three of them being bound so closely together. This was a feeling he couldn't ever imagine letting go of, not if he had anything to say about it.

Rebecca smoothed out the train of Layne's dress after they both stepped out of the white limousine in front of the Cathedral of St. Mary, the catholic church where Layne had grown up attending Sunday School. Her bestie made up the entirety of the bridal party as Layne's Maid of Honor. Rebecca was done up in a simple pale green dress, with her light blonde locks cascading down in loose curls.

Layne stood there staring at the steps laid out before her leading up into the religious institution. Given all the egregious sins she committed on any given week, it was rather ironic that she was about to step foot inside a church and have a priest bless her union with Joey in any shape or form. By all morals and religious standards, both of them were destined for an afterlife full of fire and brimstone.

Already, she could feel her heart picking up its pace; she knew the two men whom she loved unconditionally were waiting just beyond the doors for her. A part of her wanted to run straight into both their arms.

She looked up at the clear blue sky, seeing a few birds soar on by, careless and free. Everything about today felt peaceful, calm, and perfect. All the worries about having a rainy day were behind her.

Her bestie placed a hand on her bare shoulder. "You can do this. He loves you, Layne, and I know you'll spend every day loving one another for the rest of your lives. Just take a deep breath and let everything and everyone else fade away."

A soft smile crossed her face as Layne gave a small nod in response to the encouragement. Rebecca was right. Once she was on the other side of those doors, there were only going to be two points of focus pulling at her heart. She was going to pledge her life to loving both of them with all she had.

Holding tight onto the bundled stems of her bouquet's mixture of traditional white roses and the less traditional green hue of Bells of Ireland, Layne took the first step towards the stone steps that led the way to the entrance.

Once inside the church, the large and ornate double doors leading into the nave where all the guests were gathered were shut, blocking her view of what awaited her. Those doors were separating her from the two most important men in her life.

She swallowed hard, feeling the nerves vibrating all over her body with anxiety. Irrational thoughts flooded her mind. What if he hadn't shown? What if she couldn't say the words? What if this was all a dream?

Rebecca gave another fluff of the short lace train of Layne's dress before coming around to stand in front of her with a smile full of love and eyes glistening with proud tears. "You look absolutely gorgeous and deserve every bit of this happiness. I will be upfront, cheering you on. Just one foot in front of the other, okay?" She leaned over and hugged Layne.

Moments later, Rebecca disappeared beyond the doors. Layne knew there was classical music playing just inside, but she couldn't hear it over her thoughts. She wondered if her dad would have been proud and walked her down the aisle to give her away to commit her life and love to a man like Joey. She knew Liam wouldn't have.

Breaking free of her thoughts, she noticed a little old woman had her frail hand on one of the doors and was waiting for Layne to indicate she was ready. After getting a small smile from Layne, the elderly woman nodded to the man standing behind the other door. Simultaneously, they drew the doors open, revealing the sight down the length of the path she was about to walk.

The aisle was lined with flowers in various shades of green. Light poured in through the massive stained glass windows. The rows upon rows of pews filled with guests all on their feet with their eyes all looking at her. Layne could have sworn the church was void of any guests at all because her eyes immediately found her entire universe standing up by the altar. The pianist began to play a romantically slow version of *Wherever You Will Go* by The Calling.

Joey stood tall, his hands clasped in front of him. The

rich hues of his brown eyes stared at her. His dirty blonde hair was neatly styled and locked into place, and his scruff precisely trimmed. He was wearing a black tux that fit against each of his muscles and paired with a white shirt and black tie just underneath the jacket. The wings of his neck tattoos playing peekaboo just above the edge of his shirt's collar.

At his side was the other half of her heart, Gage—Joey's Best Man. His tux mirrored Joey's, except instead of a white shirt, it was all black. Gage had a hand holding onto the top of Joey's shoulder supportively and to perhaps prevent him from running to Layne to scoop her up into his arms halfway down the aisle.

The first thing Joey saw when he saw those doors open was a goddamn Irish angel. He was pretty sure that if he was ever allowed to pass through the Pearly Gates, this was exactly what he would see waiting for him. His heart damn near stopped for what felt like hours as he drank in the stunning sight, slowly walking down the aisle, moving closer and closer to him.

Layne's long chestnut locks were drawn back from her face and off of her bare shoulders. Her hair was all pulled into a loose bun at the nape of her neck, with a couple of small decorative white roses tucked into the top of the bun. The scripted letters of her tattoo, 'Luck' on the back of her neck, was on full display. Her sparkling emerald eyes left the window to her soul wide open for him to see right into everything that made her the woman Joey adored.

Her strapless white dress was a seamless blend of lace with a sweetheart neckline. Scallop-edged lace arm bands hung loosely around her trim biceps, the body of the dress hugged her petite figure and perfectly clung against the curves of her hips. Across her mid back was a band of matching lace in a design similar to the pattern of butterfly wings.

Around her throat was the thin gold chain Gage had given her just last week. She had refused to take off his discreet collar, keeping it on served as a reminder of all his promises to her. While he wasn't the man being recognized by church or state as Layne's soon-to-be husband, that necklace was his vow to have and to hold her all the same.

Joey was rendered breathless, his heart swelling so much he swore it would burst through his chest. Next to him, Gage was grinning like a damn fool at the beauty nearly at their end of the aisle. He nudged Joey to go get their girl as she reached the steps that led up to the space where they stood in front of the altar.

Layne's eyes never left Joey's face as her heart moved her feet down that aisle. Rebecca had come to ease the bouquet out of Layne's hands before Joey joined her at her side, extending his hand to her. She placed her hand in his, watching as his tattooed fingers curled over her hand as he guided her up the steps where they could turn and face one another.

The priest began to speak, and the ceremony commenced, Joey's hold on her hands being a constant reassurance of his devotion to her happiness. Soon, they were exchanging rings and saying their vows out loud to one another. Layne shifted her eyes to Gage every so often so he knew he was included in every promise she was making.

The man cloaked in holy robes addressed Layne, "Do you, Layne Nicole O'Reilly, take this man to be your lawfully wedded husband?"

She gave the widest smile at Joey. "I absolutely do."

The priest then shifted to look at Joey. "And do you, Joseph Elliot De Luca, take this woman to be your lawfully wedded wife?"

Joey squeezed Layne's hands tightly in both of his. "I do. She's mine, always and forever."

Before the officiant could complete his statement declaring them both joined in holy matrimony, Joey jumped the gun and immediately pulled Layne into his arms, crashing his lips onto hers. Layne's hands held onto the sides of his face as her mouth welcomed him, her tongue eagerly pushing past his lips to sensually dance with his. It most definitely was not a chaste kiss that most couples engaged in before such an audience.

Several drawn-out moments passed before there was a stern clearing of a throat from the priest, prompting the newlyweds to separate themselves just enough to regain their composure while they both donned giddy smiles.

"I now present Mr. and Mrs. De Luca."

Layne looked over at Gage, giving him a subtle wink. Joey wasn't the only Mr. De Luca she was tied to.

After Layne and Joey walked back down the aisle together, the formalities continued at the front of the church. Greeting all the guests on their exit from the holy building, they shook hands and shared hugs with some of New York's wealthiest and some of its most corrupt.

Once everyone cleared out, Gage nodded at them both. "I will tell the driver to meet us out front so we can get this party started." He smirked before heading out the front doors.

Joey grinned at Layne as he wrapped his hand around hers. "C'mon." He began leading her back into the expanse of the empty nave now that everyone had gone on their way.

She giggled as she had to quickly move her feet to keep up with him. "What are you doing? We have to get to the reception."

"I'm not waiting for tonight." He pulled her toward the altar.

Layne couldn't help but wrinkle her nose in confusion at the nonsense he was spouting off. "For what?"

He turned her around and pressed her back against the altar in what was probably going to be either the most holy of acts or the most unimaginable sin. Feverishly, he kissed her, bringing his body up tight against hers. His hands began bunching up her dress in his hands, exposing the lean length of her legs.

She gasped as he made it suddenly clear what his intentions were. If he was willing to go to hell, she would dive off that cliff with him any day of the week. Hell or high water, right? Overcome with desire for him, her hands pulled at the belt of his pants, her fingers going to quick work to open up his pants that were already under tension from his stiff cock.

Layne switched to helping gather all the fabric of her dress for him while Joey pulled his length out of his underwear.

He reached down and hoisted her up, separating her legs to wrap around his waist. "Hold on tight, Layney. I'm going to make sure that with God as my witness, you're screaming out His name while I fully make you my wife." Joey sinfully smirked at her as he lodged her back against the altar for support.

Her hands held onto the back of his neck as her breaths grew heavy with anticipation. She leaned over and stole a kiss from him, breaking it for a moment to whisper, "You better make it worth at least ten Hail Marys." She grinned at him, closing the gap between their lips once again.

Joey growled against her mouth as he lined up and sank himself fully inside of her. Hearing her decadent moan into their kiss, he began to hastily thrust himself inside of her. Every fiber of him needed to feel her cunt clenching around him.

Grasping onto him tightly, Layne moaned out at the movements as he needily shoved his cock into her. His arm tightly wrapped around her waist with his other around her back. He began to lay kisses along her throat with his labored breath, heating her skin while he worshiped her body.

Layne's fingers dug into the back of his neck as he furiously continued to lay his claim on her tight pussy. "God, Joey, yes!" Her body was already hanging by a thread, knowing they could be discovered at any moment.

His mouth dragged over the front of her chest, giving a

bite to the top of her cleavage that was threatening to spill over the top of her dress. Layne tilted her head back as she panted hard, trying to suck in oxygen between her moans of pleasure.

His gravelly voice spoke against the tops of her mounds, "I never want to forget this moment, Layney. You'll always be my good girl, no matter what." He groaned as he felt the swell of his cock began to throb, his release threatening to explode into her.

She cried out as suddenly she was overcome with the surge of pleasure that burst from her core. Right as her body squeezed down around Joey, he shuddered as he drove himself even deeper into her. He yelled out against her neck as he shot his cum far into the depths of her body.

They both remained there in each other's arms for several minutes. Layne provided him with several delicate kisses as they both tried to find some level of composure. After gathering themselves, they walked back out of the church to the top of the stone steps, hand in hand. Layne's cheeks still flushed from their consummation, her eyes shimmering with boundless love.

Gage was at the curb, leaning back against the side of the limo with his arms crossed in front of his chest, shaking his head. He knew that look of satisfaction from a mile away. He muttered to himself with a smirk, "Horny mother-fuckers." He fully intended to get his fill of Layne in the limo on the way to the reception. His cock hardened in his pants, imagining her dripping with their cum for the rest of the night.

There were still some guests lingering and chatting on

the sidewalk who hadn't made it back to their vehicles yet. The reception didn't start for at least another forty-five minutes, leaving everyone a little time to get where they needed to be.

Layne smiled as she used one hand to lift the front of her dress as she began walking down the steps with Joey's skull-tatted hand firmly holding onto her other. She had never expected to ever be filled with this much love in one lifetime, and she was looking forward to basking in all of it for years to come.

"Hey, Layne!" A voice shouted out to her while she and Joey were midway down the steps. The familiar voice of her brother was recognized before she even saw his face. Liam stepped past a few of the guests, his face full of a deadly cold calm. He raised his hand, and at the end of it was a forty-five-caliber pistol.

Crack!

Time stood still.

Gage began to push off the side of the limo.

Joey instinctively stepped in front of Layne.

Before there was any time to comprehend what was occurring, Layne felt the impact of the hard stone steps against her back. Joey's weight was on top of her, his back against her chest. She squirmed underneath him, struggling to get out from his expansive body that had shielded her own.

Liam paused with an evil smirk smeared across his face. He may not have struck his intended target, but he had hit the next best thing. Upon seeing Gage reaching into his jacket for a weapon of his own, Layne's brother shoved the nearest wedding guest out in front of him before turning and darting down the street. There was no hesitation as Gage took up chase after him.

Squeezing out from underneath Joey, Layne sat on the step as he lay there at her side. His hand clutched onto his chest. Panic rose in Layne's throat, the stark contrast of red quickly spreading across his white shirt. Joey winced as he gasped for a breath of air.

"Joey! Shit! God—No." Layne stammered out. Immediately, her hands pulled open his shirt and pulled his hand away from where it was clutching. Blood leaked from a hole in his chest, having torn right through the shamrock tattoo overtop his heart. Instead of inked blood leaking from the design etched into his skin, warm liquid seeped from his body. Her hands pressed down firmly over the wound despite the trembling in her body. It was all pouring out of him so quickly, her hands getting coated.

Tears spilled from her eyes, streaming down her cheeks until they fell off the edge of her face. Layne's lips quivered as she sobbed out while staring down into the pain-riddled chocolate hues, looking back up at her.

"Layne..." His voice trying to provide her some comfort.

She shook her head fiercely. "No, don't you dare. Don't you fuckin' dare. Please." Layne's heart went from feeling like it could have burst from happiness now to feeling like it was imploding on itself.

Joey coughed lightly as he raised a hand to her face. "It's okay."

"It's not... It's not okay... I'm not okay..." Both of her

cheeks shone with her flood of tears while her hands held steadfastly on his chest, getting covered in the deep crimson from his body.

He offered up a weak smile to her before swallowing hard at the pain radiating from his chest. It had all been worth it. She had been worth it. Even overcome with grief, Layne's beauty gave him comfort in those moments.

As Joey's eyelids grew heavy, Layne screamed out at him while laying herself down over his chest, wishing she could pour all the love she had ever felt for him into his wounds to mend them. She would have given everything in that moment to trade places with the man who had always completed her soul.

"I love you. Always and forever, remember? I can't do this without you, I never could." Layne kissed him several times, tasting the saltiness of her tears that were dripping over her lips. Those three words should have been enough; she desperately wanted them to be his salvation.

Heavy sobs wracked her body as she noticed his skin paling. She clung to him with every hope that she had. Her words were broken from her tears, unable to sound out any of the millions of words she wanted to say to him. Her repetitive professions of her love muffled against his chest. She didn't care that her dress would be forever stained with his blood. It all meant nothing without him.

His voice hardly above a whisper, "I'll always be yours, Layney." Joey's hand rested on the back of Layne's neck, holding her close while she clutched onto him, repeating herself over and over.

"Don't leave me, please don't leave me." Her words

overflowing with pain she wouldn't have wished on her worst enemy.

Gage had lost Liam fairly quickly after he hopped into a getaway car that had been waiting around the corner for him. Returning to the church, he was now jogging up the steps to the heartbreaking sight. Others had begun to gather around the tragedy, including Dr. Patty, who was already working her way through the crowd to try to assist. "Layne, I need you to move," the physician said as she tried to gain access to Joey's body underneath his grief-stricken wife.

Despite Gage's own emotions stinging in his eyes, he ran over to Layne, not caring who he knocked out of his path. "Baby, you need to let the doc do her work." The words pushed past the ache of his own heart. His hands tried to ease her from her position there on top of Joey. When Layne refused to budge, it took all of Gage's resolve to use his strength to pry her away from his brother's wounded body.

Layne unleashed a raw scream of protest, "NO! I'm not leaving him! No! No! No!" Her body fought against Gage's hands, trying to stay there with Joey, wishing she could go wherever he went, even if it meant the grave. Her tears never slowed their march down her face as she refused to take her eyes off of the man she so fiercely loved. That bullet had been for her, and despite it physically striking Joey, it had still managed to assassinate her heart.

Her broken sobs interjected through her screams of the worst pain anyone could ever feel. Losing the battle with herself, her struggles in Gage's arms began to slow until she didn't even have the strength to stand on her legs. He lowered her down as he felt her weight grow heavier in his hold and sank down onto a nearby step, drawing her into his lap.

Gage rocked Layne in his arms, doing what he could to be the cushion for her emotional blow. His eyes were wet with the tears he was struggling to hold back for her sake. He had promised to have and to hold her, and that meant being Layne's strength while she was in this state of utter devastation.

Joey had wanted to say so many things to her, but they got lost somewhere along the way as his pain began to ease and the world around him began to fade to black. Hearing Layne's voice replaying over and over in his mind until the final thing to linger across his senses was the faint scent of daisies after a warm summer rain. Maybe there would be a spot in Heaven for him after all.

How does it all come to an end? Find out in…

Chaos *Luck* Wrath

ACKNOWLEDGMENTS

To Nikki, my PA: Thank you for helping me wrangle my Skittles as I chose to be the ultimate chaos gremlin. Expect more insanity around the corner!

To Amanda, Melissa, and Nicole: All the damn things. I'm sorry for catapulting you off the cliff of this one so rudely. You all took it so well like the good girls you are (actually, you didn't… but thank you for taking one for the team).

To my author tribe: I can always rely on every one of you to provide insight and laughs. Thanks for letting me vent, be silly, and ask all the questions. We're all on this journey of absurdity together!

Most importantly, thank you readers for taking a chance on a newbie author and sticking with me! Thank you for being my cliff sacrifices, I promise there will be more to come.

ABOUT THE AUTHOR

Sadie Winchester is a romance author residing in the Pine Barrens of New Jersey with her husband, her son, and their two cats (Thor & Loki). She began her love for writing in high school, drafting stories on a popular internet platform.

The dream of writing and publishing a full-length novel first manifested a couple of years after she married the love of her life. However, it took a back burner as she focused on other adventures and goals. Finally, after becoming a mother and finding a way to rediscover herself, she was inspired by another new author to commit to this long-term dream.

When Sadie is not writing up her stories or getting lost in books, she is spending time with her family. She enjoys working out, cooking, visiting microbreweries, and binge-watching *Supernatural*.

You can connect with Sadie in the following ways:

SadieWinchester.com or Linktr.ee/SadieWinchester

amazon.com/author/sadiewinchester

facebook.com/sadiewinchesterauthor

goodreads.com/sadiewinchester

instagram.com/sadiewinchesterauthor

tiktok.com/@sadiewinchesterofficial

bookbub.com/profile/sadie-winchester

ALSO BY SADIE WINCHESTER

Broken Alliances Book 1: Stay In Your Layne

Broken Alliances Book 2: Layne Closure Ahead

Broken Alliances Book 3: Incoming Layne Shift

Broken Alliances Book 4: Chaos Luck Wrath